Sean Hayden

Deceptions

Book Two of the Demonkin Series

Untold
Press

www.untoldpress.com

Deceptions

Published by Untold Press LLC
114 NE Estia Lane
Port St Lucie, FL 34983

ISBN: 978-0692318829

PRODUCED IN THE UNITED STATES OF AMERICA

10 9 8 7 6 5 4 3 2 1

Dedication

For my proofreader in heaven

I miss you
I miss excitedly printing out the books I wrote and
handing you the stack of paper
I miss walking into the kitchen and seeing you sitting
in your chair with a red pen
I miss you giving them back to me and being so proud
that I had written another book
I guess what I'm trying to say
Is I miss you, Mom
So damn much

Prologue

Asmodeus brought his taloned fist down on the armrest of his throne of bones so hard the enchantments holding it together broke. The corner of the magnificent throne shattered like a crystal vase smashed against the ground. Fragments flew to the four corners of the enormous room, some embedding themselves in the granite walls of the desolate keep. Never before had Asmodeus felt such anger course through his veins.

"Vizier," Asmodeus called for his seneschal, uttering the name in the stagnant palace air.

Within moments, the misty demon appeared at his lord's feet. "Yes, my Lord," the form hissed his familiar response.

"Answer me, worm. Were you listening to my foolish cousin's accusations?"

"Yes, my Lord. I heard every word." The shadowy form nodded as he spoke, still bowing.

"What say you?" He tensed in his throne awaiting an answer. What the figure lacked in power, he made up in wisdom and knowledge exponentially. If a way existed to circumvent the law, surely his seneschal would know of it, or how to find out about it.

Vizier rose. "My Lord, I fear you must obey. To me, in this case, the letter of the law matters not. Even if we found a way around the indiscretion, you have been commanded by The All to rectify it."

"I feared as much. Go, Vizier. Go to the mortal realm and search out my offspring. I give you the image of her mother and the place I begot my illegitimate folly," he said, giving the memory to the wraithlike figure. "Find her and return. I will deal with her."

Asmodeus watched as Vizier stood to travel down the pathway to the mortal realm, the pathway that should have been open as per the decree of the messenger Raphael, but it remained as closed as ever.

Understanding quickly became replaced by rage Asmodeus slammed his hand down in frustration. "If they expect me to correct the folly, why is the pathway not open?" The crescendo of his question rose in volume until the walls of his keep quaked in resonance with his annoyance.

"Apparently, My Lord, they will not assist you in correcting your error."

Asmodeus stood. He didn't understand. The All expected him to eliminate his misbegotten child. The decree that no more of the powerful children be inflicted upon the mortal realm had stood uncontested for thousands of years. Asmodeus had devoured the soul of his latest toy. He remembered the sweetness of her fear and terror. The birth of another was his responsibility to remedy, but he would receive no aid.

Asmodeus closed around Vizier's immaterial throat. Being a wraith demon protected him from most physical attacks, but apparently his ability didn't protect him against the fury of Asmodeus.

Chapter 1

"I've told you fifteen times already, Agent Grimes, I don't know how he died. Cicero and I fought and I heard Thompson getting his ass kicked. I ended the fight as fast as inhumanly possible and rushed out to help him. That's when the cavalry came in through the proverbial window. When we went back into the office, Cicero wasn't undead anymore." I sighed as I recounted the made-up chain of events for the fiftieth time since returning to Washington, D.C.

I closed my eyes and thanked the gods the events of the past month were over. The weeks I spent working as an agent in the Chicago field office of the FBI had been pure hell. I got my partner assaulted by one vampire, and then killed by a different vampire named Cicero. The master of the City of Chicago had been a crazed lunatic and my partner paid the ultimate price. I held back the tears for my dead friend and smiled, for the gods had given me Thompson, my current partner, werelion extraordinaire, and the only reason Cicero had his ashes in a ceramic container and I didn't.

"Agent Ashlyn," Agent Grimes began and cleared his throat, "the forensic team found Cicero's body with his throat torn out and completely drained of blood. Let me get this straight, you have absolutely no idea how he became 'un-undead' as you put it?" I'd answered this question so many times I was about to snap, and how dare he quote me to myself.

"Grimes, I've explained this a hundred times and at least five of those times to you. The wounds inflicted on Cicero couldn't have killed him. Even a common

9

vampire couldn't be killed by blood loss, so I didn't kill him. Even if I had, it would have been self-defense! The deputy director himself congratulated me on a job well done. Why the sudden change?"

"It's easy. We didn't know you ate the rogue vampire, Ashlyn. You're an FBI agent, hired to police the rogue vampires. That means bringing them in so they can be incarcerated, tried by jury, and punished by a court of law!" He seemed to mean every word he said.

Was this guy joking? A vampire who kills somebody doesn't get a jury. They'd be lucky to get a cell without a window.

"Which is why I tried to non-lethally subdue him," I lied again through my teeth. The douchebag abducted my injured partner, used him to get to me, and then killed him without a second thought. If you ask me, he got what he deserved. I fought down the urge to flip my superior off and walk out of the room. "What else can I do for you, Agent Grimes? I've answered all your questions, I've filed all my reports, and honestly I don't know what else to say. If you don't believe me, the Deputy Director will have my resignation in the morning." I stood and made my way to the door, not giving the mousy man a chance to respond.

I thought the entire act of my rebellion quite debonair until I placed my hand on the knob and tried to turn the handle. I could have sworn I heard a trombone somewhere in the room going *wa-wa-waa*. Talk about ruining the moment. I watched Grimes when he came through the door. He didn't lock it, so I knew something wasn't right. I turned around and stared at the balding man sitting at the table tapping his pen on his notepad and staring pointedly at the mirror on the wall. "Sonofabitch," left my lips before I could curb my tongue.

Instead of rounding on Grimes, I walked over to the mirror. I stopped in front of it and crossed my arms. I thought about knocking on it to get their attention, but settled for my secondary idea. I uncrossed my arms and held out my talon. Slowly, I etched a circle slightly larger than my head in the otherwise perfect surface of the glass. Once it was completely etched, I rapped my knuckles against it. I smiled as the circle fell out smoothly and shattered on the floor in the tiny dark room behind the mirror.

A normal human wouldn't have been able to see in the dark room, but I didn't have a problem. I peered in and saw the Deputy Director standing next to a tall slender man I'd never seen before. I stood there staring at the both of them and waited for some sort of explanation.

"Agent Ashlyn, please meet me in my office in five minutes," the Deputy Director said without a hint of emotion or surprise.

I seriously considered telling him what he could go do with himself in his office, but I blinked and pulled my face from the Ashlyn-sized hole in the glass. I turned and strode past Grimes. By the time I reached the door, the handle was unlocked, denying me the satisfaction of ripping the door off its hinges. I snarled and made my way to the elevator.

I don't know how the Deputy Director beat me to his office, but he did. The name of the building was the J Edgar Hoover building, so I wouldn't be surprised if a series of passages wound through it, allowing the Deputy Director to add to his mysterious persona. *Yeah right, the man probably needs help tying his shoes.* I opened the glass door separating his office from the expanse of the rest of the room and nodded to his secretary.

"Go ahead in, agent, he's expecting you," she said, picking up the phone.

I sighed and made my way to the wooden door that led to my fate. It seemed too many times in my short life, fate chose to hide my destiny behind large wooden doors. Sometimes you just had to open it and see what it had in store for you.

I watched in slow motion as I grasped the stainless

steel lever. I couldn't shake the feeling of foreboding. I turned it, and without pausing, walked in and shut the door behind me. Deputy Director Sanders sat behind his desk and the other gentleman sat on a couch off to my left, resting his chin on his hand. I walked over to the desk and ignored the stranger, directing my focus solely on the man who had turned on me, or at least in my mind he had.

"Sit, Ashlyn," he commanded, leaving little room for argument. He was just lucky I *wanted* to sit.

"Thank you, sir." I gritted my teeth instead of jumping over the desk and snarling in his face, as I wanted to. I knew one thing, I wasn't going to be sitting on the couch with Mr. Mysterious, and so I opted for one of the comfortable leather chairs facing the desk on the opposite angle.

"Agent Ashlyn, I just want you to know I completely believe your series of events in Chicago," he started. "This whole inquisition wasn't for the benefit of the FBI, I can promise you. May I introduce Michael Vetters with the DHS?"

I turned toward the slender man I'd been trying my best to ignore. He didn't smile as he stood and walked to where I sat and offered me his hand. I did my best not to squeeze it like a piece of overripe fruit.

"I'm sorry to have opened an investigation, but we have a situation. We need your help and the Department of Homeland Security needed to be certain of your character."

I expected his voice to sound one way before he spoke, but the timbre of his actual voice surprised me. Some people just didn't sound like they looked. He should get a job in the radio industry.

"I'm confused, Mr. Vetters, what could the DHS want from me?" To say I wasn't feeling very comfortable dealing with somebody from the enigmatic branch of the federal government would have been an understatement.

"I'm sure you're well aware, Ashlyn, the Great State of California elected themselves a governor who just so happens to be a vampire," he began. I actually wasn't aware of it, but I nodded as if I paid attention to the news. I couldn't believe it. More so, I couldn't believe nobody found a law to keep him out of office. "The incumbent governor maintained his role while they battled the legalities of it out in court, but the Supreme Court ruled in the vampire's favor last week. He takes his oath of office on Monday."

"Exactly what does a local election have to do with the Department of Homeland Security?" I didn't see the connection and sat there confused.

"The election doesn't, but acts of terrorism do. There have been several attempts to destroy the elected governor."

I noticed his use of the word *destroy* rather than kill.

"He came out unscathed, but three state troopers assigned to his Executive Services detail didn't. We don't know who planned the attacks, but they have to stop. We need you to find our terrorists and stop them."

"Why me?" I had a feeling I already knew the answer.

"We believe the attacks have been orchestrated and carried out by vampires," he answered.

I wasn't surprised by his revelation. I turned to the Deputy Director and he nodded once letting me know he'd already given his consent to the joint operation. I gave an inaudible sigh and turned back toward Vetters.

"I'd be more than happy to help, Mr. Vetters," I lied. If they kept giving me all this practice lying, I expected to get pretty good at it. "Does this vampire governor have a name?"

"David Greer."

Chapter 2

"Special Agent Thompson and Agent Ashlyn reporting, sir." Thompson held out his meaty paw to the Special Agent in Charge of the Sacramento field office.

The name on the desk plate read James Connors, but we already knew that. We spent the better part of four days being brought up to speed by both the DHS and the Deputy Director himself. Don't ask me why, but Sanders seemed on edge about this one, almost as if he expected me to screw up.

The man rose and shook Thompson's hand, pumping it vigorously. Without even so much as a glance in my direction, he sat back down. The man either didn't like women or vampires. I wondered which one. I ignored the slight, moved to just behind Thompson, and let him do the talking.

"Glad to have you here. I'm an old friend of Reese's. He's mentioned you on more than one occasion. So what brings you to the Sacramento office?"

"Your new governor brings us here. Apparently, some folks don't take too kindly to vampires being elected as officials. We're here to make sure he stays alive."

I watched Connors' face while Thompson spoke. I doubt anyone else would've noticed the slight smirk when he mentioned keeping the vampire alive, but I did. I guessed Special Agent Connors didn't vote for Governor Greer.

"Anything you need, Thompson, just let me know. I'll have a car brought out front. I'm assuming you'll need one?" He made it a question. Thompson nodded and Connors picked up the phone and made it happen. I did my best to remain in the background.

"Thank you, sir," Thompson added when Connors set the receiver back in its cradle.

"No problem. Good luck keeping the vampire alive. God knows there are probably a million people not too happy with the fact he got elected."

"Are you one of them, sir?" The words came out before my brain could override my stupid, stupid mouth.

He rounded his gaze upon me, measuring me for all my worth. I'm sure he found me lacking. "I couldn't care less, Agent Ashlyn. The man is an elected official and none of them are too high on my Sunday golf buddy list. If you'll excuse me, I have pressing matters to attend. Good luck, both of you," he said in dismissal. Five minutes in the new office and I'd already made an enemy. *Why couldn't we all just get along?*

Thompson dramatically swept his arms toward the door telling me to lead the way. I glanced up and he winked, so I knew he wasn't too unhappy with me. Either that or he just expected my mouth to fuck things up and was letting me know I didn't. I pivoted on my heel and walked through the doorway. As Thompson cleared it, another agent shouted his name and threw him a set of keys. He didn't even slow down, plucking the keys out of the air and matching his stride to mine.

Thanks to the handy GPS unit built into the standard FBI issue black Suburban we made it to the governor's office in less than twenty minutes. Sacramento seemed quite beautiful, even at night, and I enjoyed watching the colorful buildings while Thompson drove. I relaxed and fell into the comfortable silence between us. I half expected him to at least say something about either my comment or Connors' attitude, but he sat silently, just like me.

I looked up and saw H Street on the street sign, and according to the address plugged into the GPS unit, I figured we must be close. I wondered what the vampire governor would be like. So far, I could count the number of vampires I liked on one finger. My train of thought made me think of the enigmatic Marcel in Chicago. Thoughts of him caused me to shift uncomfortably in my seat. I had officially turned eighteen last week and needed a boyfriend. If I had a boyfriend, it might make me feel a little more like a normal eighteen year old. Thinking of Marcel and his beautiful face, silky hair, and gorgeous body wasn't helping me in the least.

The car jerked as Thompson swerved and made a right turn, shaking me from my thoughts. We pulled down a small access road and stopped at a glistening, pristine white guardhouse. A man dressed in a State of California Police uniform stepped out and Thompson flashed his badge at the trooper.

"Special Agent Thompson, FBI. We're here to see the governor."

"Go on through, special agent, the governor informed us you'd be here this evening," the trooper said and smiled.

"Thanks." Thompson hit the accelerator, narrowly missing the gate arm while it made its upward arc.

We drove up to the mansion and I stared wide-eyed at its grandeur. "Our tax dollars hard at work," I muttered under my breath, but apparently loud enough for Thompson's werelion ears to pick up since he gave a short bark of laughter. Another trooper stood out front and motioned us toward an empty parking area. At least we wouldn't have to vie for the governor's attention this evening. The place looked deserted.

"Agents?" "If you would, please follow me into the residence."

"Absolutely," Thompson replied, and followed the youngish blond officer toward the door. I took the opportunity to look around. The lawn and the flowers were perfectly manicured and gave the impression of a park. I sniffed and abruptly held my breath against the plethora of pollens and scents in the night air. No breeze stirred so it lay thick over the area and reminded me of a cheap smelling perfume.

I caught up to the other two as they reached the door. The officer opened it and motioned us to go in ahead of him. We did and on the other side of the door, a beautiful woman in a gray wool skirt and jacket greeted us. Her hair was pulled up in a professional-looking style and ringlets lay on the side of her face by her ears.

"Hello. I'm Samantha Barnes, the governor's personal assistant. If you would please follow me, the governor is expecting you," she said and turned, expecting us to follow her.

"If I may ask, Miss Barnes, how did the governor know we would be here this evening?" I couldn't help but ask.

"Your Deputy Director called about an hour ago confirming your meeting with Governor Greer," she replied over her shoulder while we made our way across the marble floor and to the stairway. Pristine white wooden banners and marble stairs reminded me of the house in *The Sound of Music*. I refrained from singing. Once at the top of the winding flight, she led us down the hallway to the residential area of the mansion. She stopped in front of the first door on our left and knocked.

"Come in, Samantha," someone called from the other side of the door.

She turned the handle and ushered Thompson and me into the room. As we crossed the threshold, we stepped back in time. The décor from the wallpaper festooning the walls, the glittering wall sconces, and the ornate wood paneling from the chair rail down to the floor impressed upon the senses that you stood in a parlor somewhere in the late eighteen hundreds. I wondered briefly if the room had always been decorated this way, or if the governor decorated to his tastes. My trips to governor's mansions were been somewhat limited, so I don't know how it works.

"Good evening, both of you, and welcome to my humble home," the governor said from a leather chair facing the fireplace.

I just loved it when vampires said catchy cliché things like, "Good evening."

Thank you, Mr. Lugosi.

"Good evening, Governor Greer, I'm Special Agent Thomson and this is Agent Ashlyn. I assume the Deputy Director filled you in on why we're here?"

He rose and turned to us with a smile, setting down his newspaper on the ornate wooden table at his side. We both took a step toward him, but he closed the distance before we completed it. I guess no one filled in the governor on vampire etiquette. He stood about a foot shorter than Thompson, so I figured he was around six feet, still almost a foot taller than me. He'd been older when whoever turned him made him a vampire. Light gray streaks jutted out from the edge of his temples giving him an almost mad scientist look. If he hadn't been so damn handsome, I might have giggled a little.

He reached out and took Thompson's hand without an offer and shook it firmly saying, "Pleased to meet you," before turning to me. I held my hand out for a handshake, but he took it and pulled it to his lips, planting a small kiss on my middle knuckle. He froze at the icy touch of my skin on his lips and his eyes widened a little. Apparently, Sanders left some information out of his little phone call.

"A vampire?" At least he managed to pull his lips from my hand before asking.

"Yes," I answered and caught his scent, carefully avoiding direct eye contact. I knew from past experiences when I got close enough to another vampire I could gaze into his eyes and see his power. If I was stronger, I could easily capture his mind and make him obey me. It wasn't something I enjoyed doing, so I tended to keep my gaze firmly planted on the eyebrows of vampires I wasn't trying to interrogate. He smelled of cinnamon and vanilla and I wanted a taste, a big taste. I may not be able to eat normal humans, but vampires were definitely on the menu.

"Oh, how a vampire ended up in the employ of the FBI is simply a tale you must tell." He motioned for us to sit in the remaining chairs gathered around the massive stone fireplace.

"Another time perhaps," Thompson interjected, but took a seat anyway. "Instead, could you please tell us what's been happening?" I stifled a giggle. The concept of being polite didn't sit well with Thompson.

"Where to begin," Greer said to himself. "They elected me in November, but the two recounts the incumbent demanded took almost a month, and that's when I received the first death threat. I laughed it off, but I knew even then whoever sent the letter meant business."

"Do you still have the letter?" I doubted it, but I wanted to make sure.

"No, I turned it over to the police and their forensic team looked at it. They came up with nothing, not even a fingerprint. Let's see, after that the former governor filed an Injunction and the California courts agreed to it without batting an eyelash. I think all of the politicians in the entire state took my running for governor and my subsequent election as some sort of novelty at first, and then a joke; finally, they started to panic when I won. The death threats became more frequent and not from the same people. Many were clipped from magazines and I even received a few written in crayon." His eyes left us and traveled upward as he spoke of the incident like it was a fond memory.

"Tell us about the attack," I said, curious as to how someone would try to kill a vampire.

"It happened two weeks ago, while I sat waiting for the ruling of the Supreme Court. The State of California assigned me an executive services detail of state police officers since I had officially won the election. We were in San Francisco at a fundraiser for a local homeless shelter. Our limousine had been swept for explosive devices and pronounced clean and yet when the event ended and I climbed inside, it exploded."

The smile on Governor Greer's face vanished.

Apparently, he didn't like being caught in explosions. I can't say I blamed him. Being blown up would piss me off, too. I looked at the governor closely and didn't see any damage remaining. It surprised me. Not a lot of things could kill a vampire, but explosions and fire made the list.

"How did you survive?"

He gave me a penetrating stare I once again avoided by staring at his well-manicured eyebrows.

"I am very, very old, child. I'm hard to kill. I've never shared my true age so I don't think the people who planted the bomb could have known it wouldn't be very effective." He paused for a moment and raised his hand to his chin. "Let me rephrase that. I don't think they realized it wouldn't be very effective against me. It killed three state troopers and the limousine driver quite effectively." He gave a little sigh of sadness.

"How old are you, Governor Greer?" I didn't know if my question would offend him, but curiosity got the better of me.

"The incumbent governor used the fact that I might have a master and not be 'able to set the goals and prerogatives of the State of California above that of a vampire who might control me.' It seemed to be a major issue the Supreme Court had against me governing. I needed to produce proof of my age and prove that I had no master to them. So to answer your question, child I am very, very old," he said and smiled at me. "What about you, Ashlyn. Who is your master and why did he allow you to join the ranks of the FBI?"

"I have no master, Governor. I was free after my making to choose my own path," I lied.

"We both know, Agent Ashlyn, that's not how it works. I don't mind you not telling me, in fact I would expect it, but please don't lie to me," he said without anger. "Again, it can be a discussion for a later time. My question for the both of you is what do we do now?"

"Do you have any public appearances scheduled soon?" Thompson pulled a pad out of his jacket to write the information down.

"I am governor of the state of California, Agent Thompson. You were lucky to catch me at home tonight."

Deceptions

Chapter 3

Thompson drove the limo while I rode in the back with the governor. I shifted in my seat, quite uncomfortable under the gaze of the old vampire sitting across from me. It wasn't the upholstered leather of the seat that made me uncomfortable, Greer's penetrating stare did. I could tell he wanted to ask me a million questions and didn't know where to start. I glanced over at the mini-bar in the wall of the vehicle and wished I could have a drink. I knew last night, after we left the Governor's Mansion, I would be in this situation eventually. I just didn't know it would be so soon.

"How about those Dodgers?" I tried to break the ice. I probably should have picked a different topic of discussion than baseball, but frankly, I couldn't think of anything else to divert his interest in me.

"Baseball season doesn't start for another few weeks, Ashlyn," he said deadpan. "Would you care to discuss something else?"

"Um, how did you prove to the Supreme Court that you don't have a master?" I shocked myself with my own cleverness. *Go me.*

"The Vampire Council congregated before them and proved it without a shadow of a doubt. Who is your master?" I expected at least a brief pause before we got back onto the subject of me. Apparently, we were playing tit for tat.

"Marcel Sylvain," popped out of my mouth before I could stop myself. Thompson never put the glass divider up between the front and back, and his head snapped backward to give me a wide-eyed look.

24

"That son of a bitch finally broke down and made an offspring. It's about time!" Greer laughed and seemed genuinely happy. I needed to make a phone call. I just hoped Marc would forgive me. "Does it bother him that you're working for the FBI?"

"No, from the start he encouraged me to be my own vampire."

"I wish you'd told me last night. I need to call him to congratulate him," he said as I tried not to slink down between the seat cushions.

"We're here," Thompson called through the open divider.

Thank the gods.

I glanced out the window at The Citizen Hotel. The governor planned to give a dinner to thank all of his supporters. We tried talking him out of it, but to say a vampire could be stubborn seemed to be a bit of an understatement. The state police swept the building as well as the FBI, but for some reason I didn't think the people who wanted to see him dead would try a bomb again. The last one hadn't worked so well and the outrage people felt at somebody trying to blow up the governor flocked even more supporters to his side.

Thompson pulled the limo over to the curb in front of the entrance to the hotel. Again, we tried to convince Greer to use a back entrance, but we got the standard "I will not give in to these terrorists" speech. As soon as the vehicle came to a stop, Greer opened the door and stepped out. A red carpet complete with matching felted ropes to keep the members of the press from rushing the limo had been set up. So had the customary allotment of police officers to make sure the little fuzzy ropes did their jobs. I expected Greer to wait for me, not reach his hand into the limo and help me exit like I had the honor of being his arm candy for the evening. The press would be sorely disappointment at my wardrobe choice. My gray pantsuit and jacket looked more severe than the governor's and weren't flashy at all.

I couldn't have been more wrong. As soon as I stepped

out of the vehicle, the camera flashes started. I figured once they saw my outfit they would let out a groan and go, "Who's she?" They didn't. In fact, they recognized me from the start. They hurled questions at the governor one after another, and I hoped he would set the record straight, but he just smiled, held my hand elegantly, and walked down the carpet. A wise man once said, "Any publicity is good publicity." I think the governor held the same opinion.

By the time we reached the front of the building and a uniformed officer opened the door, if I heard one more person yell the word "Verminator" it would be a bloodbath. Images of shredded reporters filled my head and I won't lie, I started to get a little hungry.

"Verminator?" Greer apparently hadn't heard the press' nickname for me.

"Later," I replied. I really didn't want the man I'd been assigned to protect pissed off at me. It would make my job that much harder.

We wound our way through the hotel lobby, and I pulled my hand from Greer's grasp. He seemed to know where we were going, so I let him lead the way, keeping my eyes peeled for anything out of the ordinary. The hotel staff was busy wheeling in carts of what smelled like appetizers and beverages. The tempting scents only added to my hunger. *Why did human food have to smell so damn good?* I looked at the vampire at my side and felt a little jealous. He, at some point in his life, had actually tasted food. At least he knew what he was missing. On the other hand, maybe I did have it easier I tried to remember the old axiom about loving and losing, but I couldn't quite recall it. I let it go and focused on my surroundings instead.

We entered the ballroom and Greer immediately made his way to where we would be sitting. We'd arrived over an hour early, so no guests were seated at the multitude of round tables set up throughout the gigantic room. I didn't have any idea how many people supported the governor, but I'd be surprised if he filled the massive room.

I stood by his side, constantly watching while a sea of coordinators bombarded him with a never-ending stream of last minute questions. He took it all in stride, and I found myself amazed with the ease he handled the situation. I paused a moment to consider how many occupations Greer might have had before he became governor. I made a mental note to ask him about it later, along with the other question that had been nagging me. Why would a vampire want to be governor?

Time passed quickly and the guests started entering the room, introducing themselves before finding their seats. The man had charisma; I'd give him that. Most of the time, he knew the guests before they introduced themselves, and he greeted them by name. Their faces flushed with pride when he did it. No wonder the man found himself elected. What a schmoozer.

The last guests trickled in and Greer took his seat. I made my way to the top of the stage and stood against the wall behind him. A tickling sensation at the base of my skull urged me forward, planting the desire to sit next to the governor. I shook my head from side to side and that helped a little. Greer turned and gave me a wide-eyed look, like something surprised him. He stood up and walked over to me.

"What are you doing?" He looked confused.

"I'm sorry, what do you mean?" I tried not to look even more confused than he did.

"I wanted you to sit by my side so my guests wouldn't worry about their safety. A few of them picked up on who you are and it made them nervous. I could feel their fear. I wanted them to think you came here as my guest and not an agent of the FBI."

I had a nagging feeling I knew exactly where the tingling sensation in my head had come from and I wasn't happy. "Governor Greer, I am an on duty FBI agent, *not* your date," I said through my teeth.

"You misunderstand me, Ashlyn. I'm just trying to make you less conspicuous," he said with a smile. I looked across the room at Thomson, and he stood watching us. I didn't know if he could hear our conversation, but he nodded and scanned the room with his supernatural eyes. Fine, I could do it too, from a chair.

I nodded and Greer smiled, motioning me to take the empty seat by his side. If I ended up in the newspapers tomorrow as "The governor's new girl" I'd eat him for breakfast, literally. I sighed and sat. I almost laughed when I saw the fine china setting in front of us. I expected him to sit, but he made his way to the podium set up on the middle of the head table. I didn't recognize anyone at the table with us, but my knowledge of politics involved being able to pick the President of the United States out of a group of people. I knew even less about politics than I did about baseball.

As soon as Greer took his position behind the wooden pulpit, a man standing by the entrance shouted, "Ladies and Gentlemen, the governor of the great state of California." He impressed me. His voice carried over the noise of the crowd without a microphone and echoed off the walls of the room.

"Ladies and Gentlemen," Greer began. "Thank you for joining me. This evening is my way of saying thank you to all of my greatest supporters. I plan on taking our great state and healing it, but more so, I plan to usher in an era of mutual understanding and friendship between the supernatural communities of our state and the communities of my new friends and supporters. I plan to make stricter laws protecting all people and meting out harsher punishments for those who think crime is an easier way to make a better life instead of good old-fashioned hard work. So please, my friends, enjoy the bounty before you, and then let us mingle and make merry." He smiled and raised his arms to the people gathered before him. The waitstaff must have been waiting for his cue to start bringing out the delicious appetizers we'd smelled on the way in.

The people seated at the tables rose one by one and applauded the governor's short speech before turning to the company of their own tables. Utensils scraping on dishes, glasses being clinked together, and the cacophony of conversation filled the room, almost hurting my sensitive ears. Greer returned to his seat next to me and sat down effortlessly. Various members from the head table walked up to us and congratulated him on his victory once again before resuming their seats and beginning their dinner.

"So how is Marcel these days? Is he still in Chicago amassing a fortune with his chic clubs?"

"Yes, sir. I saw him about two weeks ago. Next time I'm in the area I'll give him your best." I glanced over at Thompson at his post by the entrance and he gave me a little scowl. I guess he hadn't heard our conversation earlier. "I'll be right back, Governor; I need to talk to Thompson for a moment."

I weaved through the sea of tables, ignoring the curious people casting inquisitive glances my way, and walked up to my mountain of a partner.

"Enjoying yourself, kid?"

"No, I'm not. Greer insisted I sit with him as his guest. I guess a lot of people are worried about why the 'Verminator' was here, so he wanted them to think everything was okay. You see anything suspicious?"

"No." He crossed his arms. "Just watch yourself around the governor. I don't trust him all that much."

"Shit, that reminds me. Could you step outside and call Marcel? I have a feeling Greer might actually call him to congratulate him on his offspring."

Thompson laughed. "I almost choked on my tongue when you told him that. Good thinking," he said, and pulled out his cell. "I'll be back in a minute, go watch the governor."

I nodded and returned to my seat at Greer's side. He gave me an inquisitive look I ignored and glanced down at the table in front of me. A crystal goblet with an ample amount of blood sat where my plate used to be. Greer followed my gaze.

"A little snack, I thought you might be hungry." He raised his glass. "It could be a little warmer, but it's not bad."

I raised the glass to my lips and smelled it tentatively. Shit, pure human. "Thank you, sir, but I never drink while I'm at work." I stared at his face and he gave me a curious look.

"How old are you, Ashlyn?"

"How long have I been a vampire, sir?" I wanted clarification before I answered.

"Either, I'm pretty good at math and judging people's ages," he said with his customary smile.

"How old do you think I am, Governor?" This should be interesting.

He touched the skin on the back of my hand in an intimate gesture. I thought he might be hitting on me until he closed his eyes and I felt his power pour through his fingertips. He gasped, drew his hand back from mine, and stared at it like I gave him a shock. Maybe this wasn't such a good idea.

"What happened?"

"When I tried to get a feel for your age something burned me, and I don't mean my hand. Something burned me," he said, and looked a little afraid.

"Weird. Nothing like that's happened before." I gave a half-truth. If I could count how many times strange things happened around me, I'd spend a lot of my time counting.

The rest of the governor's dinner passed quite uneventfully. The guests ate, danced, and schmoozed with the governor for four hours. Thankfully, after the little "hand" incident Greer dropped his questions about my age and everything else Ashlyn related. I don't truly believe he feared me, but he seemed more than a little wary of me. More like he regarded me as a puzzle to be solved later. I imagine when one reaches the ripe old age of very, very old you learn to be patient.

As the last guests left, Thompson breathed a sigh of relief. I glanced up at him quizzically and he just shook his head. I knew a headshake from Thompson meant "later." Greer left the final details of the dinner party to his aides and strolled elegantly back over to me.

"Are you ready, sir?"

"Yes, Ashlyn. I'm more than ready."

Thompson left to procure the limo. Before we'd even left for the gala, Thompson planned to have the limo waiting out front for the governor to minimize his public exposure time. I knew he also wanted to check for incendiary devices. In the scope of bomb detection, it usually went police dogs, electronic sniffing devices, and then wereanimals. For some reason their sense of smell rivaled even their full-blooded cousins. Sometimes my nose even beat Thompson's, but since I had never smelled a bomb, I wouldn't know what to sniff for.

The governor and I waited in the ballroom for a cell call from my partner to let us know it was safe. Thankfully, we didn't have long to wait. I nodded to Greer and led him back through the hotel. I didn't pause as the doors slid open, merely slipped between them and looked around. Not seeing anything, I waved the governor through as the flashes from the reporters illuminated the walkway. Those flashes saved Greer's life.

Very few things can kill a vampire. Fire is one, but it's often messy and causes too much collateral damage, just like the car bomb that failed to dispatch the governor the first time. You can also cut off the vampire's head and remove their heart, but you have to get close enough to do it. Security surrounding the target usually made that option pretty difficult. The only other way is silver through the heart. Every subspecies of vampire is the same, but master vampires are a little more resilient. Often a bullet won't work. They travel too fast, and even though the bullet pierces the heart, the silver exposure isn't long enough to cauterize the wound. The FBI and even local SWAT teams adopted guns that fired silver "stakes" using compressed air. They were incredibly accurate and the chances of the stake going completely through the vampire and striking someone else were slim to none. The very first time I encountered an FBI agent, I'd been in the clutches of

Cicero, the master of Chicago. The FBI had burst in, shot first, and asked questions later. I saw those weapons used up close and personal and even though silver didn't bother me in the least, I wouldn't want to be on the receiving end of the shot.

Silver is highly reflective, and as I stood waiting for the governor the flashes of the cameras reflected off a tiny little silver missile traveling through the air straight at the governor. When in fights, my perceptions often speed up, giving the things surrounding me a slow motion quality. The flash of the cameras flickered in muffled bursts, Greer appeared to stop moving, and even the sounds around me stretched. I knew I wouldn't be able to get to Greer in time to move him from the path of the missile so I did the only thing I could; I jumped in front of him. I tried to pluck it from midair with my hand, but I couldn't get to it in time. I braced myself for the impact hoping it would miss my heart. I knew it wouldn't kill me, but the last time it happened wasn't fun. I was shot in the chest with a hollow point silver bullet and it nearly shredded my most important of organs. I woke up on the morgue table twelve hours later with my chest cavity exposed and a doctor about to finish an autopsy. Not a situation I ever wanted to find myself in again.

The stake pierced my chest right between my breasts. *Whew*. It stopped as it embedded itself, and I waited for the pain to hit. I turned my head and screamed at the governor to, "Get in the fucking car," as the reporters around us began screaming. I turned my back toward the direction the missile originated so I could dive into the limo behind the governor. I felt three more stakes slam into my back before I finally cleared the door. I pulled it closed and yelled at Thompson to go. Turning to look at Greer to make sure he was missile free, I fell face first into his lap. The governor's trousers filled my vision as I passed out.

Deceptions

Chapter 4

I woke up in the back of the limo lying on the floor. The governor held my head in his lap and he was yelling at Thompson to hurry up and get to the hospital. I gave a little groan and sat up, glancing out the window and then at the governor's shocked expression.

"Are we there yet?" I started giggling at Thompson. I looked down, yanked the stake from my chest, and let it fall to the floor of the car with a sickening thud. My shirt was a bloody mess and the tip of one of the missiles that had hit me in the back stuck out about an inch through it. *Son of a bitch, they got me through the heart.* I reached up over my shoulder and could touch the stakes protruding from my back, but I couldn't reach behind me far enough to grab hold well enough to yank them out.

"Governor, would you mind?" I turned my back to him hoping he'd pull them out for me.

"What the hell are you?" He made no move to grab the stakes.

"Governor, please? They won't kill me, but they hurt like a motherfucker."

He sighed and gingerly grabbed the first stake. A sizzling sound filled the limo, but I couldn't figure out where it came from. I felt the silver missile slowly sliding back through my heart, and then with a wet plop, it pulled completely free. I closed my eyes my body started to heal itself. I shuddered at how much blood I would need to drink after I healed. I couldn't believe I woke up in the limo and not in a hospital bed. When I sustain grievous injuries, the healing process is usually a lot slower.

Greer braced his hand against my back giving him a little more leverage to work the other two missiles out. He didn't have too much trouble with the second one, but the last one seemed to have lodged itself between my ribs. Finally, he got it out, and to say I felt better would have been a major understatement.

"Thank you, sir." I lay back against the long seat running the length of the limousine.

"You okay, kid?" Thompson actually looked more worried than he sounded.

"I'll live," I said back without the strength to make it very loud. I glanced over at the governor, and he stared at his fingertips like they were covered in something other than my blood. "You okay, Governor?"

"I'm just waiting for the silver burns to dissipate. Would you care to tell me why you're still alive?" He shifted his gaze from his fingers to my face, scowling intently. *Uh oh, the gig was up.*

"I can't give you the details, Governor, but I can tell you something is different about me. I suggest you just forget about it. You did ask me not to lie to you."

Thompson gave a deep rumbling chortle from the front of the car. I closed my eyes and tried to relax. I felt the governor slide a little closer to take a look at my wounds, and when he did so, he kneeled and brought his face very close to my chest. Thompson must've heard me growl, preparing to strike, and slammed on the brakes.

"Ashlyn! Governor, back away slowly and sit as far away from her as you can. Ashlyn, listen to my voice, I'm here. I'm going to come through the window. Look at my eyes, Ashlyn. Not at the governor."

I stared at him wanting to cry. I focused on his slightly orange eyes and did my best to forget about everything else. I didn't even laugh when Thompson tried to fit his massive frame through the tiny little divider separating the driver and passenger compartments. He didn't say anything other than my name, consistently reminding me of my identity and not letting me get lost in the predator. He slid past the governor and I glanced over at him, and then I smelled it.

The fear rolled off of him like a drug. Instantly, I became addicted and a deep guttural growl began in my chest and rolled through my throat. Thompson increased the frequency and pitch of the repetition of my name to a frantic pace trying to prevent what he knew was coming. It didn't work. I lunged across the limo at inhuman speed. The fear pouring off the governor doubled. Thompson barely got his arm out in time. My waist hit it like a steel bar. He brought me down on my back, straddling me. It was one of those moments where time stopped. I stared up at him, grinning at his audacity for stopping me from feasting, and shot my arms out open-handed against his rock hard chest. He flew up into the air and dented the roof of the car before landing face down right on the spot I had been a moment ago.

I stopped a few feet from the governor and decided to slow down and enjoy closing in for the kill, letting his fear fuel the hunger to almost orgasmic heights. I stared in his eyes and saw the fear there as well, but I didn't capture his mind. If I had done that, we would have gone to that peaceful place and it would have denied me what I wanted most. I wanted him to know how it felt to be prey.

A bloody wrist appeared in front of my face. I could see tear marks in the flesh, so Thompson must have opened his own vein to feed me. There's only one thing sweeter than the smell of fear and it is blood, hot, wet magnificent blood. I forgot all about Greer and his little mewling noises and gingerly reached up to grasp the arm to test if he would pull it away at the last moment. He meant to feed me because he didn't move. I slowly brought his wrist to my mouth and gave it a sensuous lick across the wound. Thompson shuddered behind me as his chest pressed tightly to my back.

His other hand reached around and the palm rested securely on my tummy, locking me in a backward embrace, but I didn't care. All I wanted was the wrist bared open fully before me. I brought my mouth to it and my lips pulled back as my fangs sank in with a little *pop* as they pierced his skin. The blood poured down my throat, into my stomach, and created a small furnace of heat deep within me that spread through my veins like wildfire. Again, I felt Thompson shudder behind me as he gave in to the pleasure that always accompanied the bite. Whenever a vampire fed, it was pleasurable. It's the pleasure that makes humans line up like cattle at the entrance of every vampire owned establishment in the country. I read once, the effect could be likened to the initial rush of heroin, and apparently mine wasn't any different.

Thompson began to moan and grind himself into me from behind. Ecstasy filled me as well and I fought the urge to turn around and take him into me right there on the limo floor completely ignoring the company with us. Instead, I bent over slightly, never letting go of his wrist, and pushed myself against him harder. I knew he had a wife and children, but right then, right there, I didn't care, and if I had to guess, neither did he. He grew hard and long, and the length of it slid up and down the crease of my ass. I now knew what heaven could feel like.

His other hand slid lower and cupped me from the front his middle finger working itself into my other crease. I gasped at the contact and his wrist popped from my mouth with a little wet noise. Time stopped. I felt Thompson move behind me and I suddenly felt very, very awkward. I now knew what hell could feel like.

"Thompson," I said calmly and softly over my shoulder.

"Not one word kid, not one single word. This never happened," he said and slowly removed his wrist from my hand and his hand from my…um. I didn't want to even think about that one. I really wanted to take a shower.

"So, how 'bout them Dodgers, eh?" I called over my shoulder.

The belly laugh made me feel a little better about going to third base with my partner. Putting baseball out of my mind, I looked over at the governor and he simply stared at the two of us as if we'd sprouted several extra heads, each. I made a motion to go to his side to apologize, but he held up his hand.

"That's quite close enough for now, agent, if you don't mind. I need some time to process what has just happened here."

I nodded and straightened my clothes while Thompson exited the vehicle and walked around to the front of the limo. I guess he didn't feel like squeezing through the window again.

What a wimp.

He started the car and we pulled back onto the road. The governor and I didn't say anything to each other for the entire trip. The silence made me happy. The governor had more questions than before, I'm sure, and I'd officially run out of lies. That left only the truth and I wasn't ready for that, not by a long shot.

We made sure Greer got back to the mansion in one piece and went inside without any other incidents. I breathed a sigh of relief to leave the limo behind and be back in the familiar Suburban. *What a night.*

We drove in silence all the way to the Marriot where we were staying. I hoped Thompson felt more embarrassed than I did about the whole limo episode, but I doubted it. I fought the urge to cry and hide. At least we had separate bedrooms, so my crying and hiding would go unnoticed.

"You okay, kid?" He finally broke the silence as we pulled into the hotel parking lot.

"Yeah, not so much," I answered. "Sorry about that, big guy. I could say I don't know what came over me, but we both know what did. Can we just forget the whole thing happened?"

"Forget what happened?" He even said it with a wink.

I let out a breath I didn't realize I'd been holding and

gave him a weak smile before opening the door and stepping out into the dry California night. The silence returned as we walked side by side through the parking lot and into the deserted lobby. A quick elevator ride and a stroll down the hallway and we were in front of our suite. I slid the electronic card key into the lock and opened the door, practically running to my bedroom.

"Night, kid," he called out, but I was still too embarrassed to answer.

I didn't even turn on the light since I could see perfectly in the dark. I shed my bloody clothes and tossed them into the plastic lined trashcan by the bed. I thought about just slipping into bed, but I wanted to wash the blood off my chest, back, and face. I'd completely forgotten about it until I looked at the mirror on the wall. Thankfully, the lobby had been deserted. Somebody probably would have called the cops.

I went into the bathroom, turned on the shower, and slipped right in under the stream of water. I used the little hotel shampoo to wash my hair while I let the stream soak the dried blood. I stayed under the spray, rinsing my hair and relaxed, forcing the memories of the day to wash away with the blood. I shut the water off, reached out and grabbed a towel on the metal rack attached to the wall, and dried off before stepping out onto the cold bathroom tile. I brushed my teeth and my wet hair, pulling it up into my usual ponytail before returning to the bedroom and more importantly, my bed.

"Greetings, child."

The voice froze me in my tracks. Without thinking, I reached out to my side and flipped the tiny switch on the wall to my right. The warm yellow light from the twin sconces above my bed bathed the room in a soft glow, illuminating the figure sitting in a chair in the corner of the room. I hadn't heard him enter so he must have come in while I showered. I gazed at his face and let out a little gasp at his features. His black hair partially hid his face, but what I could see, he was beautiful. Piercing black eyes stared back at me, and I don't think it had anything to do with my limited wardrobe either. I felt as if he judged me with his gaze alone, and I didn't like it.

"Can I help you?" I tightened the towel around me. "Not tonight, for dawn is near. Rest well this day, child, for tomorrow you have much to explain," he said, and stood.

"Who are you?" I tried to control my anger.

"My apologies, my name is Antonio Strozzini. I will be at your door at sunset. Please don't leave without talking to me. You and I have much to discuss."

"I wouldn't miss it for the world, Mr. Strozzini," I said, and with a flurry of movement he left, which shocked the hell out of me, since I'd barely seen it. I ran over to the window he'd gone through and looked out, but I couldn't see anything. I really needed to start locking up after myself.

Deceptions

Chapter 5

I woke an hour before sunset. I wish I could say I slept well, but dreams of long-haired, imposing Italian men filled my night. I looked down at the bed and noticed my dreams had been disturbing enough for me to cut deep rivulets in the sheets and mattress with my talons. The FBI would probably be a little pissed when they got that bill. I knocked on the wall letting Thompson know I wasn't still sleeping and walked to my closet to get dressed.

Thompson wasn't happy after I told him about my post shower visitation. He wanted to be there when Strozzini came back, but I pulled a puppy dog maneuver with my eyes and got him to concede to let me meet with him alone. I knew absolutely nothing about the stranger in my room last night except his name. I don't know why, but I figured bringing a werelion on our first date would piss him off.

After getting my gun and jacket on, someone knocked on my door. I took a deep, unnecessary breath and made my way to the door. I peered through the peephole and saw Thompson standing there holding a newspaper. I smiled and turned the handle letting him in.

"You made the paper again," he said, and tossed the Sacramento Bee into my hands. I took in the picture of me going into the limo head first with several silver stakes jutting from my back with grace. The headline read, "Close Call for Governor." I read the article quickly and gave a little inward smile at the "heroic FBI agent who saved the governor" part and frowned at the "second attempt on his life" part. The rest of the article contained a brief history of Greer's political career and fight to become governor as well as the reporter's theories as to who had been behind the attempts on his life. The fact that Greer used to be the mayor of San Francisco surprised me. I felt a little miffed that he left that part out of our conversation last night.

"At least they didn't call me his girlfriend," I said nonchalantly to Thompson, and tossed the paper back to him.

"That would've been more like your luck lately. The press loves you," he said with his usual chortle. "What time is your guest coming?"

"Anytime now. You better get out of here," I said as politely as I could.

"Do I need to tell you to be careful and how much I don't like this?"

I laughed. "No, Thompson, I'll be a good girl. I promise."

He just nodded and stood to leave. "I'll be keeping an eye on the governor while you're entertaining. Call me when you're done, and I'll let you know where I am. I had the office drop off another car. Connors wasn't too happy about it, but he'll get over it. I don't think he likes us very much."

"I don't think it's you or me, I think it's vampires in general. If anything interesting happens text me or call," I said, and ushered him out the door. Once I had it fully closed, I leaned back against it for a moment. I wasn't afraid of Strozzini; I feared what he wanted to talk about.

I busied myself straightening the room. I wrapped the garbage bag containing my blood-soaked clothes and left it tied in the can. I don't know why, but I made the bed and covered up the rip marks with the thick comforter. Once they changed the linens they'd see the damage, but I didn't want my guest to get the wrong impression.

Just as I finished, a single knock sounded from the door. I sighed and peered through the peephole. Strozzini stood in the hallway. I debated not opening it and pretending I wasn't there, but he smiled at me from the other side of the door. I rolled my eyes, turned the handle, and stood aside.

Without so much as a by your leave he strode into the room as if he owned the place. I laughed to myself, for all I knew he did. I wanted some answers from my new friend. He walked to the little desk table, sat and crossed his legs. He motioned for me to close the door and join him. I glanced down the hallway then locked the door before joining Strozzini.

"What can I do for you, Mr. Strozzini?" Impatient didn't begin to describe my mood as I pulled out the heavy chair and sat.

"Please, child, call me Antonio."

"Only if you call me Ashlyn, Antonio." I smiled. The "child" thing was getting a little annoying. I didn't mind when Darenthalis, my elven instructor at Quantico called me that, but this guy made it sound a little condescending.

"Very well, Ashlyn. I have one question to start, and I beg, answer me true. When did you become a vampire?" He leaned forward, resting his elbows on the table, and stared intently at my face. I avoided his eyes, closed mine, and thought very hard on how I wanted to answer him.

I decided to stick as close to the truth as possible and tried to say, "Eighteen years ago." That was not what came out of my mouth. I heard myself say, "I've always been a vampire."

"How many years have you been this way?" Antonio continued as if it were the answer he expected.

"Eighteen years." Again the truth to his question flowed freely from my mouth before I could edit my response. "How did you survive a silver stake through your heart?"

"Silver doesn't bother me like normal vampires," I said, and froze. This had gone on long enough. I clenched my fists and my talons pierced the palms of my hands. The pain felt refreshing, almost clearing the fog that had settled in my mind. I looked up from the table and met the man's gaze.

The room fell away. We hovered a few feet apart over two vast oceans that surged and flowed against each other. Mine rolled like a stormy sea, while Antonio's surged forward, pushing against mine with incredible force. Our bodies became illuminated from within, and I spoke.

"Why are you doing this to me?"

"You intrigued me last night with your bravado and unbelievable strength. I simply needed to know the truth."

"What do you plan on doing with the information? Why do you care?"

"I don't think I'll be sharing that information with you right now, little one. You have much to learn." He smiled. His waters churned and began forcing the tide of mine back. I snarled and willed my ocean to push back, almost like a liquid game of tug of war.

His look of superiority vanished, replaced by surprise. He strained under the onslaught of my waters and redoubled his efforts, as did I. His tide fought against mine and then suddenly receded as mine pushed his forward. He gave an anguished cry, and the light illuminating him from within flared.

I came to in my hotel room, quite alone. I lay sprawled on the carpet next to the chair I'd been sitting on. Both it and the one Antonio had occupied, lay tipped over, so at least I knew he'd suffered as much as I had. I glanced around for any traces of him, but he'd apparently woken before me and fled. He could have at least left a note. *How rude!* Next time I saw him I'd have to shoot him. I owed him at least that much for the pain in my head he'd left me with. I got up off the floor and pulled out my cell phone, dialing Thompson without so much as a thought. Thinking hurt way too much. I would have to avoid it for at least the next day or so.

"Are you done, kid?"

"You could say that. Where are you?" My question came out through clenched teeth, my own voice reverberating through my head.

"Governor Greer is about to give a press conference about the incident last night. Why don't you come down to the mansion? I don't think the people trying to kill him will try again here, but you never know."

"I'll be right there."

I strode up to Thompson while he stood behind Greer who was still wrapping things up with the reporters. Walking out onto the stage had been a huge error on my part. The press stood and started shouting questions beginning with, "Agent Ashlyn," all at once. Before I left the hotel I opened my mini-fridge and downed a couple pouches of lycanthrope type A I kept stashed for emergencies. I'd started to feel better until the questions started.

I held up my hand and walked to the podium, which Governor Greer reluctantly relinquished to me. I fought the urge to rub my face and bent the microphone down to something more suited to my height.

"Ladies and Gentlemen, this is Governor Greer's press conference and I'm sure he answered any and all questions you could possibly have about last night's incident. Thank you," I said, and turned around. I expected them to be satisfied. Silly me.

"Agent Ashlyn, how did you survive being shot with silver multiple times," one reporter shouted as soon as I turned around. I ignored him and let Greer handle it.

"As I said earlier, Jim, the stakes weren't made out of silver, they were steel and meant as a warning." He fielded the question expertly. I found myself impressed with Greer's lie. I wouldn't have thought of that one.

He answered ten more questions, all about me of course. With each question, I felt a little more comfortable. Next time I found myself at a press conference, I'd have to give him a call. Some people were meant to be in front of the camera; I wasn't.

Greer ended their questions and walked off the stage. Thompson and I followed him, grateful for the end of the ordeal. I didn't like being in the spotlight, and Thompson had a natural aversion to anything that might get us in trouble. We wound our way through the bowels of the mansion and ended up in the study where we'd first met the governor. Without waiting for an invitation, I sat in one of the comfortable leather chairs.

"Won't you sit down?" The sarcasm practically dripped from his voice.

"Thank you, Governor. I've had a rough evening." "What happened?" I smiled at the concern Thompson showed.

"Antonio and I ran into a little mental impasse." I filled him in, forgetting the governor had vampiric hearing too.

"Who?"

"A vampire named Antonio Strozzini. Do you know him, Governor?" I watched his face go from pale to about three shades shy of translucent.

"Could you repeat the name?" I knew he'd heard me, but I repeated it anyway. "This isn't possible, why would The Council be here?"

"Isn't the council made up of local masters of various cities? I thought they didn't get involved." I waited for a response. Greer sat down, gripping the arms of the chair like he wanted to extract several gallons of juice from it.

"Not the North American Council, *the* Council," he said, like it clarified everything and emphasizing the word meant something to me.

"Let's pretend I don't know what you're talking about, Governor." I lowered my eyelids halfway, suspiciously.

"Marcel never told you about The Council? I figured he would since he was once one of their enforcers."

"No. After my making, he pretty much left me on my own. I'll have to give him a call," I said, and meant it. "What do you know about it?"

"I have broken enough of their laws, and if they wanted you to know, I'm sure Strozzini would have told you," he said and waved his hand dismissively.

"He didn't get a chance; he kept forcing answers as to why I lived through having a silver stake through my heart. It ticked me off, so I rolled his mind."

"You what," Thompson and Greer said simultaneously. "He kept trying to force truths from me, so I turned the tables and started asking him questions." Greer became pale enough that I worried for his health. "Are you okay, Governor?"

"Is she serious?" He asked the question without even looking at Thompson.

"I'm afraid so, Governor. Ashlyn has a very straightforward way about her, and unfortunately, her power doesn't match her experience. I've often likened it to an infant holding a fully loaded forty-five," he replied.

"I'm an infant now?" I looked at him and could feel my talons piercing the skin of my palms, but his comment stung a little.

"No, but you're young and powerful enough to scare me sometimes, kid," he said earnestly.

It made me feel a little better.

"I could see The Council checking up on me, I have taken an office in direct authority over humans, but I didn't think they would care. It's just a governorship. Their edicts clearly state, 'no title of monarch may be assumed by our kind,' but I won the election. Californians elected me as governor. That's a huge difference."

"Is it? Could it be The Council trying to kill you, Governor?"

He paled further at my questions, but seemed to assure himself. "They probably have come to question me or at least make sure the vampire community is comfortable with the idea. If they wanted me dead, it wouldn't be with car bombs and snuffers."

"Snuffers?"

"The guns that shoot the silver stakes," Thomson supplied.

"Agent Ashlyn, right at this moment, I'm more afraid

for *you* than I am with their concerns for me. You are obviously an anomaly, and the bad part is now you have come up on The Council's radar, so to speak. Be careful, and if I were you, I would hide. Go back to Chicago and spend some time with Marcel. If anyone can protect you it would be him."

"Unfortunately, Governor Greer, I took an oath to the FBI. My job is here, and I can't hide from anybody. Plus, I'm just not that type of person," I added and watched him nod resignedly

"I had a feeling you were going to say that," Greer said just above a whisper.

Chapter 6

The governor had a charity benefit to get to. I tried to talk him into riding in the Suburban instead of the dented limo, but he told me he'd already had it replaced. I sighed and resignedly sat in the back with him while Thompson drove. I half expected Greer to be afraid of me and sit as far away as possible, but it appeared he'd put last night's events out of his mind. I wished I could do the same.

Thompson put the glass partition up, which struck me as unusual, but I figured he wanted to be reminded of last night even less than I did. I doubted he'd called Marion, his wife, and told her about it. I felt horrible and resolved never to feed from him again, even if it meant the difference between life and death.

We pulled up to one of the many homeless shelters scattered through the Sacramento area. The governor would be ladling soup to wealthy individuals for the low price of five hundred dollars a bowl to support the growing needs of the shelter. I couldn't eat it, but I had a check already filled out for a donation. I knew what it meant to go hungry.

I opened the door, stepping out in front of the governor. I really hoped not to get shot tonight. I hated clothes shopping. We walked to the kitchen while Thompson parked the limo. I expected the shelter to have a particular smell, but bleach prevailed. I guess they'd scrubbed it in honor of the governor.

Rows and rows of tables occupied every square inch of the dining area, which separated it from the bedrooms. The kitchen was enormous as well. Huge kettles stood against the wall and people stirred soup and stews with what looked like small boat oars. The shelter obviously housed more people than I'd imagined. The governor met with the aides who'd organized the whole shebang and started discussing the events of the evening. I stood guard.

The whole ordeal with the governor and Strozzini put me on edge. It's hard to describe, but fear doesn't really come in to play. I honestly just dreaded anything coming in the future. I've just started my life and I already have to constantly worry about doing my job competently. Now I have this whole other world I want nothing to do with threatening to disrupt it. I wonder if they'd accept that I wanted nothing to do with them. Maybe pigs will sprout wings.

"I called Marcel," Thompson said from behind me. I didn't jump, but he scared the hell out of me. I really needed to shake myself out of the mental hole I'd dug myself into. *Concentrate on the moment.*

"What did he say?"

"He'll be here before sunrise."

"Oh, really?" I could barely keep the surprise from registering in my voice.

"Yeah, he seemed very concerned. No offense, but I'm getting kind of tired of all the vampire crap," he said with a grin to soften the blow.

"Me too, big guy. Me too." I fought the urge to cry.

I guess the bad guys took the night off because the charity event went without a hitch. Well, at least without an assassination attempt. I guess the events of the previous evening turned away a lot of potential donors who wanted to spend five hundred dollars for soup. Guilt gnawed at my insides and ended up writing a check for five thousand dollars. The governor raised his eyebrows when I handed him my check. All in all, the entire benefit raised ten. The event made the eleven o'clock news as a flop. "Danger keeps charity goers away." Reporters suck.

We left the governor tucked away safely in his mansion and went back to the hotel. Thompson had told me Marcel would arrive before sunrise, but I hadn't expected him to be waiting for us in the lobby. I held my breath when I saw him. It had been a while since I'd last seen him, and the memory of my time spent with him came rushing back However, I did resist the urge to fling myself into his arms. I hated how the whole situation made me feel, but damned if I'd let anybody else know it.

"Hello, Ashlyn, got yourself in a bit of trouble again I see," he said without any hint of smile.

I looked at his face and found absolutely no comfort there.

"Hey, Marc. Just exactly how much trouble am I in?" "Let's talk upstairs," Thompson said, and got our attention by pointing to the corner of the lobby. I looked around and saw a few people at the desk checking in, but behind them, almost out of view, stood Strozzini. He made no motion to move toward us, but his gaze focused on me intently.

Enough was enough. I scowled and turned toward my vampire stalker, but before I could walk over to tell him to leave me the fuck alone, Marc firmly grasped my arm and directed me to the elevator. Part of me wanted to protest, but the frightened child in me won the argument. We rode the elevator in silence. I hadn't wanted to, but when I opened my mouth to speak Marcel held up his hand for silence. We also passed our floor.

The elevator opened two floors above, and then sneaky Marc led us up another flight of stairs. He probably thought Strozzini stood on the first floor watching the electronic floor display by the elevator door. He should get a job with the FBI.

We walked down the hall to the last room on the right, and Marc reached into his jacket pocket and produced a key card. He slid it into the locking mechanism and the light above the handle blinked green. He opened the door and ushered us inside while watching down the hallway for any movement. I gasped when I walked into the room. It spanned twice the size of my single room, had several private sitting areas, and a sliding glass door leading out to a balcony. We had to be on the top floor of the hotel. I felt a little jealous at the luxuriousness of the room. I made my way over to a comfortable looking chair and sat down.

"What are you doing?" Marcel stood staring at me peculiarly.

"Sitting," I said more than a little confused.

"You have so much to learn and so little time. James, explain to the little one exactly what Antonio is doing right now."

"Enrapturing the mind of the hotel clerk and finding out which room the tall handsome blond vampire checked into," he said confidently.

"*Exactement*," he said, and unlocked the sliding glass door leading out to the balcony.

I glanced at Thompson, who motioned me to follow Marcel. I stood and followed him to the balcony while Marcel stood looking over the railing down to the ground. "Come on," he said, and slid over the railing like a parallel bar Olympian and fell eight stories to the ground.

"Show off," I muttered, and did the same. The air rushed up against me as I fell. I willed myself to slow at the last moment and crouched into a perfect landing about three feet from Marcel. I looked up to see if Thompson made the jump when six hundred pounds of dark werelion landed behind us. I guess eight stories seemed a little too far to jump in his human form.

"Let us go. It won't take Antonio long to figure out my ruse. My hotel is about four blocks away," he said, and took off at inhuman speed. I ran behind him and sensed Thompson close on my heels. In his werelion form, he had no problems keeping up with me, and I wouldn't have put any money on a race between us.

It took us only a few minutes to reach our destination. The Marriot we were staying at wasn't a cheap hotel. It was beautifully maintained, but the Hyatt Regency we stood in front of made me raise my eyebrows more than a little. We entered the lobby through the front doors under a concrete awning and didn't pause as we made straight for the elevators. Again Marcel punched the uppermost button, the doors closed, and the elevator began to hum as it lifted us into the air.

I couldn't remember getting off the elevator as we walked into his room. I really needed to start paying attention. I glanced around at our surroundings and my feeling of jealousy over his other room tripled. It still had a sliding glass door, but this one had been designed with vampires in mind. Instead of clear glass panes, the doors were made of opaque black glass. It was the only exterior window or door in the room. I got nosey and wandered from one bedroom door to the next, peeking in. Each had its own king size bed and bath. The rest of the suite looked just as luxurious. Comfortable couches, plasma televisions, and a large desk filled the spacious common area. I wanted to kill Marcel and live in his room for the rest of my life.

Marcel sat on one of the couches, leaned back, and closed his eyes. I doubted the run exhausted him, so he must have been thinking. I bet I could guess what about. "Thanks, Marc." I walked over to him and placed my hand on his shoulder.

"You certainly do make life interesting, little one." He smiled for the first time since his arrival.

"So what now? Do we just continue to hide until he goes away?"

"No, child, to do that would just invite the rest of The Council to hunt for you. No, we will meet him, but on our terms, and only after we have come up with a plausible explanation for your abilities." He sounded weary. "But for now, sunrise is almost here. James, take the spare bedroom. Ashlyn, please help yourself to the master bedroom."

"Where are you going to sleep?"

"Right here. I have stayed in the Regency before. Their

rooms are quite sun-proof."

"Don't be silly, Marc. There's a king size bed, big enough for the two of us," I said, trying very hard not to sound like a schoolgirl. I must have failed miserably because he opened his mouth to protest. "I insist, I don't mind sleeping in my clothes," I added.

He paused before giving me a, "*Oui*."

"In the morning, I'm going to run back to our hotel and pick up one of the Suburbans and some clothes. I shredded my shirt and pants shifting," Thompson said from across the room.

I glanced over at him, and sure enough, his pants were tattered from the knee down and his shirt probably lay shredded on the hotel room floor back at the Marriot. Hopefully, he had the foresight to take off his jacket first.

"Be careful. He might have day-friendly entities watching your room," Marcel said and stood.

"I will, Marc, go get some sleep, and thanks from me, too."

"Good day, my friend," he said, and made his way to our room. *Our room. Damn I liked the sound of that.* "Night, Thompson," I called, and followed the exquisite French buns in front of me.

"Night, kid."

I entered the bedroom, watching Marc strip off his shirt and settle himself on top of the comforter. As an afterthought, he kicked off his shoes and let them fall to the floor. He brought one arm up and covered his eyes while I flipped off the switch plunging the room into complete darkness. I could see perfectly in the dark, but honestly didn't have a clue if he could or not. I took off my jacket, lay it on the dresser, and kicked off my shoes. I had on pretty modest panties and a sports bra, but I promised Marc I would remain clothed, damn it.

I gave a little sigh and crawled onto the massive bed. The mattress seemed a little softer than I thought possible, and I sank in. I debated getting up and crawling under the comforter just to make Marcel a little more comfortable, but I really didn't care.

"Marc," I started tentatively.

"Yes, little one?"

"What's going on? Why is Antonio so interested in me?"

"That is a story too long in the telling for now. When we wake, I will tell you everything. I promise." He closed his eyes.

I sighed and did the same.

I woke with my head on Marcel's chest. He hadn't moved, but I covered him like a small blanket. I gently lifted my leg to try to remove it from his, but he shifted and smiled. His arm wrapped my shoulders and he drew me against him tighter. Chills traveled from the base of my spine all the way up and over my skull, sort of melting themselves away into my brain. I let out a little moan and rubbed my face against his chest. His arm tightened, beckoning me even closer.

The butterflies in my stomach started to form a little whirlwind as I slid over his leg, lying completely on top of him. His hand slid down and cupped the right side of my butt, pulling me up into his embrace. I couldn't reach his face with mine, but he planted little kisses on the top of my head. I brought my hand up over his chest and began to gently lick his firm flesh. I won't lie, it would be my first time, and I wanted it to last forever. I felt stirrings in familiar places as my little licks elicited a moan from Marcel's lips.

"Oh, Sophie," he moaned.

I froze. Resisting the urge to bring my knee up hard enough to drive his male parts into his stomach, I leaped off him onto the floor. "Stupid French pig," I muttered as I stormed to the door, grabbing my jacket as I opened it to leave.

"Ashlyn," Marcel called confusedly. I debated ignoring him, but I guess the whole thing had been my fault. I rolled over on him; I started licking. It wasn't his fault he was dreaming.

"Yes, Marcel?"

"I am sorry." He sounded contrite.

"It's not your fault. I woke up mid dream, too. I'm the one who should be apologizing. It won't happen again." I walked out of the room, pulling the door shut behind me.

Chapter 7

Thompson was dressed in a suit when I walked out of the bedroom. I assumed he'd picked us up a car and some clothes sometime during the daylight hours. He had the news on and sat on the couch parked in front of the television, holding a carton of Chinese food in his hand. Damn, it smelled good.

"Morning, kid. Is everything okay?"

"Peachy keen," I replied.

"Do I have to punch Marc in the face?"

"No, but you might want to smack me around a little." He laughed and resumed devouring his food. I heard the shower running so I assumed Marc wanted to clean up a little.

"Did you bring me any clothes?"

"Your suitcase is over on the other couch," he called back.

"Thanks," I said, and meant it. I slept in my clothes and they suffered for it. "I'm going to use your bathroom," I said, not waiting for a response.

Once I'd changed, I met both of them back in the sitting room. They were seated and looked like they had already been talking. Thompson had a huge frown etched into his granite features. They both turned to me as I walked toward them, making me more than a little self- conscious.

"What?"

"Field trip," Thompson supplied. "Governor Greer just called; he's heading to San Diego in an hour. An earthquake hit this morning and he needs to assess the damage. Pack your stuff; we're flying down with him."

"That's a good thing, isn't it?" If we were leaving Sacramento, then surely Strozzini wouldn't be able to find us.

"It would be if Strozzini hadn't made contact with Greer and introduced himself as part of The Council. He's going to be Greer's shadow, too. He's to determine if by assuming the office of governor, Greer has not broken any Council laws. We need to come up with a cover story, little one, and fast. One strong enough to explain your anomalies to Strozzini so he won't run back to The Council to report what he's found. At this point, I'm open to suggestions." Marcel spoke exasperatedly and ended with a little shrug of his shoulders.

"I told Greer you sired me. Could we stick to that?"

"If I had talons and slit pupils, maybe. I don't think Strozzini would believe it though."

"What if we told them the truth?" We both looked at Thompson.

"Absolutely not, my friend. To tell them she has always been a vampire would be akin to telling the government she landed here from another planet. They would dissect her to see how she worked. We need something better."

"Could we bribe Strozzini?" It's not like I had enough to bribe him with, but I wanted to know.

"He is a creature of The Council, no we cannot."

"Could we kill him?" The question hung out there in the air; I just didn't realize it had come from me.

Let's hear it for self-preservation.

"I've already resolved to do that as a last resort," Marcel said deadpan. A chill ran along my spine for the second time in one evening. I liked the first one better.

"How about if we threaten him?" Thompson seemed to realize the futility of it as soon as the question left his lips.

What would keep him from telling us what we wanted to hear, and then blabbing about me once he touched down in Europe?

"Never mind," he finished.

"I wish we could just tell him I wasn't a vampire," I said, thinking aloud.

The silence in the room made me look up. Thompson and Marcel sat on the couches staring at each other with raised eyebrows. "We couldn't blame it on lycanthropy," Thompson said.

"But she had a mother, and she does work for the U.S. government. She could have been the result of a genetic experiment. She could be a cross breed of lycanthrope, vampire, and human. Ladies and gentlemen, we have our answer," Marcel said with a smile.

"Oh, joy. I get to be an experiment!"

We pulled up to the Governor's Mansion, and I fought hard not to start shaking. I wasn't afraid, or at least I didn't think I feared Strozzini, but I wanted nothing to do with The Council. I just wanted to be left alone in my own little world. I don't mind what I do for the FBI; it kind of offers a buffer between me and the vampire world. I'm an outsider keeping an eye on them; I don't want to be one of them.

"Remember, Ashlyn, stick to the story," Marcel said before he opened the door and stepped out into the night air.

"I'm a genetically engineered mutant. Got it," I said to myself, but Thompson must have heard me because he gave a rough bark of laughter.

I opened my door and followed them up the hewn granite steps to the front door. Before either of them could knock, the door opened and Samantha Barnes, Greer's personal assistant and aide, stood there waiting. Without so much as a hello, she led us up the stairs to Greer's office. I half expected her to take us to his study.

"Go ahead in, he's expecting you," she said, and left us. Thompson opened the door and went in first, leaving Marcel and me to follow. I couldn't see the governor or Strozzini until Thompson sidled out of the way. When he did move, I spotted Greer at his desk on the phone, and Strozzini standing behind him staring at Marcel. At first he looked surprised, but I recognized hatred when I saw it. I glanced to my right and saw the same look etched on Marcel's face. I coughed in an attempt to break the staring contest, and Marcel looked at me with a small smile.

The governor set the receiver into the cradle and stood to greet us. "Welcome back, agents. A helicopter is on its way and we should be in the air in about fifteen minutes. May I introduce Antonio Strozzini of The Council," Greer said with his usual charm.

"We've met," Strozzini and Marcel said in unison. "Marcel, it is very good to see you again," Greer greeted Marc.

"You as well, David. It has been a long time." Marcel replied but never took his eyes from Strozzini. "What brings you to California, Antonio?" Marc turned the focus of his conversation to the Italian vampire.

"The Council has concerns regarding David taking a position of authority over the human population. They sent me here to investigate when I came across the little treasure you've been hiding."

I'm a treasure? I tried not to laugh.

"A treasure indeed, Antonio, but be wary of her. She not only has her own protections, but also that of the United States government," Marcel informed the smug vampire.

"You will have to explain all of this to me, in great detail," Strozzini shot back.

"All in good time. Right now agents Ashlyn and Thompson have the governor to attend to," Marcel replied.

"Oh, this is a story I can't wait to hear," Greer Chimed in.

I'll have to say no to that, Governor." Thompson spoke for the first time. "Ashlyn is a puzzle wrapped in an enigma, and the U.S. government wants to keep it that way. We received special dispensation to share her secrets with The Council to keep them placated, but that's it. I'm sorry, Governor," he added almost as an afterthought.

The governor gave a sheepish nod, but Strozzini stared

at us with open disbelief. I would bet even money he wasn't going to buy Marcel's story. He opened his mouth to say something, when Marcel held up his hand indicating he should wait. He nodded and moved from his spot behind Greer.

"I do have to ask you something, Mr. Strozzini," I said. "You said you were here to make sure the governor's oath of office didn't break any of The Council's rules. You wouldn't know anything about the attempts on his life, would you?"

"No, I don't. I know a vampire used a gun that shoots the silver stakes, because I saw him on the rooftop of the building next to the hotel. I became so engrossed in watching you I didn't look for him until later. He fled, taking everything with him, so to answer your question, no, *il mio piccolo tesoro.*"

"Thank you," I said politely.

Vetters had been right. It seemed a vampire, or vampires, wanted Greer dead. I just needed to figure out why. I tried every plausible avenue I could come up with mentally and rejected each one. "Who would want to kill a vampire governor? We know it wasn't a human, so we can rule out any extremists who didn't vote for him. A vampire took the shot. A vampire wants him dead."

Thompson looked at me while I pondered aloud. "But why kill another vampire? Maybe it's not because he's governor," he added to my train of thought.

"Maybe it's because he's the master of Sacramento?" I tossed out there.

"I'm not the master of Sacramento. I'm the master of San Francisco," Greer spoke up.

Thompson looked at me and me at him. It couldn't be that simple. I knew from my studies that vampires were highly territorial, to say the least. If this boiled down to a turf war, I would be pissed. Either way, we had our first lead.

"Who is the master of Sacramento, Governor?"
"Ramon Santiago," he supplied.

"How does he feel about you being in his territory?"

Thompson continued the questioning.

"He's not happy about it, but he understands the necessity. We have a meeting scheduled next week. I offered to give him some sort of compensation for my being here. That seemed to make him happy."

"Maybe not happy enough, Governor. Where can I find him?"

"I can take you to him," Strozzini said, moving closer to where I stood. I really didn't want to have to spend any time with him or be indebted to him in anyway, but what the hell.

"Ashlyn, can I talk to you alone for a minute?"

I looked at Thompson and nodded. I made my way to the door. Thompson beat me there and opened it, giving me a scowl as I passed through. Once out in the hall, I spun to face him, but he walked past me to the stairwell. Apparently, he didn't want anybody to hear us. He stopped at the top of the landing and turned.

"I want you to go with the governor; I'll go with Marcel and Strozzini," he said, leaving little room for argument. Of course I did anyway.

"No." I shook my head.

"This isn't open for discussion. You're going with Greer."

"I would, if I weren't better suited to questioning the vampire suspect and you know it. Plus, I want to, actually let me rephrase that, I need to be there when Strozzini gets his explanation. I know my body better than anyone, and if he has questions, I'm sure I can come up with answers."

"Ashlyn, I want you to trust me on this."

"Thompson, I need you to trust *me* on this."

He paused to think about it, sighed, and nodded. I couldn't believe I won the argument. I was proud of myself, but didn't jump around like I wanted to. Instead, I closed the distance separating us and threw my arms around the mountain of man. "Thanks, old man," I said, and released him before he became uncomfortable.

Chapter 8

Marcel, Strozzini, and I stood by as the helicopter lifted off the ground carrying Thompson and Greer to San Diego. I didn't have a clue when they'd be back, but Thompson told me he'd call when they touched down. I just hope they stayed safe.

"Are you ready?" I didn't know if my question was meant for the two vampires standing next to me or myself.

They nodded and we walked to the Suburban. I pulled out the keys Thompson gave me and clicked the unlock button. The hazards flashed, and I opened the driver's door. Climbing in, I needed to scoot the seat forward all the way. I cursed being short as I started the ignition.

"We have time to talk before we get to Santiago. I want to hear your explanation," Strozzini muttered from the back seat before I even put it into reverse. I opened my mouth to tell him to go to hell, but Marcel beat me to it.

"Just remember, Antonio, what we are about to tell you is one of the largest secrets the US government has at the moment. To spread this information is to make yourself a target. You may give the gist of it to The Council, but I wouldn't go into detail. Please also remind them seeking to harm Ashlyn in any way would bring about retribution," he began solemnly.

"Is that a threat?"

"One does not threaten The Council. I am simply warning you. To touch Ashlyn would be considered damaging government property. They don't think of her as a person; she is their creation," he said, and paused to let the information sink in to Strozzini's head. It didn't take long.

"*Perdono?*"

"You heard me. Ashlyn isn't a vampire, or not entirely. They genetically engineered her to be as she is."

"Engineered, like Frankenstein's monster?"

"*Exactament*, they wanted a way to fight back against us, and she's it. They tried to make more, but have been completely unable to duplicate the results. She's one of a kind so far," Marcel said, and gave me a wink out of the eye Strozzini couldn't see from the back seat.

"I don't believe you, she's pure vampire. I felt her in my head."

"Show him your claws, little one," Marcel bade me.

I released the steering wheel with my right hand and reached behind me, exposing my talons to Antonio. He took a deep breath and tentatively reached out to touch one. I wanted to pull my hand back and clean it with something, but I let him explore their strength and sharpness.

"I still don't believe it. How did they do it?" For the first time I thought maybe we could pull this ruse off.

"They added vampire and lycanthrope DNA to a human embryo. I don't know the exact details, but it worked. The only problem is they can't reproduce the effect. Ashlyn is effectively a new type of being, both lycanthrope and vampire, and neither at the same time. That is why I warn you, if any harm comes to her the United States government will be very, very unhappy," Marcel finished.

"Would they permit The Council the opportunity to meet her? If I promise no harm will come to her?"

"I can't promise anything, but I will ask," Marcel told him.

I hoped he was joking.

"And what is your involvement in all of this anyway?" Strozzini asked, eyeing him suspiciously.

"Where do you think they got the vampire DNA?" Marcel lied smoothly.

"Pull in the parking area on your left," Strozzini called from the back seat. He'd been giving me directions for the past half hour while we made the drive from the Governor's Mansion to the downtown Sacramento area.

I did as he said and pulled in, finding a spot in the back. The sign by the road stood nearly thirty feet tall and illuminated the name, "Bare Fangs." I didn't get it. I assumed it had to be some sort of nightclub.

The name became clearer once we walked inside. Little leather chairs surrounded a raised platform complete with three brass poles. A statuesque vampire danced quite provocatively on the stage without a stitch of clothing. The meaning of "Bare Fangs" became quite evident.

"Welcome. There's a ten dollar cover for each of you," a large human-seeming bouncer said from the counter to our right.

"Agent Ashlyn with the FBI," I told the man. He didn't seem shocked when I flashed my badge. "We're here to see Ramon Santiago. Is he around?"

"Have a seat, he should be back shortly. I'll let him know you're here," he said, and motioned us through. I would've taken the closest set of chairs, but Strozzini walked down by the stage and sat at one of the smallish round tables right at the edge. I let out a sigh and followed him with Marcel right behind me.

I tried not to face the stage, but Marcel pulled out the chair closest to it for me to sit. I didn't want to be rude so I sat, trying to stare off into the distance. It became extremely difficult to do so when the blonde vampire ambled her way to where we sat. I caught her movement out of the corner of my eye and turned to look. I gasped as I saw everything the gods had given her just a few short feet away. I tried to turn away in embarrassment, but she squatted down right next to me, opening her legs and giving me a clearer view.

I couldn't look away. The smoky smell of the

club faded away, and I caught the scent of vanilla wafting from her skin, which happened to look like unfinished marble. I had the strongest urge to reach out and run my finger along the vein glowing just under the skin of one of her thighs. The vanilla smell became stronger until it filled my senses. I wanted to taste it. I could smell when a vampire or lycanthrope was afraid. I didn't know, until that moment, that I could smell desire. A low rumbling growl started in my throat as I stared at her thighs and what lie between. I've never wanted anything more.

She interrupted my view as she cupped herself and ran her hand along her sex, letting her fingers part her flesh. My gaze followed her hand as it ran up over her belly and then her breasts. She brought her fingers up to her mouth and sucked them in making a soft, slurping noise as she did. Her lips were painted red, a beautiful contrast to her pale skin and green-hued eyes. I caught myself licking my lips as she put on her little show. She smiled at me, stood, and turned around giving me a view of her buttocks before bending over and looking at me from between her legs.

I expected her to dance away, but our gazes met. I could feel the pull of her power drawing me in. I fought the pull and remained in the real world while the beautiful vampire licked her lips, making me want to taste her. She brought her lips together into a little O and blew a puff of air across her mound and into my face. Marcel's hand slid down my arm and over my wrist and he squeezed painfully, breaking me out of the trance I'd slipped into. I blinked my eyes several times as the girl vampire gave a throaty chuckle. She then stood up straight in a sensuous movement and continued her dance for the remainder of the patrons.

"Are you all right, little one?" Marcel placed his face perilously close to mine.

"I will be in a minute; could you please give me a little space?" I closed my eyes, trying very hard to get the dancers natural perfume from my mind. Strozzini, from the other side of the table, gave a little chuckle. I flipped him the bird, which turned his chuckle into laughter.

"She is quite beautiful. It's okay," Marcel said, and I held my hand up to him asking for silence. Reminding me of her beauty probably wasn't a good idea right now.

"He's here," Strozzini said, nodding at a darker skinned vampire who walked in. I looked up as the bouncer who'd told us to sit mouthed something to Santiago and pointed to us. He nodded and strode through the club to our table.

"I'm Ramon Santiago. You are looking for me," the vampire said in a deep voice when he got close enough for us to make out his words. Even with vampiric hearing, the music levels made casual conversation next to impossible.

I stood and held out my hand to Ramon and he readily took it. "Do you have someplace we can talk?"

He nodded and motioned us to follow him. He deftly led the way through the sea of tables toward the rear of the club. We went up another raised dais that held a multitude of leather couches and large upholstered chairs. I glanced around and noticed several more vampire strippers giving private dances. One difference stood out from every other vampire club I had ever been to. Usually humans congregated there to feed the vampire patrons, but at Bare Fangs, the patrons fed the employees. I watched as naked and near naked vampires ground themselves against the laps of the male–and one female–patrons while feeding. Moans from the customers filled the room and it drove my previous state of arousal up another notch.

We passed through another door Ramon had to unlock. I assumed we were at his private office. He pulled the door open and ushered us in and we stepped into old California. Frescos of Mexican villas and pueblos adorned every wall. Red clay tiles lined the floor. Even the ceiling looked like clay roof tiles. I ran my finger along the wall expecting textured dry wall, but Ramon had spared little expense and used real stucco to complete the effect.

"What can I do for you folks?" His voice seemed much more pleasant without the blaring hard rock music prevalent throughout the club.

"I'm Agent Ashlyn, FBI," I said, and produced my credentials for him to look at. He declined, so he must have believed me.

"I saw you on television; I know who you are, agent. What can I do for you?"

"I'm sure you know Governor Greer. Do you know who's trying to kill him?" I tried my best to make him think I suspected him.

"Yeah, I saw that on the news, too. I have no idea," he said calmly. "I have no beef with him. He encroached on my territory, but he offered me compensation."

"What sort of compensation."

"I don't know yet. We have a meeting to discuss that next week. Agent, I don't mean to be rude, but I have a lot to do. Is there any way we can speed this up?"

"Make him tell you the truth, *il mio piccolo tesoro*," Strozzini chimed in from behind me.

Ramon seemed to notice him for the first time and frowned.

"Who are you? I only know of one vampire who works for the FBI. She has dispensation to be in my territory, you two do not."

"I am sorry," Strozzini said in a sarcastic voice. "I forgot to introduce myself. Antonio Strozzini at your service."

As soon as he said it, Ramon stood from behind his desk and bowed low to Strozzini. "It is I who am sorry, enforcer. I had no idea The Council had sent an envoy. My territory is yours."

I stared open mouthed at both of them. Marcel reached over and pushed my chin up, effectively closing my mouth. When I looked at him, he gave me a little wink. I had so much to learn about the vampire world.

"It is quite all right. I am not here for you. I am here for…other reasons. Are you sure you have no idea who tried to kill the governor?"

"You have my word, enforcer," he said, and bowed again.

"He had nothing to do with it," Strozzini said to me as he turned.

I remembered the first time he questioned me. I had been compelled to speak only the truth. I so wanted to learn how to do that.

"Thank you, Mr. Santiago, I appreciate your honesty," I said both sarcastically and emphatically, a fact not wasted on Marcel who gave a short chirp of laughter.

"Please, won't you all stay and be my guests?"

It was a little hard to say no, but I didn't trust myself in the strip club either. I hadn't eaten for two nights and the chances of me trying to satisfy my hunger with one of the naked dancers seemed pretty high. "I'm sorry, Mr. Santiago, I'm afraid I'm going to have to pass. I have more work to do, and I must feed. I thank you for your cooperation and your hospitality," I said, and reached out to shake his hand.

"You cannot thank me for my hospitality, agent, until you accept it. Please, I insist on you all staying as my guests this evening," Ramon said, and closed his eyes.

"It would be our honor, Master Santiago," Strozzini and Marcel said in unison. It came out like a well-rehearsed response that I didn't get. I turned to Marcel and he glanced from me back to Santiago like he wanted me to do something. He mouthed the exact words he and Strozzini said and gave a small flick of his finger to point at me.

"It would be my honor, Master Santiago," I said, trying not to make it a question.

Marcel gave an almost imperceptible nod from his spot to my right. I knew I responded appropriately. Santiago opened his eyes and smiled at me. "It is the honor of the host to provide for his guests," he said, and Marcel and Strozzini bowed low. I did the same.

The door to Santiago's office opened and a tall vampire walked in. He stood well over six feet and a spidery air clung to him like a shadow. Long spindly legs propelled him across the room to the master's side. "Yes, my master?" The man bowed and stayed in that position.

"Raul, we have honored guests. Tonight we shall have a feast in their honor. Please make it so," Santiago told the gangly man. He stood and I could see the excitement in his eyes. I had a bad feeling about it.

Deceptions

Chapter 9

The spacious underground room looked as if it had been hewn from the rock by hand. Score mark, upon score mark marred the granite walls not leaving a smooth surface anywhere. I marveled at the difference between the room in which we sat and the expertly crafted hidden entrance we were led through to enter the vast catacomb-like area beneath Santiago's club. Gone were the sounds of the club, replaced by the subtler sounds of acoustic Spanish guitar in the background.

A wooden table, easily forty feet long sat squarely in the center of the cavern. Wrought iron candle chandeliers hung from the stone ceiling over different segments of the table, as well as candles in wall sconces illuminated the room and casting flickering shadows everywhere. The effect seemed positively medieval. I liked it. I doubted I'd be decorating an apartment in D.C. like it anytime soon, but I liked it.

"Please, make yourself at home, the master will be joining you shortly," Raul said and gave a curt bow, leaving us to explore the room. I wandered to the far wall and sat down on a mahogany colored leather couch. Marcel and Strozzini did the same.

"I apologize for the wordplay in Santiago's office, Ashlyn. There is so much you need to learn about being a vampire," Marcel said, and sat next to me, leaving Strozzini to either sit somewhere else or continue standing. "When the master of the city offers you hospitality, you are under obligation to accept. It is one of our oldest laws," he continued, and Strozzini nodded as he stood a few feet away from us.

"He could have taken offense, but I think he is a little confused as to your office," Strozzini said. "Remember the words we spoke, for it is almost a ritualistic response, the same for Santiago's acknowledgement of our gratitude."

"Well at least I don't have to remember Santiago's response. I have no inclination to ever be master of any city," I said with distaste, earning me a short burst of laughter from Strozzini, but not Marcel.

"Take care when you speak out loud so the fates may overhear, *il mio piccolo tesoro*. Sometimes the fates take great pleasure in heaping on you that what you wish for least," Strozzini said with a sad smile. It sounded as if he spoke from experience.

"What does *il mio piccolo tesoro* mean?"

"My little treasure," he replied offhandedly, like he had more serious thoughts running through his head.

Santiago chose that moment to enter the dining hall. I hadn't even imagined vampires gathered for meals. I did however have a feeling of what would be on the menu. I just didn't know how I would get away with not partaking in the feast.

"I hope you are all comfortable. The others should be joining us shortly," Santiago said, and as if on cue, one by one, came the rest of his entourage. They took their seats around the table and left spaces at the head for Santiago and us. The men talked animatedly about the state of affairs of the Sacramento vampires, and I listened disinterestedly as the vampires filled the spaces around the table. Most of them seemed comprised of the workers from the club upstairs. My suspicions were confirmed when the tall blond dancer who'd captured my attention onstage sat in one of the seats closest to where we would be sitting. I'd just have to make sure I sat on the opposite side of the table from her.

"It is time," Santiago said, and raised his arms. He walked us over to the table and pulled the seat out by the blonde exotic dancer, staring at me expectantly.

Well, crap. "Thank you, Mr. Santiago," I said.

"Ramon, please, Agent Ashlyn. We are all friends

here," he replied, bowing his head.

I smiled and took my seat with Marcel sitting on my left. Santiago sat at the head of the table with Strozzini taking the seat opposite Marcel. I gave a shy smile to the beautiful vampire sitting next to me and blushed. When she entered the room, I thought she'd dressed herself in a silk dress of the darkest green I had ever seen. Her modesty impressed me. Sitting next to her, I saw my mistake. While the gossamer gown looked modest from a distance, from a foot away with the light of the overhead candles radiating on it, I realized it didn't hide anything. It looked like it'd been spun from spider webs and then dyed green. I could see every slope and curve of her breast and every ridge and bump of her nipple. I didn't dare glance down to her slightly parted thighs. I began to doubt if this evening would ever end.

"May I introduce myself, mistress?" The sultry dancer's timid English accent came from somewhere very close to my ear. I hoped she didn't hear my audible gulp of air.

"Hi, I'm Ashlyn," I said formally, and held out my hand for her to shake. She didn't. She very gently took my hand, turned it knuckles up, and brought them to her lips. Her fingertips gently caressed the palm of my hand as she sensuously parted her lips and pulled my knuckle between them with just the slightest amount of suction. I gasped as her tongue darted out and gently lick the skin of my hand. I barely stifled the moan threatening to escape my throat before pulling my hand from her mouth.

"I'm Victoria," she said, not releasing my hand. Her skin felt cool in mine, and I sighed, trying to relax. I'd always dreamt of holding hands romantically for the first time, never having thought it would be with another woman. I stopped to think if it bothered me and realized it truly didn't. She might not be a guy, but I knew how looking at her made me feel. Giving her hand a tentative squeeze, she returned it. My smile waned just a tad when I thought how hard it would be not to make her my next meal. I definitely needed to start carrying a little extra lycanthrope blood in the back of my vehicles.

I glanced to my left and saw Santiago conversing with Strozzini about happenings with The Council. I looked at Marcel and expected him to be engrossed in the conversation as well, but he stared at my hand, in Victoria's, with a curious smile on his face. I gave him a little eyebrow raise, and his smile got a little bigger. He probably would have laughed, but Santiago stood and clapped his hands once. The sound echoed in the cavern like a gunshot.

"*Mi familia*," he began. "Tonight we have honored guests. Let us make them feel welcome into our home and shower them with our hospitality."

The vampires at the table with us gave a round of applause that seemed genuine. I guess they didn't get much company. Even Victoria released my hand to join in the applause. I quickly lifted my hand above the table before anyone besides Marcel noticed. I probably should have left it there. When she finished clapping she brought her hand back down and gingerly placed it on my thigh and gave me a private smile that brought a flush of blood up to my ears.

The round of applause must have been a cue for somebody to bring in dinner. A line of twenty wide-eyed and excited humans entered the room. This wasn't good. I assumed they were the patrons of the club upstairs brought down to feed the vampires, but a mix of males and females. I'd been one of the few females in the club not dancing, so they must have been brought in from somewhere else. Maybe one of Santiago's other businesses. Either way, the humans knew they'd been brought here to be dinner, and they liked it.

They spread out and fanned around us, stepping in between the seated vampires to sit on the table. Some disrobed as they sat, not exposing themselves completely, but rather exposing as much flesh as possible. A tallish man with short brown hair stepped in between Marcel and me and pulled off his shirt. I looked over as a short girl who looked like she'd just enrolled in college slipped between Victoria and the other woman vampire next to her. Well, at least I didn't have to share with Victoria. That should make faking it easier. I planned to just bite the human since I couldn't really drink his blood. I didn't want Santiago asking why I wasn't eating.

"Hi, I'm Steve," the man between Marcel and I said shyly. "Where would you like to bite?" He stared at me as he asked the question.

"I'm not picky, Steve, the wrist is fine," I answered, and watched as he brought his wrist up to my lips, looking to Marcel to see what his preference would be.

"The wrist is fine with me, too," he said nonchalantly, like he'd done this a million times before. Hell, for all I knew he had.

Marcel took Steve's wrist into his mouth and bit down. He glanced at me out of the corner of his eye and made a motion toward the wrist in front of me. I tried not to laugh as "Daddy" told me to eat my dinner. He knew I couldn't really, but to not fake it would be rude.

I pierced his flesh and heard his intake of breath. I thought I might have hurt him, until I saw his face. He stared at me with utter ecstasy etched upon every inch of his face. His body went rigid and his breath came in shallow gasps, like he'd started hyperventilating. I concentrated on not drawing the blood through the wounds I'd created. Even the small amount that got on my tongue had a numbing effect. The blood tasted lifeless and strange. I shuddered to think what would happen if I swallowed any.

When I felt like I'd pretended long enough, I pulled my fangs out quickly. I made sure to run my tongue over the wound and let the healing properties of my saliva close it. Steven immediately stopped his rapid breathing and looked at me with pleading eyes. "Please, don't stop," he begged, but I couldn't do it anymore. The taste of his blood didn't agree with me. Marcel redoubled his efforts and Steve closed his eyes in blissful ecstasy, getting me off the hook for now.

The sounds of the vampires feeding filled the room

along with moans of pleasure from the humans providing the meal. I felt oddly out of place sitting there, the only one not eating. I considered rejoining Marcel and pretending to feed from Steve again when my new friend Victoria released the thigh of the woman she had been feeding on with a soft pop. She gave the young girl a brief smile and a briefer pat on her leg and surprised me with a heartfelt, "Thank you."

I stared at the wound on the girl's leg and watched, waiting for it to close. It didn't. I kept staring at it, as if it meant something, when it dawned on me. Victoria wasn't a master vampire. I looked from the wound to her face and saw something I didn't expect, embarrassment. I gave her a quick smile and licked my finger before running it gently across the wound. My effort made the girl still being fed upon by the vampire on the other side of Victoria moan a little louder and spread her thighs apart. I glanced up at Victoria and she looked at me a little funny.

"What?"

"Your eyes," she said, and drew her face a little closer. "Your pupils are like a cat's, but why?"

"Honestly, it's too long to get into, but they've always been like that. I'm a little different in other ways, too." I held up my hand, not high enough for anybody else at the table to see, just enough for Victoria to give a little gasp. She reached up tentatively to touch them and stopped short as if to ask for my permission. I nodded and felt her cool skin touch mine as she grasped my hand and gingerly ran the fingers of her other hand over my talons.

"They're beautiful," she said, and I gave her a patronizing little smile. My talons were many things, but beautiful wasn't one of them. I appreciated her little lie though.

"How long have you been a vampire?" I saw her face darken as I asked. "I'm sorry," I said immediately, hoping I hadn't made a faux pas in vampire etiquette.

"No, it's okay. It'll be three years in May. I hated

London and thought San Francisco would be a nice change. I used all my savings to pay for the move and wanted to go to college, so I took a job at a club out there to pay for it. The club attracted a lot of vampires, and most of them were pretty nice, even the one who turned me. I didn't want this; I never wanted this. One night Sam offered to take me home. He hadn't been a vampire long and still kind of nerdish and gangly, but he seemed nice enough. I'd been fed upon a few times and liked it, so I asked him to come up for a drink." She paused as if relieving the night. "Sam couldn't control himself and severed my jugular. In a panic, he turned me. He saved my life, sort of."

I didn't realize it, but as she told her story, she moved a little closer and her face was only a few inches from mine. Her vanilla scent magnified several factors from her proximity. I closed the last few inches and whispered, "I'm sorry."

She turned her face until her lips brushed mine, and I saw reddish tears leaking from the corners of her eyes, staining her pale skin darker. A little jolt of electricity ran from my lips to places I'd rather not mention, just from that little innocent brush. I'd like to say she pressed her lips against mine, but I know in my heart it happened the other way around. I even removed my hands from hers and slid them over her sides and up her back, pulling her closer into my embrace.

My lips opened as she molded herself against me. Her tongue gently slid between my lips and over my fangs. She tasted so sweet. I needed to draw her in closer because I couldn't get enough. Her hands began to roam and ended up on the back of my neck, begging me not to let the kiss end. The entire room dropped away until Victoria and I sat alone at the monstrous table. She intensified the passion of her kiss as her tongue slid over the tip of my fang. The vanilla of her scent faded away and the taste of her blood filled every one of my senses.

The smell of her blood filled my nose. I reveled in the wetness and magic of it with my tongue the roar of her blood in my ears. Her blood became the sweetest drink I have ever experienced. A low growl started in my chest as I broke our kiss to have more. I licked a trail down her jaw and kissed along her neck until I could feel her artery beneath my lips. Vampires don't have a heartbeat, but I could feel the ebb and flow of her lifeblood pass through that fragile little tube. Before I knew it, my fangs pierced the flesh of her neck and my mouth filled with honey sweet nectar.

Victoria began moaning and writhing beneath me. Her arms tightened around me, pulling me even closer. When she realized the impossibility of it, she slid her hand down my chest and cupped my breast. The sensations drove me wild and I pulled her blood even faster into my mouth. Her strength flowed through me as it left her body. Then I reached the point I had with Cicero. I could either stop, or pull the last dregs of blood through the wound, and with it the magic that kept her alive, that made her a vampire. My body wanted her magic so badly I didn't think I *could* stop. Someone tried to pull me from Victoria, but I didn't care. Nobody else could keep me from my meal and I wasn't sure I could either.

With Cicero it had been very different. I wanted to end his life for killing my partner. I willingly sucked the life right from him, but the creature in my arms wasn't anything like him. She'd been nothing but sweet to me. I couldn't end her as I had him. I forced myself to stop drinking, pulled my fangs from her flesh, and licked the wound closed. Her hands had fallen from my neck and she didn't move. She nudged the collar of my suit jacket away with her mouth and gingerly licked my neck. I gasped at the sensations running through my body from that tiny lick. When she started suckling at my neck, my eyes started to flutter. When Victoria pierced the flesh of my neck with her fangs, I fell to the floor, with her cradled into my arms.

The pleasure began overloading my senses. A thousand tiny bursts of electricity sparked from my toes up to my face and everywhere in between. I didn't want it to stop, ever. Victoria's jaw worked as she sucked my blood into her body, and with each draw the fireworks exploding in my body started all over again. She pushed her leg in between mine and pressed against my mound, which only added to the sensations threatening to overwhelm me. No wonder humans lined up in droves for this.

I felt strength returning to Victoria as she pinned my arms against the cool stone floor. She continued feeding and brought her other leg in between mine, forcing them apart. She lay completely atop of me and started grinding against me, threatening to destroy my sanity. I couldn't take the pleasure anymore. I struggled and she released my arms, allowing me to wrap them around her and roll her onto her back with me on top.

"Victoria," I said softly. She made a moaning noise, so I at least knew she could hear me. "Victoria, stop." As soon as the command left my lips, her jaws froze. I leaned away from her, breaking the connection of her fangs with my neck and knelt over her. She raised her arms above her head and stretched like a cat, complete with tiny mewling noises. Victoria opened her eyes and looked up at me. She smiled.

"Amazing," she said, as I saw her focus on me coming back to reality.

I smiled back at her until I saw her pupils dilate completely, and then the sides close together, forming a tiny black slit in a sea of blue.

Deceptions

Chapter 10

I blinked and shook my head to confirm what I thought I saw. Sure enough, my eyes stared back at me from Victoria's face. "Well this wasn't in the manual," I muttered, and stood up, offering Victoria my hand. She took it, and I glanced down, looking at her fingers as she did. I sighed with relief when her normal looking fingernails briefly reflected the room's candle light, rather than showing dark talons like I had.

A soft cough from my left reminded me we weren't alone in the room. At least forty sets of eyes, both human and vampire, stared at us. I turned to Marcel and saw something dark in his, Strozzini looked angry, and Santiago looked incredulous. I tried to meet Marcel's gaze, but he shifted away focusing instead on Santiago and gauging his reaction.

"What?" I didn't get it. I expected someone to answer me, but no one did. A hushed silence fell over the room and nobody moved an inch. Santiago closed his eyes and tilted his head backward a fraction of an inch. He stood frozen for a moment, and then opened his eyes looking at Marcel.

"This is how you repay my hospitality? You come into my home and steal one of my people. Did you plan this all along?"

"Ramon, I assure you it wasn't our intention. I don't even think the child realizes what she has done. Look at her, she is completely confused." He held up his hand in my direction.

"What are you talking about?" I was just as confused as Marcel said.

Opening my mouth probably wasn't the wisest of ideas. Santiago bared his fangs, letting out an echoing hiss that left the rest of the guests rubbing their arms or holding their heads. I probably should have kept quiet, but Santiago pissed me off. *How can he be so angry over something I didn't even know I did?* I crouched a little and hissed back, narrowing my eyes.

"Fuck," Marcel turned to look at Santiago. In the split second it took him to turn, Santiago swung his arm fully into Marcel's chest, sending him flying off to the side. He lunged at me and had his hands around my throat faster than I had ever seen another vampire move.

The force of his attack knocked me back a few feet and sent Victoria to the ground. I brought my arms up in a two fisted attack, punching him squarely in both shoulders simultaneously. It freed his grip from my neck, but I felt where his nails ripped through my flesh. The remainder of Santiago's people attacked.

I took a blow to the back of my head and heard the crunch of wood. I spun and saw a male vampire holding a broken chair with a dumbfounded look on his face. In a flurry of movement, I grabbed the remaining leg of the chair from his hand and drove it through his neck in a spray of blood. His eyes rolled and he went down hard right on top of Victoria. She cursed and threw him off, jumping to her feet. I half expected her to attack, but she smiled and spun, putting her back toward me to fight off the vampires rushing us.

I turned to put my back against hers when Santiago caught me in the jaw with an uppercut. My head snapped back and something crunched in my neck. He'd broken my neck. I just hoped it healed fast enough for me to keep fighting. I tried to hold still for a moment, but Santiago had other ideas. His hand closed on my windpipe as he drew his other hand back to strike. I looked down and started to lift my head when Marcel tackled him from the side, driving him into the massive oak table we'd been feasting upon moments ago.

I gently lifted my head and it worked. Marcel had bought me the few precious seconds I needed. I rolled it from side to side and everything snapped back into place, as the gods had intended. Marcel had Santiago pinned, his hands crushing his neck as if he meant to rip it off the vampire's shoulders. Strozzini kicked Marcel in the face, freeing the master of Sacramento.

"This is her fight, Marcel. She committed the crime; she has to pay. You know the laws. If she lives, you need to teach them to her apparently." Strozzini spat contemptuously.

"There are too many," Marcel pleaded.

"Enough." Strozzini crossed his arms, finishing the argument.

I spared a glance behind me. Two of Santiago's vamps had Victoria held upright between them while two others pummeled her faster than she could heal the damage. The rest of them surged forward to subdue me. I knocked the first two away and gouged the third in the face before the others surrounded me. Once they did, I fought them off for a few minutes before they finally had my hands and arms pinned to the ground. I'd officially gotten my ass kicked.

I lay on my back when Santiago finally walked over and kicked me in the face. Victoria's curses turned to whimpers as her beating continued. I think her cries of pain hurt more than the kicks I received from Santiago. Victoria hadn't done anything wrong, and hell, I didn't even know what I'd done to deserve this, but after several minutes, the pain turned to anger as they lifted me off the ground and held me. I had a vampire on each arm and one had me in a headlock forcing me too look forward as Santiago leaned in and punched me right in the face.

My body trembled as my anger turned to hatred. A growl started deep in my chest, getting louder with every passing moment. I could feel my fangs grow longer, as well as a peculiar sensation in the tips of my fingers and toes. It had happened before when I fought the master of Chicago. When I became angry enough, my teeth and my talons extended themselves, and judging by Santiago's face, two small horns had sprouted from my forehead.

I leaned my head forward and then slammed it back against the face of the vampire who held me in the headlock. The satisfying crunch of bone filled the room, and the arm around my neck fell limply away. I let out a guttural scream that echoed off the walls as I bit into the shoulder of the vamp holding my right side. My fangs slid through his shoulder, and I bit down until my incisors hit his collarbone. With a quick jerk of my neck, the bone tore free, causing the vampire to scream in agony. I spit out the bone, along with a chunk of flesh and looked around. The vampire holding my other side had let go and backed up a few feet.

I considered letting him go, but my body had other ideas. I spun and brought my right arm down in a sweeping arc. My talons ripped out three quarters of his throat in a spray of blood that splashed the wall and floor like a gruesome piece of artwork.

None of the other vampires were attacking, so I focused on Santiago. He let out a snake-like hiss, and I returned it with a leonine roar. He charged, and I charged him right back. Our collision sounded like a train wreck. His fist connected with my face as I shoved my hand through his chest. From the strangled cry he let out, he felt the excruciating pain as I grabbed his heart and held it as my fist passed through his back. Without a second thought, I crushed the organ to a pulp and dropped it to the ground with a sickening thud.

I held my arm straight as his very dead body slid backward and off with a wet plop. He hit the ground and the room stopped moving. I turned and saw Victoria, expecting her to be a bloody mangled mess, but she stood whole between the two vampires who held her. She still had a good coating of blood on her, but her wounds had healed. She gave me a triumphant smile, and I realized something. I could feel her in my mind. I closed my eyes, and where she stood, I could see a small crimson glow. Now I understood what Santiago had meant. Victoria belonged to me, and no matter where she went, I would see her and feel her.

Glancing around the room, I felt the other sparks that belonged to Santiago's vampires. I'd killed him and released those tied to him as master of Sacramento. They stood there, free for the taking. It would be so easy to reach out and pluck those little sparks of power, making them my own. Unfortunately, I had no desire to be the master of any city. I gently pushed each one away with my mind, but the amount of them nearly overwhelmed me. I'd freed a lot of vampires with my actions. I briefly wondered what would happen to them, but at that moment, I didn't care.

The quiet sound of Victoria's bare feet as she crossed the room broke me from my mental state. I reached up to push away the stray hair that had fallen around my face and rubbed my fingers across my once again smooth forehead. My horns had receded. Thanks be to the gods. I would have had a hard time explaining them if they'd stuck like that. A mental image of me shopping in the Home Depot for a grinder crossed my mind and made me laugh.

Remembering Marcel and Strozzini, I looked around for them, but they were nowhere in sight. I had a bad feeling. As a matter of fact, there wasn't a human in sight either. None of the vampires made a move to go anywhere though.

"Did you see where Marcel and Strozzini went?"

"No, master, I didn't."

"Stay here, don't let anyone else leave," I took off as fast as I could back up the way we'd come.

I burst through the open hidden door and into the almost empty club above Santiago's lair. I found them on the dance floor, but they weren't dancing. Strozzini held two wicked curved silver blades and fought to hit Marcel with them. Marcel expertly blocked every strike with what looked like part of a stripper pole. "Fuck," I said quietly, and attacked.

He'd been too engrossed in his fight with Marcel to notice me attacking from behind. I jumped and landed on his back and did the only thing I could do. Reaching around, I latched on to his chest with my talons and bit him in the neck. His blood hit my tongue and I groaned. Immediately, he let his blades fall to the ground as the pleasure of my bite spread through his body. Marcel dropped his makeshift weapon and watched me as I fed.

"You need to make a decision, little one. He no longer believes the story we concocted. He ran away to get word to The Council about you. You can either let him go and deal with The Council, turn him like you did the other, or kill him" Marcel sighed resignedly.

The vampire fell limp in my arms. If I kept drinking I could take his spark, but I really didn't want another death on my conscience. What I did to Victoria, I would never do again. I had trouble enough taking care of myself. To be someone's master wasn't something I would ever want. I knew in my heart I'd have to deal with The Council sooner or later. Making my decision, I stopped drinking and let Strozzini fall from my grasp onto the dirty floor of the strip club.

"I won't kill him. Hell, I didn't want to have to kill Santiago," I said more to myself than to Marcel.

He nodded and drew me into a hug. I wrapped my arms around him as far as I could and he kissed the top of my head.

"You have so much to learn, and I'm running out of time to teach you. You keep fumbling through a world that has rules older than I, and you don't know the basest of laws. I will teach you, or find someone who can." He sighed into my hair, "It would have been much simpler if the FBI hadn't been so eager to use their new weapon."

I just tried not to cry.

"I'm sorry, Marcel. I promise to learn as fast as I can," I said earnestly.

"I know you will, *mon enfant*." He stepped away

from me. "Go collect your new second. Take my hotel key and wait for me there. I will find my own way. Should you talk to James, don't mention anything about what happened here. Tonight didn't happen. We came, we talked, and we left, *bon*?"

I nodded and ran back to where I'd left Victoria. As soon as she saw me, she moved to my side.

"Stay here," I said to Santiago's vamps, or the ones left standing anyway. "Marcel will be back down shortly and take care of you. I'm sorry," I added almost as an afterthought.

I didn't look back as we got into the suburban and drove back to the hotel.

Why should I look back? Marcel would fix it. Marcel fixed everything.

I woke not remembering going to bed. I was completely under the comforter and enjoyed the feel of soft skin covering most of my body. I opened my eyes and Victoria's head rested in the crook of my shoulder. She hadn't stirred yet, so I kept my movement to a minimum. Laying there holding her felt quite relaxing, and after the night we'd had, I deserved to relax a little. I moved my fingers to her hair and began to stroke its silky smoothness. "Good Evening, master," Victoria said without lifting her head. She tightened her arm around me and her cheek shifted as she smiled against my shoulder.

"Good morning." I stretched. You never see vampires stretching, and I liked to think it set me apart just a little more. The more I learned about the vampire world, the more I looked for little differences to use as insulation between us.

Victoria untwined her legs from mine and rolled over on her back, giving me the freedom to either stay where I lay, or get up and start my night. As much as I wanted to stay, I needed to talk to Marcel. He either hadn't come back to the hotel or slipped in after I had drifted off to sleep.

I pulled back the covers and rolled out of bed, giving a little gasp as I realized I was very, very naked. I looked over at Victoria and she lay there exposed completely as well. I ignored the blood rushing to my face and tried not to stare while I walked to the bathroom to take a shower. I didn't close the door behind me as I wanted to, but reached in the shower, starting the water while I brushed my teeth. Water temperature meant absolutely nothing to me, but I wanted the water as hot as possible to wash away the remains of the previous night.

I shut off the sink and stepped under the spray, immediately letting it flow over my hair and face. I grabbed the little bottle of hotel shampoo and poured it directly into my hair. I stepped forward to give my head a quick rinse so I could work it through my hair. Victoria's hands reached up and started massaging the soap into my scalp. I closed my eyes and concentrated on Victoria, feeling her spark just behind me. I tilted my head and let her work her magic on my scalp. She pressed against my back as she worked, and I reached behind her and pulled her tighter against me.

The suds from the shampoo trapped themselves between us and made the sensation of her naked body sliding against mine quite pleasurable. I lay my head back against her shoulder and her face pressed against mine as she worked the lather over my skin. She cleaned every inch of me and I shuddered under her touch. When she finished, I did the same for her. She looked at me, surprised when I started, but I enjoyed bringing her pleasure.

We shut off the water still giggling and dried each other off completely before slipping back into the bedroom to get dressed. I couldn't in good conscience let Victoria slip back into her transparent dress, so I loaned her a pair of jeans and a T-shirt I'd brought with me.

"Do you live around here?"

"I have a room at Santiago's. Most of the dancers live there," she said solemnly. I realized I didn't want her going there for any reason.

"Well, we'll go shopping later. I'll buy you some new clothes."

"Thank you, master." She bowed low.

"Hey, Vic. Do me a favor, don't call me that."

"If it's just you and I, I will call you whatever you command me to, master, but in front of others it is my duty." She bowed again.

I had a lot of work to do.

"Call me Ash or Ashlyn, whatever you prefer."

She bowed for the third time, and I refrained from saying anything about it. I stepped over to the bedroom door and she opened it for me without me asking. Maybe she had more work to do on me than I did on her. I'd never get used to being waited on hand and foot.

Thompson sat dressed on the couch with his feet propped on the hotel coffee table, television remote in his hand. When Vic and I walked out of the bedroom, he hit the power button and crossed his arms without getting up. I did however get one raised eyebrow.

"What?"

"What the fuck happened last night, kid? Do you know how many phone calls I've ignored from Sanders? He's the fucking Deputy Director of the FBI. You better have something good to explain it." I had never heard him yell before, and I didn't like it directed at me.

"What are you talking about?" I stared at him in confusion.

Hadn't he talked to Marcel at all?

"Where's Marcel?"

"I'm talking to you right now. What happened last night?"

"We met with the master of Sacramento and questioned him. He didn't have anything to do with the attacks on the governor so we left. Why? What's going on?"

Thompson gave me another dirty look before he got up and walked over to the desk. He picked up a newspaper that looked like it had been read, reread, crumpled up, and read again. He spun it as he tossed it to me, and the front page landed in my hands face up. A picture of a large fire stared back at me, and I recognized it at once. Bare Fangs had been reduced to a cinder. I read the caption underneath the picture, and then read the article twice before dropping it on the table Thompson had been using as a footstool.

"What happened last night, Ashlyn? You were the last one to see those twenty-seven vampires alive."

"I told you, we talked to him and that's it. By the way, I wasn't the last one to see them alive. Whoever killed them saw them for the last time." I had a sinking feeling in the pit of my stomach.

"I spent the entire night with my master, she didn't kill anyone." Vic chimed in next to me with the worst imaginable timing ever. I needed a story to explain her, and I hadn't come up with one yet.

"I'm sorry, who the fuck are you?"

"Thompson," I snapped angrily. "She's mine." I clenched my teeth.

"Excuse me?"

Fuck, I need more time. Why couldn't you have stayed in San Diego for another day?

"It's a long story," I started as the door beeped merrily and Marcel entered the room. Thank the gods.

"Welcome back, James," he said, and sat down on the couch where we were having our discussion. "What's going on?" He spoke as if he didn't have a clue. As far as I knew, he didn't, but the nagging feeling in my stomach begged to differ.

"This is." Thompson picked up the front page of the newspaper and handed it to Marcel. "Care to tell me what happened last night?"

"*Oui.*" Marcel glanced through the paper. He tossed it back down on the table and stared Thompson. "Where should I start?" He looked up at the ceiling dramatically. "Oh yes, I know. Your stupid FBI found themselves a new kind of vampire. You trained her how to be an agent, but she has no fucking clue how to be a vampire. She needs to be trained and she needs it now. Last night she broke one of our oldest laws, and she didn't even know she had done anything wrong! She accidentally ended up not only binding one of the master of Sacramento's vampires to her, but she also turned her into whatever she is! To top it all off, she blew apart the story we concocted for Strozzini. He ran off to tell The Council all about it. Do you think they will let her stay alive?"

Disbelief laced his voice. So much for his plan that last night never happened. He must have been really pissed off.

"Marcel, what did you do?" By the look on his face, he must've had the same sinking feeling in the pit of *his* stomach.

Marcel sighed. "The only thing I could, my friend. I ended Strozzini's life and the lives of all the other vampires who witnessed what happened. When I finished, I burned their bodies and set the blaze to destroy any evidence we had been there. Now the North American Council needs to find another master of Sacramento," he finished nonchalantly.

"You killed the master of the city, too?" Thompson groaned.

"*Non*, that one I cannot claim. He attacked our girl, and she defended herself to the best of her ability, unfortunately for Santiago." Marcel gave me a little grin I didn't return. He pissed me off. I'd decided to let Strozzini live, and yet he took it upon himself to end his life, as well as the rest of his vampires.

"Next time you tell me nothing happened, I'm going to swat you in the head." Thompson sat down rubbing his face with his meaty paws. "What the hell am I going to tell Sanders?"

"Tell him the truth. Maybe it will convince him I need time with Ashlyn," Marcel answered. "Or tell him she had nothing to do with it and she has a witness to prove it, and let her continue stomping all over the vampires of this country. I really don't care. She wanted me to let Strozzini go and let him run back to The Council. After she left and I looked at his prone form, I realized I couldn't let that happen. I lost the woman I loved to their fears and jealousies, I couldn't let it happen to Ashlyn, too." He slammed his fist down in frustration.

"Jesus, Marc, you killed twenty-seven vampires. How the hell can I forget about that?" Thomson cried in anguish.

"Ask yourself this, what would you have done? I've seen the lengths you have gone to protect her. Would you have done anything different?"

Thompson leaned back against the couch and stared up at the ceiling before giving a simple, "No." My chest caught a little and my anger toward Marcel vanished. "No I would have done the same. I just would have hid the bodies a little better."

Chapter 11

I stared at Thompson. He'd smoothed things over with Sanders after a four-hour conversation, but as soon as he clicked the end button–

"What do you mean we're going to Los Angeles?"

"Greer is going to be hobnobbing it down in L.A. for a week. Sanders got a call from the governor himself asking for more protection. Made us look like a couple of rookie assholes by not going through us. No offense, kid," he added.

"Why would he ask for more protection? Doesn't he realize it's not our job to protect him, but to find the people trying to kill him? I took those stakes because I knew he couldn't, not because it's my job."

"He doesn't see it that way. In fact, he doesn't want us to leave his side while we're down there. If you ask me, he sounds a little paranoid about going to L.A. Sanders said good work, by the way. Apparently, Greer couldn't go on enough about how you saved his life. Wants you to get a commendation, too." He smiled.

"Fuck off, Thompson." I stormed to my room to pout a little.

I shipped Vic off to go buy new clothes and anything else she might need. Marcel volunteered to go with her, leaving Thompson and me alone in the room while he called the Deputy Director. I'd pulled my bankcard out of my wallet, but Marcel refused to take it. He was the first man I've ever known who wanted to go shopping.

Darkness filled my bedroom like a comfortable blanket, and I refused to turn on the light. I didn't need it anyway, so I jumped on the bed, turning midair to land on my back on top of the fluffy comforter. I stared at the ceiling. I couldn't keep going the way I had been. I'd end up getting myself, or someone else, killed. The FBI had been very eager to use me, and for the millionth time since I started the job, I doubted my effectiveness. In Chicago, I made a million rookie mistakes and indirectly my first partner died. I'd been told it wasn't my fault, but doubt still nagged at me every day.

Now, here in California, my utter ignorance of the vampire world had gotten twenty-seven people–vampires–killed. That didn't nag my subconscious; it cut my soul every second. I counted myself as one of the good guys, but I didn't feel like it anymore. I felt more like a self-serving prick. Tears welled in my eyes and I let them fall. The drops hit my chest, sounding like a soft drum to my vampiric ears. Without realizing it, I let out a soft sob, and it quickly developed into a fit of body-wracking convulsions.

Thompson knocked on my door and let himself in without so much as a sound from me. He flipped the light switch and walked to the bed while I lay there crying like a five year old whose puppy just got ran over in the street. He didn't say anything, just sat next to me. Finally, he lifted me into the crook of his arm, positioning my face so I could literally cry on his shoulder. I flung my arm over him and held him like a giant teddy bear. Okay, maybe a giant stuffed werelion, but I clutched him just the same.

The sobs slowed to whimpers, and then the whimpers faded into silence. The whole time Thompson didn't say a word, simply comforted me. Long after the tears stopped falling, he shifted, freeing me to wipe the tears from my face.

"Thanks, old man," I said, and meant it.

"Don't make it a habit, kid," he said with a cheesy smile. "If the shit that happened last night didn't bother you, I'd be worried. Ash, you're a good kid. Don't ever forget it and don't let the vampires change you.

I'm not saying to do exactly what you have to do to survive, but always let it bother you. The minute you don't is when you become one of the monsters. I hope you don't mind the advice."

"You know what? I don't mind, and in fact, feel free to drop it on me anytime. Honestly, I don't know what I'd do without you. Thanks for putting up with me."

"All right, enough with the Hallmark bullshit, we've got work to do. Come on." He led me out to the other room. He then sat at the desk and called Greer, getting the details of our flight out tomorrow night, the name of the hotel, and all the pertinent information we might need. I found myself hoping Victoria would be okay without me, but I knew she wouldn't mind spending a few days in the hotel. Maybe I could talk Marcel into staying with her.

I sat around, vaguely listening to Thompson on the phone. I knew we had seats on the governor's helicopter and that someone from the L.A. field office would be meeting us when we landed. I also knew we were staying at the Kyoto Grand hotel along with Greer and his aides. After his forty-five minute conversation that had been all I'd caught.

As if on cue, as Thompson hung up from booking our reservations, Marcel and Vic walked through the door. Both of them looked like they'd won a shopping spree at the mall. Each carried at least fifteen bags with a different store name blazed across it. I rolled my eyes and gave a little smirk at the bliss plastered on Victoria's face. It pleased me to see her happy.

"Did you kids have fun?"

"Yes, ma'am." Marcel laughed, dropping his share of the loot on the floor by the door. "We got you two presents, too," he said, grinning.

"Did you get me a G.I. Joe with the kung fu grip?" I turned to Thompson and he had a serious look plastered on his face. Damn he could act. Or at least I thought he could until Marcel reached into a bag with a clown stenciled on the front of it and pulled out an action figure. He tossed it to Thompson who plucked it out of the air and started laughing.

"Really," I said in complete disbelief. They had to be kidding, right?

"Old joke from many years ago, young one. Your partner doesn't play with action figures, right, James? James? *Jim*!" He kept repeating uselessly.

Thompson merely sat engrossed reading the back of the blister package. I started laughing and couldn't stop. It beat the hell out of crying.

Vic dropped her packages on the ground and started rooting through them, searching for something in one of the larger bags. I had no idea what she could be looking for, but walked over to her anyway. She found whatever it was and held it out to me like a kid giving their parent a Christmas present. I furrowed my brows and gave her a disapproving look, gingerly taking the long white box from her outstretched hands. I pulled the lid off and saw a chain of thick silver links with a green gem in the center. I peered closely and saw it had a line through it, giving the gem a cat's eye effect, or my eyes. I gasped and gently plucked it from the box and held it in my hand.

"Do you like it, master? It's called a Cat's Eye. I loved wearing silver as a human, and now I can again." She held out her wrist. She wore the exact same bracelet, but hers had a blue gem set in it.

I looked up at her and smiled. "I don't think I've ever had a more thoughtful gift." I wrapped my arms around her, gave her a hard squeeze, and kissed her cheek. "Thanks, Vic. I love it." I held it out for her to put it on.

My skin tingled every time she brushed my wrist with her fingertips, but the effect lasted only as long as it took her to get it on. I sighed in disappointment when she finished. She beamed with pride and held hers up to mine for a moment to get the full effect. She gave me another hug before gathering the rest of her bags, taking them into the room.

"Thanks, Marc. That meant a lot to her."

"Little one, when you have lived for centuries, money

usually isn't an issue." He started rooting through his bags. He pulled a large wooden box labeled "Cohiba" and took it to Thompson. He dropped the action figure to take the box from Marcus' hands reverently.

"Oh-ho-ho-ho." He tore away the paper seal with his thumbnail and pried the box open. Immediately, I smelled tobacco. I walked over to peer inside, and there amidst torn up tobacco leaves lay twenty-five hand rolled cigars. Or at least that's what the top of the box said.

"You smoke," I said disgustedly.

"Only the finest of cigars when Marcel buys them for me," he said. "God bless you, Marcel."

"A small repayment for the grief I caused you last night, old friend. I just wish I could find Cuban's in the mall. I'll give Fidel a call when I get home and arrange for a few boxes."

"You actually know somebody in Cuba named Fidel? That's funny." I started to laugh. They didn't join in.

"You know him, too, little one. He's been on the news enough." He returned to his bags.

I stared at his back, sure he was teasing me, but Thompson merely gave me an affirmative nod. I shook my head in disbelief and went to check on Vic. I knocked on the doorframe as I entered. She glanced up from putting clothes in the dresser, giving me a peculiar look.

"What?" I stared at her, uncertain as to why she looked at me the way she did.

"Master, um…can I tell you something?"

"Of course," I said, my confusion growing.

"I haven't been a vampire long, so I remember what it's like to be human. Please don't be mad at me for saying anything, but you're too polite." She moved to me, putting her hands on my shoulders. "I am yours, body, mind, and soul, if I even have one. You need to stop treating me as if I could ever say no to you. Do you get it? You could slap me in the face with a two-by-four, and I would be happy you noticed me. You don't knock when entering your own room."

"It's going to take me a while to get used to this, but thank you for your honesty."

She rolled her eyes. "See?" She then gave a throaty chuckle. "Trust me, master, I don't mind, but watch how you treat me in front of another vampire."

"The other vampires will make fun of me?"

"No, they'll think you are weak and attack."

"She's absolutely right, little one," Marcel called softly from the door behind us. "Between your young Victoria and me, I think we might be able to turn you into a proper vampire. You left before I could give you your gift," he said, changing the subject.

"Marcel, you didn't–"

He held up hand. "A gift isn't something you give out of obligation. A gift is a token of love, appreciation, or esteem." He picked up a large, wrapped box from outside the door, handing it to me.

I ripped off the large ribbon and slipped the large cover off. Inside the box, a large expanse of black silk wrapped in tissue lined the bottom. I gingerly picked up the corners and lifted it free. The dress, as it turned out, fell to the floor and shimmered under the overhead lights. I gasped.

"Marcel, it's beautiful." I stared, too stunned to say anything more.

"When you are presenting yourself to a master of the city, it is proper to dress nicely. Plus, I noticed in your closet that your wardrobe needed a lot of work." He sniffed disgustedly.

I flushed before running into the bathroom to try it on. I took my clothes off and pulled the dress over my head. Looking at myself in the mirror, I got the shock of my life. I'd never considered myself beautiful. Pretty maybe, but never beautiful. The black silk dress made me look like a woman. I tried to imagine what I would look like with my hair done and makeup on. How had Marcel gotten the size right? I barely knew it.

I debated taking it off and putting my skirt and shirt, but figured Marcel would want to see what his gift looked like on me. I held on to the doorknob and counted to ten to build up my courage before stepping out into the room. Marcel's eyes grew wide over Victoria's shoulder. Seeing the change in his expression, she spun and gave me the biggest smile I've ever seen in my life.

"Master, you are beyond beautiful." Vic moved over to me and gave me a warm hug.

"I am going to have to agree with young Victoria. You look amazing, little one," Marcel said from his spot by the door.

"Thank you, both." I tried really hard not to beam. It's a shame they were the only two people who would get to see me in my beautiful dress, unless... "Hey, Thompson and I have to leave for a few days. In fact, we're leaving tomorrow night, but we seem to have the evening off. Would you like to do something?"

"I want to go dancing," Vic said sheepishly.

It kind of surprised me; I didn't think anybody who danced for a living would get any pleasure from doing it in their time off. I glanced over at Marcel and he nodded affirmatively at her suggestion.

"You two go, enjoy yourselves. I think I shall stay here and rest." Marcel gave a small smile.

"Hey, Thompson," I hollered through the door. "We're going dancing. You wanna go?" I never expected a response.

Deceptions

Chapter 12

I glanced up at the name of the club and made a face that caused Vic to laugh next to me. NOS4A2 Nation glared at me in gothic styled neon. I glanced over at Victoria and rolled my eyes. "Are you kidding me?" I pointed at the sign above the door.

"Be nice. I used to come here a lot before Santiago gave me a job at the club. The nosferatu that own the place are cute in an ugly sort of way, and they have killer, killer music." Vic opened the heavy glass door letting said music hit us full force. Not a fan of techno, I avoided rolling my eyes at her a second time and strolled into the club.

My mouth dropped open in surprise. The building housing NOS4A2 Nation looked nondescript and almost shoddy in appearance, but when you went through the door, you literally stepped into another world. Since I joined the FBI, I've been to some remarkable places and some pretty cheesy clubs. This one topped the remarkable ones exponentially. The far wall of the room wasn't a wall at all. Whoever decorated the club imported enough stone to build a castle, literally. It wasn't a fairy princess castle either. Imagine the gloomiest castle in all of Europe, and then make it tenfold darker. I expected the dark knight to come charging from its depths, but it was just a façade that stretched thirty feet in the air.

The dance floor sat nestled about three feet below the main entrance in a sunken pit. I don't think one more person could have occupied the floor without a good coating of butter. A sea of people undulated to the throbbing pulses of the trance music pumped out through speakers that looked like they'd been ripped from a major league baseball stadium. My ears hurt, but I found my head bobbing to the music. I gained a little insight into Vic's fascination with the club.

Vic grabbed my hand, led us to one of the very few unoccupied spots at the rear of the club, and parked her butt on a stool at the high top table. I half expected her to drag me out on the dance floor and gave her a quizzical glance. She held her hand up and began looking around for someone, or something.

I decided to engage in a little people watching. Quickly, I realized I should have just kept my eyes in my head and saved myself some serious embarrassment. Every guy within a ten-table radius stared at Vic and I as if we were a couple of T-bones. I felt more than a little self-conscious and wished Marcel or Thompson had deigned to come with us.

I glanced back at Vic and she smiled and waved at someone. A tall, gangly, bald man, who could only be a nosferatu, waved back and hobbled his way to our table. I could only stare more as he got closer to our table. I'd seen pictures of the elusive nosferatu, but never met one in person. The pictures didn't do them justice. They weren't ugly, but they were scary. Even when he smiled at Vic, it didn't erase the fear factor from his face.

"Viktor," Vic said with a little squeal, and launched herself into his arms.

I giggled a little at the "Viktor, Victoria" thought that flittered across my mind and smiled at the utter exuberance Vic showed at seeing her friend. Then jealousy reared its ugly little head. Only for a moment, but I recognized it at once and mentally swatted myself.

"Hello, sunshine," Viktor replied with a deep accent and a small smile. I tried to place the accent with little success. It wasn't Russian, and for some reason it struck me as older, much older.

"Viktor, come meet my *new* master." She released the nosferatu, dragging him closer to the table. I walked around the table, holding out my hand.

"Hi," I said.

The smile faded from his face as he stared into my eyes. He slowly raised his hand and grasped mine without ever taking his gaze from me. Before I could feel his cold flesh, the club fell away. I broke my cardinal rule. I never looked vampires in the eye anymore; when I did, bad things happened.

The club vanished and Viktor and I hovered in the air, illuminated from within. As usual, I floated over the massive body of water I'd learned was the embodiment of my power. Every other vamp I captured with my gaze usually did the same, hovering over their own ocean, lake, or pond depending on their strength. Viktor was floating, but it was over a dry, barren desert, bereft of life. The waves of my power lapped at his sandy beach. He gazed around him and sighed. Just when I formed the first of my questions, he disappeared.

I came to standing in the club with the mysterious Viktor still holding my hand. I avoided his eyes and stared down at our joined hands. My talons I'd seen a million times before, but *his* hand I stared at intently. It looked like somebody had taken every bone in his hand and fingers and stretched them until they doubled in length. His handshake literally wrapped around my hand. His skin held a rough quality, and if anything, his body temperature appeared colder than mine. The nosferatu held the honor of being the oldest of the vampire races, and now I understood why people truly thought us the undead.

"Pleased to meet you," Viktor said, and turned around, walking into the crowd of people I'd completely forgotten about.

"What just happened?"

"I don't know." Victoria gave me a small smile. "I'm going to find out." She left quickly, following Viktor into the crowd. That left me sitting at the table, alone.

"Great." I sighed and took my seat while I waited for Vic to come back.

I avoided any more people watching and found myself

faking great interest in the surface of the table I sat at. Mid stare, I heard them come in over the droning noise of the music.

I glanced up and saw at least thirty vampires pause at the entrance. They looked around the club as if they owned the place and tried to find a spot large enough for their party. The lucky streak that had been following me all night held as they found the few empty tables in the club that happened to be in the area I sat. Many of the patrons of the tables vacated their spots as the small army of vampires approached.

I debated doing the same, but the small stubborn streak inside held me rooted to my spot. I glanced up, using only my peripheral vision, and held my breath. The sickly sweet smell of so many vampires really started bothering me. It also made me more than a little hungry. In human years, the vamps around me looked rather young. I wondered if they all were the result of an overzealous vampire in a fraternity house. The thought made me giggle a little. I fought not to look up from the interesting nick I'd found in the table's surface. I started prying at it with the tip of my talon. A hand closed over my shoulder.

"Excuse me, beautiful. Would you care to dance?"

I stopped playing with my little hole in the table, and in one motion, turned, grabbed his hand in a vice like grip, and snarled in his face. He backed away wide-eyed and tripped over his feet, ending up on his butt on the dirty floor. His friends erupted into laughter as he got up and brushed himself off. I hoped he would run away, but being surrounded by his friends made him bold and stupid. Instead of going back to his seat and brushing the incident off, he advanced on me and made a grab to pull me from my seat when Victoria appeared between us.

She grabbed his throat and neatly lifted him from the floor. I could see his eyes over her shoulder, and he didn't look surprised–he looked pissed. She pulled his face closer to hers and whispered something into his ear I couldn't catch over the music before she dropped him to the floor for the second time that night. His friends started to stand up, but he held his hand up, motioning them to stop. That may have been the first smart thing he'd done since coming into the club. He lifted himself off the ground and walked back to one of the other tables.

"Thanks, Vic." I gave her a grateful smile as she turned and sat back down next to me, never taking her eyes from the group of vamps around us.

"Do you want to find a new table?"

I rolled the idea around in my head and figured any show of weakness would just invite more trouble. I shook my head. "No, I'm fine. Do you want to dance?" I really didn't want to, but it would be a good reason to get away for a little while without looking weak.

"I thought you'd never ask." She reached for my hand. I took it and followed her into the sea of dancers while trying very hard not to look around at every set of eyes I could feel staring at us.

Vic led us to the exact middle of the floor and turned to face me. A wicked grin played across her lips. She closed the distance between us and put her hands on the silky material covering my hips.

Slowly, she started to undulate to the beat of the rhythmic music. It throbbed in the very bones of my body. I offered a delicate smile and matched her movements as best I could. I might be a vampire, but Vic was a vampire who worked professionally as an exotic dancer. I tried not to feel outclassed as she snaked around me in suggestive movements, caressed me in places that shouldn't be touched in public, and basically let everyone in the club know I was hers. I didn't know how to feel about that.

She must have felt me stiffen because she paused in her more suggestive movements and looked straight at me. My eyes widened in panic, not wanting to enrapture her, but I could gaze into her icy blues without any problems. "What's the matter?" More comforted by the fact that I could share something as simple as eye contact with her than the level of discomfort I felt from her being a woman, I let a big smile creep onto my face as I pulled her closer.

"Absolutely nothing," I replied.

"You've never been with a woman before," she said in my ear, guessing at what caused my initial discomfort.

"I've never been with anybody before." I felt her stiffen in my arms.

She pulled back and stared at me with a cute little incredulous look on her face. "Truly?"

"Truly."

I expected her to pull away, but her sultry smile crept back and she hugged me close again. "We're gonna have so much fun later," she whispered in my ear, and gave my neck a little lick. I shivered and felt a chuckle rumble in her chest that just happened to be pressed as close as possible to mine without being naked. A blush crept up to my face, and I buried it in Vic's shoulder as she held me tight in the middle of the dance floor.

We walked back to our table, giggling. The group of frat vamps still occupied all the tables around us, and I tried really hard not to let it affect my mood. We sat down and a small waiter eased his way up to our table.

"May I offer you refreshment?" I tried not to laugh at his voice. Fangs occupied most of his mouth.

"Yes please, Drago," Vic replied automatically. He nodded and scampered off.

"They serve blood here?"

"No, but he'll bring us some willing food," she replied nonchalantly.

I looked at her eyes and a peculiar feeling settled itself in the pit of my stomach. Her eyes had changed to match mine when I fed her, and fed from her, making her mine. I looked down at her normal-looking fingernails and wondered if she would have my particular dietary requirements. I opened my mouth to break the news when Drago returned with a nervous human behind him. He looked like a college student, but unlike the frat brother vampires around us, this one belonged in a dorm room studying astrophysics. Horn-rimmed glasses perched precariously from his beaky nose as he clutched nervously at the yellow knit cardigan sweater covering his skeletal frame. I looked in vain for a plastic pocket protector.

"Here you are, ladies," he said with more than a little difficulty.

Vic gave him a cursory once over and a little shrug. She held out her hand and nerdy guy handed her his wrist. Looking away, she brought it up to her mouth and bit down. I heard the little crunch as her fangs pierced his skin and saw the look of horror as she pulled back and spit out the blood she collected in her mouth.

"Damn." I covered her hand with mine.

"What just happened?" She let go of her food and stared at me. He held out his other wrist to me, and I shook my head, telling him to leave.

"You're like me now, Vic. We can't eat humans."

"What do you mean?" She narrowed her eyes suspiciously.

"How hungry are you?"

"Starving," she replied.

"It's a long story, but trust me when I tell you that from now on you won't be able to eat humans anymore. Vampires yes, lycanthropes yes, but not humans." The suspicion in her eyes transformed into confusion. "I don't know what to tell you. I'm not a normal vampire, and it would appear that I passed it on to you." I removed my hand from hers.

"Master." She took my hand as I pulled it away. "Don't be sorry. Do you know how happy I am? For the first time in my life, I'm happy. You've made me strong, stronger than I could ever have imagined. So, what are we gonna have for dinner?" She gave me a little wink.

"Don't worry, I'll think of something." I squeezed her hand. Actually, I'd brought some lycanthrope "juice pouches" with me, but I saved those for emergencies. It wouldn't be enough for the two of us. Just my luck

I'd ended up with another mouth to feed.

Lost in my ponderings, I missed the concern on Vic's face and the sound of a heated arguing behind me. It wasn't until Drago landed in a heap next to our table that I snapped out of it. I reached down from my stool and offered him a hand, which he accepted with skepticism as his gaze flittered between my face and hand. I lifted and pulled him from the ground into a standing position.

"You okay?"

He nodded. Getting knocked on your ass wouldn't hurt a vampire, but I still asked. I turned around and looked behind me. Of course it had to be the Abercrombie vamps. Every last one of them was laughing and high fiving each other like little boys. Maybe they did all belong to the same fraternity. I sighed and stomped over to the one I'd dumped on his ass earlier. Before he even turned to acknowledge me, Vic slipped up behind me like my shadow.

"Is there a problem here guys?" I tried to sound bored, but I think it came out a little waspishly. Oh, well.

"No problem, girlie. Funny fangs over there tripped," he replied, closing his eyes halfway in annoyance.

I gazed down at his brown loafers and then let my sight travel upward to just above his eyes. He stood while I gave him my visual sweep and towered over me by a good foot and a half. I still avoided eye contact. I didn't want this creep in my head, even accidentally. I knew he was full of shit, but I didn't want to get into a fight.

"Drago," I called over my shoulder, "did you trip?"
"Yes, miss," he replied, but I could hear the hesitation in his voice.

"Are you sure, Drago?"

"What's it to you, girlie?" Abercrombie looked at me like I'd grown an extra head.

"It's my job." I reached for the badge that I'd left in the hotel. *Bad FBI agent, no cookie for me.* I realized I'd seriously screwed up and vowed to get one of those neck thingies. I never carried a purse and without jacket pockets, I hadn't even thought about taking my ID with me.

"Sure, beautiful. Why don't you go back to your own table and mind your own fucking business." With each word he stepped closer to me and finally bent over until his face was a few inches from mine. He was close enough that I could smell him without all the overwhelming scents of his friends. I took a tentative whiff and tasted the anise in the air.

"What's your name?"

He blinked in confusion and sneered before giving me a hissed, "Lord Steve."

I fought really, really hard not to laugh. Victoria didn't fare so well and her musical giggle wafted behind me. That pissed Steve off and he glared at her over my shoulder.

"Who's your master, Stevie?"

He shifted his glare back to me. The rest of his seated crew stood and closed the distance between us, fanning out behind their leader.

Steve laughed. If anything, it was higher than Vic's laugh, but instead of having a musical quality, it grated on my nerves, like talons on a chalkboard. "Nobody is my master. Can't you feel it you stupid bitch? We're free. We're all free." Steve's speech started to take on a maniacal sound, and it worried me. I thought about backing up, but figured that would have been bad, very bad.

"Steve, you need to listen to me. Calm down and leave. Go home, Steve."

"Fuck you." He lunged.

The world slowed. As he brought his hands up to grasp my throat, I reached up and grabbed his. I squeezed hard. His face went from pure anger to pure anguish as I crushed his neck. I felt the tiny little pops as my talons pierced his skin, and I could smell his blood as it started to flow free. Steve's strength seeped into my hand, and it didn't impress me. I could have ripped his head off, torn it free with one swift jerk of my hand, but I didn't want to. He didn't disgust me anymore. I pitied him.

"Take him home, and so help me gods, if I catch any of you in here again, I will kill you," I spat over Steve's shoulder to his friends.

They all stared at Steve's dangling form in my hand. I was inhumanly strong, but lifting someone who's six feet tall when you're only five feet tall is damn awkward. I heaved Steve backward to his friends who caught him and scrambled for the exit. I thanked the gods it hadn't escalated to a full-blown brawl.

I turned and a smiling Vic nodded at me. Drago still stood next to her, and the mysterious Viktor had joined them. He had a hard look on his peculiar face, and I don't think he wanted to thank me for bouncing the Abercrombie vampires out of the club. Some people are just way too serious, and for some reason I think Viktor fell into that category, head first.

"Sorry about that," I said to him, and walked over to my seat.

"There is nothing to be sorry for. It is I who should be thanking you, warrior." He bowed a little. I guess he wasn't as angry as he seemed. I still got the "I don't like you" vibe from him, but hopefully I wasn't right about that either.

"It's my job," I said, trying not to make a big deal out of it.

"You are a protector?" He sat down at our table. I watched Vic slide gracefully into the seat next to him and Drago scampered off toward the back of the club.

"You could say that." Vic gave me another of her smiles that warmed me as well as doing a few other things I'd rather not mention.

"I'm afraid things are going to get worse. Apparently, the master of Sacramento ended up dead last night. Nobody controls the lesser vampires now, and they seem to be taking advantage of their new freedoms," Viktor rubbed his chin thoughtfully.

I sat in shock. Everyone who had done any sort of publication on the mysterious nosferatu painted them as unintelligent monsters whose hungers needed to be controlled by others. The conversation with Viktor left me a little bewildered. I could see the intelligence in his eyes, and his mannerisms were straight out of eighteenth century Europe. It put me on guard and eased my tensions at the same time.

"What about you, Viktor?" I opened my mouth without thinking.

His spine straightened as he stiffened in his seat. "I am nosferatu. We do not answer to the self-proclaimed masters of your cities. We have our own king and we answer to him," he answered somewhat condescendingly.

The term "racist" seemed a little too apropos at the moment. Vic's face darkened, and I realized I'd fucked up, royally.

"Viktor," I started contritely, "I'm sorry and I hope you will forgive my ignorance. The amount of information I have about nosferatu is limited at best." I felt extremely small and I meant my apology whole-heartedly. I felt myself slinking into my chair.

He stared at me before nodding, and I felt the anger leave him. "I apologize, as well. Most modern vampires care little for our kind. I assumed you to be the same," he said. "I must ask though, who is your creator to give you such unusual eyes and hands?"

"My master didn't survive, so I don't know if he passed on the trait or if I'm some sort of anomaly." I answered his question without batting an eyelash. It amazed me how easily the lie flew from my lips.

"Interesting, and now the beautiful Victoria has your eyes." Viktor stood. "Ladies, I apologize I must leave. The club will be closing soon, as sunrise approaches. I bid you both good day." Before he walked away, he took Vic's hand in his and gently kissed it. I found myself staring and blushed when he nodded at me before walking away.

"Enough fun for one night?" I suddenly had an urge to go home and crawl into bed.

"Yes, master," Vic said with a smile, and led the way.

Deceptions

Chapter 13

Again I rode in another limo. I'd ridden in more limousines in the past week than I had in my entire life. I wasn't getting used to it either. I sat back in the gray leather seat and kept my hands folded in my lap to stop me from pushing buttons, rooting through the mini bar, and playing with the sunroof. I didn't even pay attention to the Hollywood skyline as it zipped by the limo window.

Thompson had the gas pedal of the limo floored. We didn't want to miss the governor's first stop in the city of Los Angeles, a worldwide movie premier. The movie's stars already strolled down the red carpet during the waning sunlight hours of the day. Since a variety of celebrity vampires would also be in attendance, the premier had been scheduled right at the brink, allowing the human guests to arrive first and the vampires after the sun settled in the western sky. Governor Greer ranked among the celebrity vampires.

I wanted to walk down another red carpet, paraded in front of the press, like I wanted to spend a sunrise on the beach.

I'd rather be back at the hotel with Marc and Vic.

A stabbing pang of jealousy surged through my chest. The fact was I trusted Marcel with Vic more than I trusted Vic with Marcel. Maybe spending a few days away from her would help me get my head back on a little straighter.

"Put your happy faces on. We're almost there," Thompson called from the driver's seat.

I sighed resignedly, and Greer laughed a little at my discomfort as the limo slowed and pulled over to the side of the road. I looked outside the window at the sea of people standing around and gawking at the line of limo's parked waiting for their chance to drop off their cargo at the famed red carpet. I tried really hard not to cry.

"I'm surprised Strozzini didn't want to accompany us to Los Angeles. I'd hoped to procure his services in smoothing things over with Claude," Greer said to me while our limo waited in queue.

"Claude?" I made the name a question.

"Claude Wagner, the master of Los Angles. Or Vahgner as he prefers." He made a dismissive motion with his fingertips.

"I take it he's not too happy with you being in his territory."

"He's not my biggest fan, that's for sure." Greer looked out the window toward the line in front of us. "Being a vampire governor in a state full of territorial master vampires often makes my job a little difficult. Santiago's murder isn't making things any easier either. Nobody has come forward to take his place so I'm acting as interim master until the council can approve a replacement."

I shifted in my seat in what I hoped wasn't a nervous gesture. I turned to see how much longer we had to wait. The conversation wasn't going well, and I didn't want it to continue any longer.

"We're next." Thompson looked me in the eye through the rearview mirror.

"Thanks," I said with as little sarcasm as I could, and scooted closer to the door. I wasn't going to take any chances with Greer's safety tonight. I would go out first and block the door until I felt it would be safe for the governor to come out behind me. I wasn't dressed for combat, but my skirt and suit jacket were made of silk and a little classier than my normal fare. I wanted to go for classy and dangerous.

"Wait for my signal." I grabbed the door handle as the limo pulled forward to the cordoned off red carpet.

As soon as the car stopped and I opened the door, the flashes from the paparazzi's cameras started. I got out and blocked the door. Time didn't slow as I let my eyes roam from face to face and then up over the top of the theater entrance. Reporters started calling my name and shouting, "Verminator," over and over. I let them fade into the background. A few faces caught my eye. I could feel their power even from a distance. There was a chance they were reporters who happened to be lycanthropes, too. Even though it would make my job easier, I couldn't just go around swatting every supernatural being in the area.

Reaching behind me, I motioned the governor to come out. We agreed he wouldn't move to my side until we safely reached the inside of the theater. He slipped out of the limo, and I let out a little sigh when he stuck with the plan. I don't know why, but I expected him to move ahead of me and start waving to the crowd. Walking forward, I could feel him moving along with me, never closing or opening the three-foot space between us. Good governor, he gets a cookie.

Between the lights of the camera flashes and the cacophony of questions shouted at us, I couldn't detect anyone who might be a threat. Eager faces of photographers glanced down at the velvet rope, no doubt wondering if they dare cross it. On a whim, I bared my fangs. I didn't mean it as a hostile gesture, rather parted my lips and exposed them, reminding the photographers what I could be capable of. I saw more than a few take large gulps of air and step back.

I tried to close my ears to the raging sounds around us and continued up the carpeted pathway to the rear of the line. Twenty or so people stood in front of us having close up snapshots taken for the national news while being interviewed by entertainment shows from around the world. My stomach settled somewhere around my larynx. I didn't like the press, and to date, my experiences with them had been pretty crappy. Oh well, I could ignore them as long as they ignored me. I continued to keep an eye on the crowd as the governor left his place behind me and settled on my left. So much for following instructions.

"Do you see anything?"

"Not yet."

"I think you can relax, Ashlyn. We're safe now."

I didn't even dignify it with a response. The line shifted forward as the B-listers in front of us made it through the press gate with a modicum of questions.

"Your last movie actually lost money, how do you feel about that?" I tried not to laugh. We still had a few minutes before we would be safely inside, and I promised myself not to let my guard down. I didn't want to screw this up. Having a nice, uneventful night would really make my day. Okay, maybe week.

I watched as one of the interviewers looked up and noticed the governor and I standing in line a few couples down from their current interviewee. I didn't recognize anybody in front of us as being famous, and I don't think she did either. She actually halted the human-looking man mid-sentence and ushered him and the remainder of the people ahead of us through.

The other reporters and cameramen stared at her like she'd lost her mind, until they saw us–actually I prayed it was the governor–and formed a semi-circle around the entrance. Cameras pointed at us as we strode forward.

"Governor Greer, Ashlyn, are you excited to see *BloodLust*?" The first question came before we even made it to the entrance. I didn't even know the name of the movie, so I let the governor answer the question while I turned my back and watched for bad people pointing weapons at us.

"Absolutely! When I received the invitation, I just knew I couldn't pass up the chance to see it in all its glory," the governor replied.

I could barely stand listening to him. His voice held a lot of power and its sickly sweetness almost stifled the air in the room. I turned back and saw the reporter rubbing her arms and smiling like a small child. I rolled my eyes and continued to watch for the bad guys.

"Verminator," the reporter said, trying to get my attention. It worked, but not in a good way. My head snapped to the side and my eyes narrowed as I looked at her like a chocolate covered éclair. I couldn't eat her, but she didn't know that. "Ashlyn," she started over, "are you here as the guest of the governor, or is he still in danger?"

"I really can't say." Let her make what she wanted from my statement.

"I don't think they'll try any funny business tonight. If any assassins did show up, they'd probably be too engrossed in the movie to try anything." Greer's talents were wasted as a governor. He should be in public relations.

"We agree! Thank you for your time, Governor. You too, Ashlyn." The reporter backed up, allowing us to enter the theater, finally.

Greer sat to my right in the crowded auditorium. I insisted on the aisle seat in case I needed to get him out of there quickly. He seemed totally engrossed in the cheesy movie shining on the glistening screen. Trying not to barf, I kept an eye on everyone and everything. I don't think I've ever been so bored in my life. I should have stayed outside and looked around, and let Thompson sit in the theater with the governor.

The thing that really bothered me was the smell of popcorn permeating the air. I stopped breathing about the time we hit the lobby, but the scent still lingered in my nose. Imagine going to a theater and not being able to eat popcorn, not fun. I don't think any human food ever struck me as so enticing before, and I sighed at the unfairness of it all. From now on, I'd stick to DVDs.

Finally, after what seemed like days, the movie screen faded to darkness and the credits started rolling on the screen. Everybody in the theater began clapping, and I joined in, although my reasons probably differed from everyone else's. The governor moved from his chair while I stepped out into the blue rope-lit aisle and made room for him. He began talking animatedly to the couple on his right though, probably discussing the merits of the fine film. *This should be a short conversation.*

He finally turned and beamed at me. I fought not to roll my eyes as I made a "this way, Governor" sweeping gesture with my arms. I wanted him safe just as much as I wanted the evening to go off without a hitch. A dead governor would definitely ruin that. I flipped open my cell and texted for Thompson to bring the car around. I could almost taste victory.

With Greer behind me, we skirted around the other patrons and exited into the brightly lit lobby. The others who left before us began milling about in small groups as the rest slowly followed. There must be some sort of after movie party, but so far the governor had not yet received an invitation. My plan was to get him out of the theater before it happened. He called the shots, but that didn't mean I wouldn't manipulate him when I could.

"Ashlyn, I need to pay my respects to Wagner before we leave. If I don't it might make things more difficult."

I stopped and saw the hope in his eyes. I guess he could manipulate me, too. I didn't like it, but I understood his need.

"Absolutely, Governor." We waded our way over to one of the columns littering the lobby, giving us something to put at our backs.

"Thank you."

We waited where we stood for the better part of ten minutes while the crowd slowly exited the theater. I tried really hard not to fidget as I expected danger to come from everywhere and everyone. I'd need a vacation after this assignment. My nerves of steel felt a little more like tinfoil from all the stress. Finally, Claude Wagner, the master of Los Angeles, appeared with his entourage.

I expected… well, honestly I didn't know what to expect, but Claude overshot the mark by a mile. He had to be at least seven feet tall. Okay, maybe not that tall, but when you're barely five feet, really tall people look like giants. He wore a black tuxedo that must have cost a fortune just from the amount of material alone. Long blond hair flowed unfettered around his head like corn silk, and the model beauty of his face made him quite alluring. *Quite* alluring. Too bad the appearance of Governor Greer darkened his features. He didn't seem happy at all to find us waiting for him.

I'd give him credit though. If I saw somebody waiting for me who I didn't want to talk to, I'd pretend I didn't see them and run for the door. Wagner didn't do that. He steeled his obvious distaste and strolled elegantly to where we waited, motioning for his followers to stay where they were.

"David, how good to see you," he obviously lied as he approached us. His smile more fake than his girlfriends' boobs. Yes, I meant girlfriends, as in more than one. Claude appeared to be quite the slut.

"Claude, it's good to see you, too. I apologize for encroaching on your territory unannounced, but the duties of governor are as widespread as they are many. I hope you can forgive me?"

"Just don't make a habit of it, and all will be well. I understand your new role will cause a lot of friction, but a phone call would have been nice."

"Again, my apologies, but I seem to have misplaced your number…"

Claude laughed and rolled his eyes at Greer's obvious attempt at humor. "Everyone is headed to my home in the hills for an after-party celebration. Would you and your…guest care to join us?"

"We would be delighted," Greer said with obvious interest. I groaned quietly. Not quietly enough, apparently. Wagner gave me a quick glance and a brief nod.

"Not interested in a party, Verminator?" Claude said it surprisingly amicably. Like he thought the name I had earned was a joke. It made me like him a little more. I thought about the party and all the possible security threats to Greer, and this time, my groan wasn't very quiet.

Deceptions

Chapter 14

The limo traversed the winding driveway behind the twenty-odd other limousines. The whole scene seemed snake-like, or funeral-like. Take your pick. The one thing the procession didn't resemble was anything I wanted to do before I died. Nope, going to an after premier party wasn't on my bucket list. Go figure. Most eighteen-year-old girls would give their firstborn for the opportunity. I, on the other hand, would have traded anything to get out of going. So far, I'd managed to keep the governor safe for the entire evening, not killed anyone, or gotten anyone else killed. It was a record for me since Thompson and I touched down at LAX. I wanted to keep it that way.

Thompson stayed in line and gave Greer and me the rundown while he waited for the opportunity to dump his passengers at the front door of Wagner's mansion. Stay away from the windows, don't drink anything given to us (apparently it was chic for vampires to serve blood in goblets), and don't get dead (his words not mine).

"Agent Thompson, since we didn't know we would be attending this party, how could anybody else?" Greer sounded smug from the back seat. I sighed and refused to backhand him for being stupid. I hope Thompson appreciated my restraint.

"Governor, twenty black limousines traveling in a line from the premier might have given someone a clue. Please be careful." Even Thompson kept it together enough to be polite. I appreciated it.

Our turn came up, and just like at the premier, I stepped out of the limo first and took a look around before motioning Greer to come out after me. I didn't expect any danger at Wagner's home (If he wanted Greer dead he could have ripped his face off at the theater), and put the governor in front of me. I just hope nobody opened fire. I'd grown pretty tired of taking silver stakes for the man. They hurt like a bitch.

We wound our way up the steps from the covered drive, through the frosted double glass French doors, and into the marble-floored Mecca of California wealth without incident. Waiters with little silver serving trays wandered through the forest of people with tall glasses of champagne and thick, red liquid I didn't think was Kool-Aid. My stomach rumbled a little, but I told it to be quiet, remembering Thompson's party rules. *He says I never listen, sheesh.*

Greer mingled and schmoozed while I stood behind him with a wary eye on the exits and the guests. I kept in contact with Thompson via text messages. He sat outside the mansion keeping an eye on things. I thought about it a minute, and I felt safer with Thompson outside than I would if there were an entire field office of FBI agents instead. That said a lot about Thompson. I just hoped he shared my feelings. Since I was usually the one *causing* problems, I doubted it. It didn't stop me from wishing it.

The man of the house finally arrived. Nothing says fashionable like showing up late to your own party. He practically glowed from within, though the girls with the breast implants accompanying him to the premier seemed a little drained and pale. *Wonder what he did in the limo on the way home?* I felt a little jealous. My hunger kept rearing its ugly little head, and Wagner looked more like a nice juicy T-bone every minute. I should have eaten something before we left the hotel. Sometimes I just wasn't the brightest bulb on the string. Maybe I should start keeping a "to do" list in my pocket.

1. Eat

2. Protect Governor Greer from bad vampires

Then again, maybe I shouldn't.

Greer gave a little wave to Wagner as he strode into

the party. Wagner tried to keep his meal down.

Why would he invite Greer if he holds such an obvious distaste for him?

I wondered if his distaste was strong enough to murder for. Maybe he invited Greer here to make it easier to kill him. If he could do it in such a manner that he could get rid of Greer and still seem innocent in front of all his guests, Wagner would be in the clear. *Oh, shit.*

My fingers flew over the keys of my cell. I had a very bad feeling in the pit of my stomach, or at least the big empty hole where my stomach used to be. I wanted to call Thompson, but Greer stood right by me and Wagner moved closer with every step. Probably not a conversation he would want to hear. Finally my message reached completion, and I hit the little send button. I shoved my phone in my pocket and smiled at Wagner as he approached. His blond hair looked truly amazing, and I wondered what it would feel like in my fingers. Wagner's hair saved Greer's life.

His hair was so fine, the tiny dot of laser light shining on it made almost all of it glow red. Somebody had been targeting Greer, and Wagner stepped in the way, fouling the shot. I grabbed the governor with my arm and pushed him behind me to keep him safe.

The horror on my face must've clued in Wagner as to what was happening. He spun, searching for danger just like I had. The laser had to be coming from somewhere; I just couldn't spot the location. Wagner crouched, and I fully expected a shot to ring out, or a silver stake to come crashing through one of the multitude of windows in the mansion.

I didn't expect a small explosive tipped projectile.

Everything in the room slowed. I followed the trail of the tiny missile, but couldn't move to stop it. I assumed it would sail over Claude's head and take out the governor and myself, but it didn't. It impacted full force in Wagner's chest, and before it could lift the enormous vampire off his feet and hurl him backwards, it exploded.

A rhythmic tempo on my cheek woke me up from my missile-induced slumber. I drew in a deep breath and opened my eyes to find Thompson kneeling over me, slapping me lightly on my cheek. "You okay, kid?"

"Huh?" I saw his lips move, but I couldn't hear a word.

"Are you okay?"

This time I heard him. It sounded like he was talking underwater, but I could hear. *Yay.*

"I'll live. How's Greer?"

"Fine, between you and the tall vampire, he lucked out enough to be almost completely shielded. I got your text in time to make it to the front door and watch the fireworks. Ambulance is on its way. Good thing the missile didn't pack that much explosive. There was only one fatality. The humans in the room might take a while to get over the shock and flying debris, but they'll be okay."

"Wagner?" I had to ask, knowing the answer before I made his name a question.

"Yeah, he didn't make it."

I nodded and tried to stand. I failed miserably, but I'd tried. Thompson's gigantic paw of a hand made an appearance in front of my face so I grabbed it and hauled myself up. The room spun for several minutes, but it finally ceased its rotation and I got a good look around. I thought my vision had gone red, until I realized Wagner pretty much coated the room. Guess he wouldn't be getting a decent burial, unless somebody got a squeegee.

Eww.

I looked down at my black silk suit and realized I'd probably need one, too.

The room started to strobe in reds and blues and the muffled sounds of sirens filled my ears. The cavalry had shown up. They entered through the front door with guns drawn. EMTs with stretchers and orange tackle boxes full of medical supplies followed right behind. Thompson and I pulled out our badges and let the police know what happened while the governor stood behind us looking rather green and somewhat grateful. If I were him, I'd be grateful I didn't get blown up, too.

By the time the house cleared out, Thompson and I ushered the shaky governor back to the limo. We went straight back to the hotel. The police had asked us so many questions I'd lost count. I didn't even know what time it was, and I didn't have the energy to reach into my pocket to pull out my cell phone and check. So much for breaking my "haven't gotten anybody killed today" record, life can be a real bitch at times. I'm pretty sure most of the pieces of Claude Wagner would agree with me.

I woke in the hotel the next evening praying to all the gods that I'd dreamed the entire night before, but the smell of blood coming from my silk outfit on the floor told me I hadn't. Even after being blown up, Claude smelled yummy. I needed to eat, but not yet. Shower first and then food. Sometimes, I had good plans.

I washed myself and stood under the spray, replaying the events of the night before over and over in my head. Claude had ducked; the missile should have hit us.

Don't get me wrong, I wasn't upset; I just couldn't believe we were that lucky. I could sustain a hell of a lot of damage, even silver, but I sincerely doubted I could survive being blasted into Ashlyn kibble. Nobody is that good, or lucky. Nobody. I gave a grateful sigh and shut off the water. I still didn't feel like moving, so I let the water bead up on my skin and fall slowly to the shower floor. Almost dry, I finally mustered the energy to slide back the curtain and grab a towel.

"Hurry up, kid," Thompson called from the other side of the door. "The governor is going to hold a press conference before we head back to Sacramento."

"Oh goody," I called out to him. Just the thing to top off the perfect trip, a press conference full of reporters who would probably have a million questions I didn't have answers for. I needed to quit my job and move to Alaska. I could find some magic bears to eat I'm sure.

I sighed, got dressed, and met Thompson in my room. With a brief stop to meet the governor at his room, we went to the limo and sped off to yet another press conference. I could barely contain my excitement, and I think the governor and Thompson knew to leave me alone because we rode in silence the whole way. I stared out the window and watched the contrasts of Los Angeles. If I had to use one word to describe the city, it would be surreal. Parts of it looked like a theme park. Other parts were so destitute you would swear you were driving through a third world country.

We pulled into the parking lot of a nondescript, gray building, and I silently cursed myself for not paying attention to the sign as we pulled in. Thompson parked and we pulled the usual, stand in front of the governor in case there were bad guys with guns–or rocket launchers– waiting to shoot him. Don't tell anybody, but I kind of hoped there were. I was getting tired of protecting the little weasel more every day. I stopped in my tracks when I realized what had crossed my mind. He'd been nothing but polite to me since our arrival, and I had no reason to dislike the man. Then it hit me. All of this was his fault, not directly, but still his fault. Because he'd insisted on not hiding until we could figure out who was trying to kill him. He had caused the deaths of those around him. His guards and now Claude, hell he had even gotten me shot. Small wonder I didn't like him. I started to feel a little better.

Before Greer got to the center of the stage, the press had already started bombarding him with questions. Most of them weren't very nice either. It's kind of amazing, most masters of the city are tolerated if they behave themselves and do a good job of keeping the vampires of the city in check. Some, like the master of

Chicago, were outright criminals. Claude Wagner had been one of the few beloved masters. He'd held the status of iconic celebrity and had been featured in more celebrity magazines and television news casts than Brangelina. His death would probably cost the governor more than a few votes at the next election. If he remained alive long enough to run again.

One of the bolder reporters shouted a question at me. I held up my hand and motioned to the governor, letting them know he had called this conference. I wanted no part of it. I thought it a great plan until the reporter asked Greer why I failed to save Wagner. I rolled my eyes and shook my head, expecting the governor to make a long speech about the sanctity of life, yada, yada, yada. He surprised me by saying exactly what happened. How I had been expecting the attack, but due to the unfortunate turn of events, I wasn't in a location to save Claude. He lowered his eyes and actually looked saddened by his loss.

The press ate it up. They began asking about the extent of Greer's friendship with Claude and how much he would miss him. I smiled at Greer's back when he began hamming it up. I refrained from shaking my head and laughing outright. Sometimes, I never ceased to impress myself. The torrential downpour of bullshit coming out of Greer's mouth threatened to bring up my morning meal. Opportunist: Noun, see Governor Greer. *What a douche*. I silently vowed to sidestep the next bullet that came our way.

Greer finished up, and said, "No more questions, please." He closed his eyes and bowed his head before exiting the stage. I gave a quick sigh and took my usual spot behind him. We walked the entire way to the limo with cameras pointed at us and reporters trying to get in a few more questions. I didn't relax until the door shut behind me. Now all I had left to do was try not to kill Greer on the way to the airport.

Deceptions

Chapter 15

It felt good to be back in Sacramento. Dropping the governor off at his mansion–even better. Back at our hotel, we relayed the entire story of what happened to a concerned Marcel and a very concerned Victoria. Finally, we said goodbye to the guys, and she and I retired to our room. She held me the entire day, and I can't even begin to describe how much I enjoyed it. I felt a little guilty because I was "her master," and yet she comforted me without asking anything in return.

When the sun dropped below the horizon, I woke to find her still sleeping. Her arms wrapped around me like a cocoon, and I basked in the feeling of being safe. The governor would be spending the entire evening in his office doing governor things, so we sort of had the day off. Well, we didn't have to play body armor at least. Does it make me a bad person to hope somebody blew up the mansion? That way we wouldn't get blamed, and we could go home. I missed my small apartment in DC. I just hoped Vic would like it.

"Morning, master," Vic whispered in my ear, giving it a little kiss. A shiver ran from my earlobe, down my neck, and straight down to lower things. I smiled and gave her a quiet thank you. I couldn't come up with a better way to wake up, until my thoughts drifted to Marcel. *What the hell is wrong with me?*

Vic released me and got off the bed. I slept in my underwear and T-shirt. Vic must have crawled into bed with me buck-naked. I hadn't even noticed I'd been so tired. I noticed now. As she bent over to retrieve her clothing from the floor, I caught sight of her magnificent body and felt a slow, hot blush creep up into my cheeks. I resisted the urge–with some difficulty–to run my hand over her ass to see if it was as soft as it looked. Don't get me wrong, there isn't a spot on her that isn't incredibly muscled, but her skin had an almost glow to it. She must have been even more breathtaking when she could tan.

Wonder what she'd looked like as a human.

A knock at the door broke me from my reverie. "Who is it?" I expected it to be Thompson.

"It's me, *chere.* May I come in?" Marcel's voice sounded slightly muffled.

"*Oui,*" I answered jokingly. Vic stifled a giggle.

The door opened and he stepped inside. I shot a quick glance at Vic who still hadn't dressed, nor did it appear she was in a rush to do so. I guess working at a strip club will get you over any nudity issues you might have. I wish I could. I didn't even like to be naked in front of myself. Maybe hanging out with Vic would rub off on me.

"Still in bed? I thought the youth were supposed to be full of energy."

"Not after the night I had, Marcel. What did you need?"

"Yes, I can see how you might be a little drained. I wondered if I might take my leave. With Strozzini gone, you don't really need me here right now, and I have some urgent matters to take care of back in Chicago."

I turned and gave him a concerned look. I understood his need to leave, but I didn't like it at the same time. I wanted to plead with him to stay, but said, "Sure."

"Would you promise me one thing? When you have some time, please find me. There is much I need to teach you. Your *premier enfant* understands much. She will keep you safe while I am gone."

"Marcel, I can't begin to thank you enough. My ass would have been grass if it weren't for you."

He stared at me before glancing down at my comforter-covered butt. I guess he was wondering what it would look like green.

"Just promise, come as soon as you can."

I pulled myself out from the covers and walked to him. He refused to lower his gaze below my neck. I felt a little pride at standing in front of him in just my underwear. I leaned in and wrapped my arms around. He made a little *harrumph* noise, and I thought I might have been embarrassing him until I heard his rib creak a little. *Oops*. I guess I hugged him too hard.

I pulled away, and he touched the back of his fingers to my cheek. He nodded once at Vic and gave her a quick, "Keep her safe." I didn't turn to see if she responded, but he gave Vic another of those melt your heart, make you swoon, grins. He needed to bottle those. My heart did something a little funny when he turned and left, pulling the door closed behind him. I decided I better get dressed and figure out what Thompson planned for us to do today. If he suggested a movie, I would punch him in the face.

The helicopter touched down in the arid San Jose night. I'd have preferred going to a movie rather than being quickly shipped ninety miles to see a dead vampire. What was the old saying about being careful what you wished for? Such is life. Apparently, somebody killed the master of San Jose. With the death of Claude Wagner and now this, the Deputy Director feared somebody was targeting all the influential vampires in California, and not just the governor. Thompson actually asked me if I wanted to fly solo on this one. He would stay and guard Greer, and I could come and check the body to see if I could find a connection. I wanted away from Greer for a while anyway.

The pilot shut down the rotors, and the rhythmic *thwump, thwump, thwump* of the blades moved slower, halting their spin. "You can exit now if you want, agent." The pilot spoke to me through the intercom in my helmet.

"Thanks, Charlie," I shot back, and began to unstrap my harness before taking off my helmet and opening the door. I watched two people dressed in black suits rushing across the landing field. *They must be my babysitters in this strange land.* Even though the rotors of the chopper had almost completely stopped, they still ran hunched over. I never really got that. The blades of the helicopter are almost fifteen feet off the ground. Even a professional basketball player could stand with another professional basketball player on their shoulders and not worry about decapitation. Yet whenever humans get near one, they instinctively hunch over like they have appendicitis. It'd be funny if they did it with ceiling fans, too.

I stepped off the edge of the door, dropped the few feet to the concrete pad, and stood proudly straight, *I ain't afraid of no chopper.* I could have started walking forward, but the agents went through all that trouble to face their fear of having their heads detached to meet me, so I let them come.

"Ashlyn?" The taller of the two made my name a question. I didn't like that he left off the "agent" but I let it go. "I'm Special agent Devries. This is Agent Mahoney. We're supposed to take you to see our dead vampire?"

"Lead the way," I said in a little bit of a snit. *They get titles, and I don't? Oh well, maybe I was just being childish.* I tried not to let it get to me as I followed them to their black SUV. They weren't running, so I fell into step behind them. Devries Slipped into the driver's seat and Mahoney rode shotgun. I opted to sit behind him.

"Don't know what you expect to find here," Devries said as he started the vehicle and drove out of the helipad parking lot.

"I don't know either. We've had a lot of dead masters in different cities popping up. Just making sure they're not related." I experienced a little twinge of guilt since the master of Sacramento definitely hadn't been murdered by the same people who murdered Claude and attempted to murder the governor.

"Well, I'll take you to the body and let you

decide. Warning you though, it isn't pretty."

"It never is." My reply made Devries shift his gaze from the winding road to me in his rearview mirror. I could have met his eyes and not enraptured his mind, but I stared out the window and pretended not to see him looking at me.

"So, why did the Deputy Director send you? Do you have crime scene forensic experience?"

I gave a little bark of laughter and didn't take my gaze off the road. "You could say that." Apparently, Devries and Mahoney didn't know who or what I was. Sometimes I think Sanders did stuff like this on purpose. I mentally clicked him up a notch on my people who annoyed the crap out of me list. "Let's just say I have special abilities that help out from time to time."

"You're a supe?" "Yes. Yes, I am."

We rode in silence after that. Finally, after about twenty minutes, we pulled into the parking lot of a bar. *How come Claude Wagner seemed to be the only vampire who lived in a house?* Vampires are just plain stereotypical. I caught the name on the sign and chuckled. Bloody Mary's wasn't the most original name for a vampire bar. Especially when you considered some of the ones I'd been to.

"Come on, Ashlyn, your body awaits," Devries opened the door, letting the dry, hot air back into the Suburban.

I didn't say anything in return. Devries plucked a nerve in me, and I tried not to let it show. I could be a good little agent and play nice in the sandbox. I could.

Devries and Mahoney practically ran through the parking lot to get out of the heat. I didn't mind it. It felt like something inside me had gotten a little warmer. *I could get used to this.* I finally reached the glass double doors leading into the bar and pulled the right one open. The blast of arctic temperature air instantly washed my newfound warmth away.

Dead silence filled the club, no pun intended. I half expected the bar to be full of police interrogating witnesses and crime scene investigators looking for tiny shreds of evidence, but the club sat deserted, completely. Devries waited for me at the far side of the large room by a door leading to the back. I crossed the floor quickly and waited for him to either lead the way or open it for me. He walked in first.

The door opened to a stairwell going down. I should have known. The master of San Jose hadn't been killed in the middle of his club. Somebody had gone hunting for him. That differed from all the other attacks. If they were the same people responsible, maybe the governor wasn't safe tucked inside the mansion. I pulled my cell out and texted Thompson. Better safe than sorry. I even managed to go down the stairs while texting. I have talent.

The stairs ended in a large underground facility. Apparently, the master had felt safe behind his big metal door. Usually, the lairs of powerful masters were a little more secure and hidden. Maybe the master of San Jose had a learning disability. When everybody really is out to get you, it's not paranoia.

Devries' feet echoed throughout the cavern as he strode across the empty area to what looked like a living room setup toward the back. Couches, sofas, and huge ornate chairs spread out across the area nestled on rugs of various sizes and shapes. Everything was beautiful and ornate, just horribly mismatched. Oranges, blues, reds, and yellows all clashed and assaulted the eyes like a movie made in the seventies. The Technicolor living room smelled funny, too.

The closer I got, the stronger it became. It smelled like nothing I'd ever encountered before. I couldn't even begin to describe it. I smelled blood, and that I knew. I smelled fear and death, and those I knew. Finally I had to ask, "Devries, what is that smell?"

He saw my crinkled nose and chuckled. "Don't tell me you've never smelled weed before, Ashlyn?"

"Oh." I shook my head. I've seen hundreds of movies and videos with people smoking it, but I'd never smelled it or seen it in person. It was really unpleasant. The smell filled the air like a pungent perfume. I didn't know vampires smoked pot. *Would it have any effect?*

I moved around the couches and saw the body sprawled out on the nicest one. The silver stake in the middle of her chest probably put a damper on her festivities. A lighter and paraphernalia on the floor indicated she'd been mid puff when she died. "Where's the master's body?"

"That's her, Mary Moore."

Duh. I'd automatically assumed the master of the city would be a man. Not in this case. She'd probably been beautiful before somebody put the huge chunk of metal through her heart. Long blonde tresses had been tied up with a strip of leather. The rest of her attire looked Native American, but a cheap imitation. Long dangling strips of leather hung from her arms and legs, decorated with cheap shiny beads. *Hippie.* I closed the distance and bent to examine the body a little closer.

Her head was turned so I couldn't see her right eye from where I stood before. I'd missed the silver stake embedded in her brain. I should have known. If you're going to take out somebody strong enough to be master of the city, silver through the heart wouldn't always do it. The stakes were the kind fired from the snuff guns the FBI used. Whoever killed her had not only been a professional, but a damn good shot.

"I have a feeling it's the same vampires who killed the others and tried to kill the governor."

"How can you tell?" In the distance, footfalls echoed. I turned and saw Mahoney joining us. I guess he didn't want to wait in the car anymore.

"Because I took three of them in the back while protecting the governor," I told Devries.

"You took stakes for that bloodsucker? You should have ducked. Undead fuckers running for governor, what's next?"

I so couldn't resist. I turned toward him and flashed my fangs. "I know, right? Next thing you know they'll want to join the Bureau."

He turned from red to white and back again while the implications flashed through his head. He started backing away and tripped on one of the rugs, landing hard on his ass. Priceless. I ignored him and snooped around some more.

If there had been any other evidence around, the CSI team had been very thorough. I looked with my vampire eyes for anything they might have missed and came up empty. I could smell the clove scent from the dead vampire, along with the smell of about fifty other vampires, but I had no way to tell which one belonged to our killer. Mary probably just entertained a lot.

"Were there any witnesses?" I turned to Devries who had picked himself off the floor.

"Not that we know of, agent." Oh, look who turned into Mr. Formal.

"Great. I think I've seen enough. Would you mind taking me back to the helicopter?"

If I thought the club had been dead silent, the ride back to the chopper was worse. I didn't even get an apology. Not that I wanted one, but still. Some people could be so rude.

Chapter 16

"I'm sorry, the what?" I stared at Thompson incredulously.

"Governor's Ball," he enunciated slowly like I was the village idiot.

"I know what it is. I just can't believe you agreed to it. How the hell are we supposed to keep him safe?" I tried really hard not to slap some sense into him.

"You know Greer. 'I shall not be deterred by these terrorists.' I tried to talk him out of it."

"Yeah well, you shoulda tried harder. I want it in our file that I think this is a horribly stupid idea."

"Me, too, kid." Thompson took his size fifteen shoes off the coffee table in our hotel suite. With Marcel's departure, I worried that we would have to go back to our meager hotel rooms, but Thompson assured me Marcel insisted we stay right where we are. His treat.

"Where's Vic?" Thompson hit me with the news about the ball as soon as I'd walked into the suite. I guess he wanted to get it out of the way.

"She said she was heading to the ugly vampire club."

I laughed. "They're called nosferatu, Mr. Kittycat. Don't be rude."

"Whatever, all you bloodsuckers look the same to me." He winked.

I smiled at him. With Thompson, I didn't mind the vampire name-calling. I'd filled him in on what happened in San Jose on the phone once the helicopter landed. I left out the part about Devries' comments, and I debated telling him now. I'd been pretty opinionated about vampires myself–until I found out I could be counted among their ranks. Maybe I should just leave him to his prejudices. If I told Thompson, I'm sure he'd make a big deal about it and try to get Devries reprimanded. I didn't want that. The guy was a complete jerk, but he'd probably be a bigger one if I got him in trouble.

"Did you get my text about the governor's safety at the mansion?"

"Yeah, I doubled the guards and made sure there were plenty of supes to help out. Turns out he has some werewolves on the state trooper detail. Shame they weren't working when his limo blew up. They might have survived it."

I nodded and debated what to do for the evening. Vic was out dancing and having a good time and Thompson seemed content to sit and flip channels between the dozen or so national news networks. My gods, he was boring. I debated sneaking up on Vic and having fun with her, but maybe she wanted a little time away from me. Then I thought of my seriously depleted closet of clothes without blood or holes in them. Maybe now would be a good time to replenish. I've never been a huge fan of shopping, but this time the thought of it didn't scar my soul.

"I'm going shopping. You wanna come?" Thompson laughed.

The Arden Fair Mall seemed like a logical choice for shopping. I parked the big SUV in the tiny mall parking spaces and tried to seem inconspicuous as I strolled through the glass entrance. I passed by a Sears and decided to forgo looking for clothes in there. All the suits I owned that hadn't been destroyed seemed kind of reserved. I wanted to start dressing a little nicer. Kinda like Will Smith at the end of MIB. I wished Marcel hadn't left. I had no idea what fashionable meant, let alone how to dress that way. Marcel had more fashion sense in his little pinky than most people in the fashion industry combined.

I stopped and got my bearings. Sears was behind me, and the closest stores ahead were someplace called Wet Seal and Chico's. I peeked through the window of both, and while the Wet Seal appealed to my jean and T-shirt persona, neither exactly screamed business attire. I walked the entire length of the mall only to stop briefly at the counter at Starbucks to sit there and smell the coffee. I would give an appendage to try coffee. Finally, after what seemed an eternity I came across Macy's. *Jackpot.*

Several hours later, as well as several armfuls of bags, I reached my limit. I carried the items out to the car and loaded it up. Thankfully, I put the last bag in and shut the monstrous trunk when I dropped my keys. The simple fumble saved my life, or at least a pain in my neck. I mean that literally, the silver stake that shot through the window of the Suburban would have pierced my neck.

I crouched low and spun around. I looked everywhere before I spotted him on the roof of the mall. *Motherfucker, how the hell did you know I would be at the mall?* Even I hadn't known I would be at the mall. I ducked between my SUV and the next. As soon as I stepped out to run over to the building, another stake buried itself partially into the asphalt in front of my foot. Seconds later, I heard the telltale *snuff,* of the air-powered rifle. At least he wasn't running. That gave me a shot of catching the bastard.

I backed up a step and ran with all my vampiric speed. I heard *snuff, snuff, snuff* and the sounds of the stakes hitting around me, but I moved too fast for him to pick me off. Finally, I reached the exterior wall of the mall. The outside was entirely constructed of large blocks of stone. I'd never been rock climbing before, but I figured I would give it a shot. There wasn't enough purchase to grab on to the stone, so I made holes with my fingertips to pull myself up. The stone made a peculiar crunching noise as I dug the little holes into it, like puncturing Styrofoam. Within a few seconds, I flipped myself over the ledge.

The first stake caught me in the shoulder; the second

one caught me in the thigh. Then my mysterious sniper's gun clicked empty. I saw him at the far edge of the roof. He'd backed up and hid behind an air-conditioning unit while I made my climb. I roared and charged. He threw his weapon at my head. It was a good shot. I'd give him that. If I hadn't held up my hand to deflect it, I'd have a snuffer rifle handle-shaped dent in my forehead. As soon as he threw the weapon, he jumped over the ledge. By the time I got to where he'd been standing, he disappeared from sight. I had zero chance of catching him with a silver stake in my leg.

I gave another roar of displeasure, hoping he could hear me, but I doubted it. He'd probably made it to Mexico by now. I reached down with my good hand and pulled the stake from my thigh. I was so pissed I almost forgot the one in my shoulder. With a horrid slurping sound, I freed that one, too, and held onto both stakes in my right hand while I dropped off the side of the roof and down to the ground. I probably should have waited for my leg to heal. The pain that shot through my thigh reminded me to take some don't-be-stupid lessons later.

But my mind was on other things. I wanted to know how he found me. The only thing I could think of was that he had gotten lucky and trailed me here from the hotel. *The hotel. Oh, shit.*

I grabbed the cell out of my pocket and frantically dialed Thompson's number as I ran for the Suburban. My first dial went straight to voicemail. So did my second, third, fourth, and every other time I dialed on the way back to the hotel. Of course, the traffic would be horrible on the way back. Nothing ever goes the way you want it to. Everybody was probably pulled over to rubberneck somebody changing a tire. As it turned out, I'd come to the wrong conclusion. They had slowed to look at the burning hotel. My hotel.

I drove the SUV up onto the curb and ran the rest of

the distance to the hotel. People standing around gawking barely noticed the breeze as I passed by, but by the time they looked around I was gone. I was still far enough away that it took me a few minutes to get there. I stopped at the police barricade and flashed my badge. The officer holding back the perimeter lifted the tape, and I ducked under. He looked like he knew about as much as I did so I darted around searching for somebody barking orders.

Ah, he'd be the one in charge. I found him coordinating with the fire department. As I ran up to him and his hand went to his gun instinctively. I held up my badge when I got close enough for him to see, and he relaxed.

"Are you in charge?"

He nodded and eyed me warily. "I was until you showed up. What can I do for you?" Apparently, he'd met somebody from the FBI before.

"My partner was in our room, have you seen him? He's about six-five and 300 lbs. He's a big black guy who goes by the name of Thompson." *Please let him say yes.*

"No. Most of the hotel guests made it out okay; the flames seemed contained on the top floor for the better part of the fire. It spread lower, but they're getting it contained, slowly."

"Fuck." I bolted past him. He yelled after me, but I ignored him. I burst through the door into the smoke-filled lobby. Remembering my lessons, I avoided the elevator in case of fire and bolted for the stairwell. It would be faster anyway

Floor by floor sped past me as I took the stairs by threes and fours, and I made it to the top probably in record time. I held my hand against the fire door and heard a faint sizzling. It was hot, damn hot. I heard firefighters on the other side yelling as they tried to contain the blaze. I flung open the door and a burst of flames enveloped me. It singed my skin in a searing wave of heat. I closed my eyes and jumped through to the hall.

No lights were on, and the smoke was unbelievably thick. A group of firefighters at the end of the hall held a hose and soaked whatever they could, trying to douse the flames. I could vaguely make out the door of our hotel room, or most of it, anyway. It looked like it had been blown apart from within. Thompson was either in deep shit or dead.

I ran the length of the hall and came up behind the firefighters. One of them turned, saw me, and did a double take. He tapped the lead hose man and shouted something in his breathing mask. The man turned and aimed the hose at me after lessening the force of the water. The cold water doused me and I looked down. Most of my skirt had burned away, as well as my suit jacket. Gratefully, the water put me out before the flames burned through my white shirt.

I made a "move out of my way" motion with my hands and they stepped aside. I jumped through the jagged remnants of the door and rushed into the hotel suite. The blast had started in the living room and the rest of the apartment was ablaze. It had to be a couple hundred degrees in the room. Something cool touched my back. The firefighters stayed at the door and blasted me with as much water as they could. If Thompson had been in this room when the blast occurred, he was dead. I tried to swallow past a lump in my throat, and then a thought crossed my mind. I gave a silent prayer, to whoever would listen, that he hadn't. *Please let him have been on the shitter*. I kicked what was left of the door to his room open.

Flames shot out when the oxygen filled the room. The bed was a mass of cinders and my heart leapt at the fact he wasn't in there and sank at the fact he wasn't in there. He had to be in the bathroom. I sped through the room and opened the door. He lay in the shower with the water running full force. He'd put a wet towel over his head, but he wasn't moving. I ran to him and grabbed his hand. Again, he didn't move. Without thinking, I pulled. I'm strong, but I'm tiny. It became a problem of leverage. I propped him against the wall and pushed my shoulder into his stomach. I let him flop over onto my back and lifted with my legs. I had him, but I could barely keep my legs from slipping out from underneath me. The floor was too wet. Carefully, I kicked off my inappropriate rescue shoes and hoped my feet would get a little better traction.

They did. The difference was marginal, but it helped. I carried Thompson as quickly as I could through the bathroom door and the apartment. When they saw me, my firefighter friends doused us both with water, keeping the flames from igniting our clothes. I could barely make out their faces through the plastic of their breathing apparatuses, but I did see their surprised looks. I could only imagine what the scene looked like to them. I desperately tried not to slip as I walked past them.

"Let us help," came a muffled yell from the man with the nozzle.

"Just keep the fire away from me until I get him to the stairs!"

He nodded and maneuvered the hose back around and settled it on my back. I wanted to run, but I didn't think I could with Thompson on my back. The walk took hours, or maybe it just felt that way. Finally, we reached the door and safety. The stairwell had been constructed entirely of cement blocks with metal stairs. There wasn't anything to burn; the problem was the smoke. I didn't need to breathe, but Thompson did. I don't think you could kill a lycanthrope with smoke inhalation, but I'm sure he wouldn't be a happy camper if and when he woke up.

Shut up, Ashlyn. He would be all right. He had to be, or I'd kill him myself.

Carrying Thompson on my back through the hallway was difficult. Carrying Thompson on my back down stairs proved fucking insane. The floor was dry, so it minimized my chances of slipping, but just the sheer awkwardness of the situation started jerking on my sanity. I had inhuman strength and speed, but I couldn't use the speed or I'd drop him. I needed to get him out of there and I didn't know what to do. The firefighters couldn't help, Thompson was out cold, and I was alone. Panic started to flow through me like a small electrical charge. It thankfully ignited a fire under my butt. I leapt from mid-stair down to the landing, and we hit with a large thud. Thompson didn't fall. This I could work with. I gripped him a little tighter and tried it again, but this time I jumped the stairs.

My flight from the landing above to the landing below, echoed through the well. Loud and effective I could handle. Finally, I got the rhythm down enough I didn't have to stop long between jumps. I could only imagine what the *thump, thump, thump* would sound like to anybody who happened to be close enough to hear it. I'll be honest, I didn't give a fuck. Getting Thompson out of there occupied every thought process I had. I couldn't lose another partner, I just wouldn't. I was going to find the fucker who'd shot me, and the bastard who blew Thompson up, and I was going to shred them like pulled pork, cover them in barbeque sauce, and serve them up for Sunday lunch.

The panic surging through me gave way to anger. My talons grew longer and I sprouted bone-like protuberances (sounds way better than horns) from my forehead. I can't explain it, and I hate to even think about it, but as the anger flowed through me, I could feel it happening again. The thumping noise of my landings on the metal stair platforms gave way to *thump, chink* as my talons struck milliseconds after my feet. The fangs I'd been born with grew a little longer, and I had to open my mouth so they didn't pierce my bottom gums.

Normally, I would take time to calm down and let the changes revert to normal, but I didn't care. My only thoughts were of the man on my back and his safety. I hit the bottom landing of the stairs, kicked open the fire door and charged through the lobby like a raging bull. I didn't even bother with the front door. When I got close enough, I jumped through the plate glass hotel lobby and landed amid a shower of glass and fire.

Everyone stopped to stare at the diminutive monster with the massive bulk of man on its back. From behind the police barricade, the *click, click, click* and a multitude of camera flashes started slowly, but increased in frequency as I carried Thompson over to the EMTs stationed by the fire trucks.

Nobody said a word as I handed Thompson over and slumped down on the asphalt, truly exhausted. My clothes hung in tatters, but I didn't care as I brought my knees up to my face and cried. I heard the paramedics working on Thompson, and I even heard the word defibrillator. I sat quietly and let them do their work as I prayed. I prayed to everyone and everything. *Let him be all right, please.* Someone took pity on me, and covered me with a gray woolen blanket. I didn't even say thank you. At some point, I drifted off to sleep.

Deceptions

Chapter 17

I woke up in the hospital alone. Usually when you wake up in the hospital, the curtains are drawn and the door is wide open, but my door sat shut, drowning out most of the noise coming from whatever hospital I'd been admitted to. I looked down, expecting to see my clothes or a hospital gown, but somebody had dressed me in surgical scrubs. Maybe I did it and don't remember, I'd been that exhausted. The last thing I remembered was slouching down on the ground by the hotel.

The room was windowless, so I had no idea how much time had passed. A little weird to explain, but I could usually feel the sun. No matter where it was in the sky or below the horizon. I closed my eyes and felt nothing. Maybe I was still too tired.

My legs slipped over the side of the bed, and I followed them, silently dropping to the floor. I walked over to the door and grasped the handle, pulling it open. Two gentlemen in black suits stood in front of the door facing outward. *Guards?*

"Excuse me, gentlemen," I said softly to their backs. One of them turned his meaty head over his shoulder and looked at me through his sunglasses. I expected him to let me through, or say something at the least. He didn't. *Uh oh.* "Can you please move?"

"You're to remain here until the Deputy Director joins you, *agent*," he said, making my title a sneer.

Well doesn't that just chaff your nuts? What the hell did I do?

"When will that be?"

He didn't even reply. After the night I'd had, I

developed a sudden case of *fuckthisshititis*. When push came to shove, I did. Hard. The two guards at the door landed on their stomachs and slid the remaining distance until they collided with the nurse's station. I debated leaving, but I didn't have anywhere to go. They got the point, so I closed the door and went back to bed. I flipped on the television and watched cartoons. Yes, I said cartoons. Little talking yellow sponges are very therapeutic.

Fifteen minutes into the show, the door opened without so much as a knock. Without looking up, I pushed the power button on the television remote and set it on the wheelie cart next to the bed. I smelled the Deputy Director's aftershave before I heard his first footfall.

"Why didn't you tell me?" He took a seat on one of the padded pleather chairs that comes standard in every hospital room.

"Tell you what?"

"That you were some sort of demon."

"What?" I stared incredulously. If there had been any glass in the room, I think I might have broken it with the high C my question ended on. "Nobody has seen a demon in a millennium, why would you even remotely think I was one?"

"Here." He pulled a folded up newspaper from under his arm and tossed it right in my lap. I didn't even have to open it to see my picture on the front page with Thompson on my back and horns–I mean bone-like protuberances–sticking out of my forehead. I gulped a little at the ferocity of my face. My eyes even glowed a little. A shudder started at the crown of my head and traveled down my spine.

"I don't know what to tell you, sir. Your own medical people classified me as a new type of vampire. I am definitely not a demon."

"Then how do you explain the horns?"

"I prefer bone-like protuberances, and the answer is simple. I don't know. When I get extremely angry, they sort of pop out." I considered telling him about the talon and fang lengthening issue too, but something inside me said to keep my mouth shut. "Am I fired?"

"No, not even close. You ran into a burning building to save your partner's life and succeeded. The problem is everybody else in the world. We concocted a story to explain how a vampire came to be in the employ of the FBI, and now that story has some serious holes in it. Do you know how many blogs, discussion groups, and conspiracy theory websites now feature you as their major topic of discussion? I'll give you a hint. If you could sing you'd probably have a record contract right now. You have gone viral, Ashlyn."

I stared at him, and my mind swam with the news Thompson was all right, thank the gods. I looked down at the picture again. The horns were clearly visible. Blaming it on poor lighting or smudges of dirt probably wouldn't fly. The first tear rolled down my cheek. Sanders walked over to the bed. Deep down I expected him to ask for my badge and gun, but he didn't. He placed his sweaty palm on my clasped hands and gave them a little squeeze.

"We'll figure something out, Ashlyn. We worked too hard to train you. I'm not going to lose you. My only fear is that we won't get to keep you. Now that your secret is out, everybody and their mother is going to want you. The Department of Homeland Security already borrowed you, and I didn't particularly care for that. However, if it wasn't for you, the governor would be dead. Good work, by the way. I'm tempted to let the governor fend for himself and bring you back to Washington until this blows over."

He paused like he was seriously considering it. I briefly pictured myself locked in some room under the J Edgar Hoover building until everybody forgot about the horns. Goody. "I wish we could blame it on some sort of mutation. We need to call Marcel. He knows more about vampires than anybody I've ever met. He'd know what to tell the press."

"Yes, your friend Marcel is very interesting. If

Thompson wasn't such an effective babysitter for that temper of yours, I might consider offering him a position at the FBI. I'm currently thinking about making him a regularly paid consultant. Maybe he can help you with your vampire relation skills."

My mind and something in my chest fluttered at his words. I looked around for my cell phone, but didn't see any of my possessions. I'd find it later. I needed to get my SUV and my bags of clothing from the street. Hopefully, somebody had tracked it and taken it back to the local field office. I didn't want to go shopping again.

"Sir, someone attacked me last night at the local mall. When I came out there was a sniper on the roof with a snuff rifle."

"I know. About twenty witnesses called it into the local police department. One of them recognized the Verminator. The Sacramento field office got the call. They dispatched agents, but you were already gone. I'm assuming you headed to the hotel?"

"Yeah, I figured if they knew where I was, they knew where Thompson was. By the time I got there, the fire had gotten out of control. I'm just glad I got him out okay. Is he bad?"

"Some serious smoke inhalation scarred his lung tissue, but he seems to be healing quickly. He's been asking about you a few octaves lower than his normal speaking voice. Don't tell him I said so, but with the oxygen mask on, he sounded even more like Darth Vader."

Sanders cracked a joke. Surely the world would end tomorrow.

After a quick visit with Thompson, Sanders drove me to the Sacramento Field Office to retrieve my SUV full of brand spanking new clothes. At least I wouldn't be working in scrubs. On the way, he even gave Marcel a call in Chicago and offered him the consultation position. I heard a lot of "uh huh" and "yes" on Sanders part, so I could only imagine what they were talking about. Finally, Sanders got around to asking him about the picture of me in the paper.

The silence in the car was deafening. I think at one point I tried to lean over in my seat so I could hear the conversation. Usually, I have no problem picking up cell phone conversations, another benefit of being a vampire, but I couldn't hear anything from Sanders' phone. I glanced over at it and it wasn't like any other cell phone I'd ever seen before. It was a smartphone, but the back of the thing looked like hexagonally molded plastic tiles had been fused together, giving the impression of snakeskin. I made a mental note to ask him about it later. I loved toys.

When Sanders finally pulled into the parking lot at the local Bureau, he had just hung up with Marcel. He pulled into a spot and turned to me. "It would appear that Marcel is upset with us. Apparently, you are an excellent agent, but your vampire skills 'leave something to be desired.' Effective immediately, your new home office will be Chicago. Get this mess taken care of and head back there. I'll inform Reese."

"How long am I going to be there, sir?"

"Indefinitely."

I fought hard not to smile and ended up just nodding. *Thank you, gods.* Once Thompson heard the news, I'm sure he would call his wife, Marion, and give her the good news. She'd stayed in Chicago with the children, waiting until school finished for the year before moving to Washington. None of them had been looking forward to the move. "Thank you, sir. I've been screwing up a lot around the vampires and all their rules. Marcel will be invaluable."

"Next time you have a problem, call me, please. I'd rather know immediately than find out from somebody else. You're young, Ashlyn. I understand that. I also asked your friend what he thought about the article in the paper. He's trying to come up with some explanation to feed the press."

154

"Thank gods," I said with honest relief. Thinking about shit like that hurt my head.

"Gods, Ashlyn? I pegged you for a good catholic girl. You might be a lot of things, but you're obviously Irish."

"So Irish my aunt and mother were of the pagan variety."

He nodded and held out his hand. For the first time in my career, I had an appreciation for the Deputy Director. I reached out, took his hand, and pumped it vigorously. He gave me a little smile and I stepped out into the Sacramento night.

"Ashlyn," Sanders called before I could shut the door. "One more thing, next time I ask people to keep you somewhere so I can get to you, try not to throw them across the room." He gave me a little wink.

"I'm sorry, sir. I had a rough night."

"I had a feeling. Here's my cell number." He reached into his suit jacket, pulled out a gold embossed business card, and handed it to me. "You are the best thing that's happened to the Bureau in a very long time. If anyone else in this agency isn't courteous to you, please let me know.

"Thank you again, sir. I'll do that." I softly shut the door. I needed to get my SUV and clothes and head back to the Marriot we had been staying at originally before Marcel moved us. I crossed the parking lot and slipped inside.

Entering the building and heading to the office in scrubs wasn't the easiest of things to do. Luckily, I had my badge. The leather case I had it in got a little singed in the fire, but the hospital staff managed to save it. I needed another gun though. I'd left that in the hotel room, and I doubted it survived the fire. I just hoped my cell phone was still in the Suburban.

I walked into Connors' office, who was busy on the phone. I didn't want to be rude so I hovered around the door until he finished. "You look like hell, agent. Have a seat," he said when he hung up the receiver.

"Thank you, sir. It's been a rough week."

"I heard. That was probably the bravest thing I've ever seen. Just happened to flip on the news last night and saw the whole damn thing, including your spectacular exit.

Damn. "I–"

"Don't. I saw what I saw and I'll be honest, I don't give a shit. You ran into a burning building to save your partner. The rest doesn't matter."

I smiled and gave him a heartfelt, "Thank you."

"Anytime, good luck with everything. If you need anything, don't hesitate to call." He handed me a business card from the nifty black holder on his desk. I was going to need one of those business card wallet thingies if this kept up. "Your SUV is out in the lot. Keys." He tossed them to me from the top drawer of the desk. "I have two agents outside Thompson's hospital room, just as a precaution. If I ask you if you want a couple, are you going to say no?"

"Yes."

"Yes as in you're going to say no, or yes as in you want the agents?" He grinned as he said it.

"Yes to the former and no to the latter," I replied, thankful for his attempt at humor. "I really appreciate it, but I can take care of myself."

"I can see that, agent. You be careful."

"I will, sir."

Deceptions

Chapter 18

Thankfully, my cell phone was in the cup holder of the Suburban. I knew Victoria must be a frantic mess, but I didn't have a way to get hold of her. I needed to get her a cell phone. She'd probably gone back to the hotel, saw it in flames, and had a meltdown. I don't even know if she knew we'd been hospitalized.

The first place I checked was the cordoned off hotel. There weren't any lights on inside, and the only illumination outside were several police cars with their lights on in the parking lot. On a whim, I pulled up to the first police car and waited patiently for him to roll down his window. When he did, I leaned out mine.

"You need to move along, miss. This is a crime scene," he said before I could even spout out a question.

"I know, officer, I'm with the FBI." I pulled out my badge. "I'm looking for a girl vampire who was a guest at the hotel with me. Have you seen her?"

"No, ma'am, I just came on shift about an hour ago. If I see her, I'll let you know."

"Thanks." I gave him my cell number before pulling out of the lot, and headed for the Marriot. Vic didn't know we had rooms there, and I took my frustrations out on the steering wheel. She wouldn't go back to Santiago's since it lay in ruins. The only other place I could think of to look for her was the nosferatu club we'd gone to. Maybe she'd be waiting there for me. I tried to remember the rule about getting lost, but all I could come up with was start at the beginning.

The closer I got to the club, the *righter* it felt. If I closed my eyes, I could almost sense her sitting at the table in the club, worried about me. I stepped on the gas, and the Suburban sped forward. Before I concentrated on Vic, I vaguely recalled where the club sat nestled in the rundown area of Sacramento. Now I knew exactly where I was heading, guiding the SUV like I had a built-in GPS unit. Finally, after the longest drive of my life, I saw the neon lights of the club in the distance.

I pulled up on the curb and flew out the door. Without pausing for the bouncer, I jumped the velvet rope and rushed into the crowd. I spotted her before she spotted me and stopped. She sat there looking like somebody had run over her puppy. Sadness radiated from her. It washed over me where I stood. Tears started flowing down my cheeks. Without even thinking about it, I gave a little pulse of power. Vic lifted her head and started looking around the club as if she smelled somebody baking brownies. I gave a little laugh, and I swear she heard me. Her eyes focused and her head snapped in my direction. When she finally saw me her eyes lit up .

Her stool hit the ground as she launched herself toward me. I braced myself for the impact, and it was a good thing I did. She hit me with the force of a speeding freight train and sent me skidding back a few feet. I'd expected a, "Hello," but she locked her lips on mine. I could feel everybody's eyes in the club focus on the two of us as Victoria kissed me with an intensity I'd not known in my life. My very short life, but still.

The sound of somebody clearing their throat behind us stopped Victoria's welcome. I actually felt a little more relieved than disappointed. Victoria had the honor of being the greatest enigma in my life. Even after such a short time, I would die without her. She'd become more than a friend, but I didn't know if I loved her. I needed to figure that out, quickly.

"I told your young friend if anything had happened to you, she would have been the first to know. Yet, when she couldn't find you, she fell into despair," Viktor said softly with the tiniest of smiles, and something else. It almost looked like jealousy.

"Tomorrow I'm taking her to buy a cell phone. I woke up in the hospital and had no way to get a hold of her. I'm sorry, Vic." I turned toward her. I couldn't do anything but laugh. Gone was the dead puppy look on her face. Instead, she radiated joy and happiness. She held my hand, and I gave hers a little squeeze.

"When I went back to the hotel last night, it felt like a nightmare. I tried to ask the police about you, but they started questioning me about the fire. I don't think they like vampires."

"Yeah, I've had that happen to me a couple of times over the past few days, too," I said with an ironic little smile. "Thompson got caught in the fire; he's in the hospital still."

"As long as you're okay, master." She hugged me again.

"Excuse me. Can I have your autograph?"

"I'm sorry, what?" I pulled away from Vic. She looked almost as confused as I did.

"Can I have your autograph?" I turned to see a young guy who looked like he'd barely reached drinking age standing in front of a triangle of people. They all had the same eager expression on their faces.

"Why?" To say I was confused would be the understatement of the century.

"You're d-demon girl aren't you, the Verminator? The guys back at the dorms won't believe I saw you here." Realization hit me. They'd seen the news.

"I don't really…" I trailed off. "I don't have anything to sign."

"Oh, my god, wait here, I'll be right back!"

He took off and miraculously the horde behind him followed out of the club. I stood there dumbfounded. Well, that was simple. Now I just needed to get Vic out of there in case they came back. I so wasn't signing autographs.

"Come on, Vic, you ready to go?" She stood there with the most curious look. Viktor's matched hers perfectly. "It's a long story. I'll tell you later."

"They saw you?" She had seen me transform into my worst, so she knew exactly what the guy had been talking about.

"It's worse than that. The news filmed me. Please, Vic, let's go. I really don't want to be here when they get back."

"It's too late for that because here they come," Viktor piped in.

I groaned as my autograph hounds rushed back in through the entrance. There must have been a newspaper machine somewhere outside the club. Most of them held a brand new newspaper. Thankfully, the machine must have been only partially full. I winced as they bobbed and weaved through the club, making their way back to where we stood.

I felt ridiculous as the ones with papers lined up in front of me. I wasn't a celebrity, nor did I have any desire to be one. The gods of irony were probably sitting around wherever the gods of such things do and having a good chortle at my expense. I debated running, but I just couldn't. I said I would do it, so I would. I reached out my hand to my original stalker and took the newspaper from him. I thought he had been clever and come up with the demon girl name all on his own. He hadn't. It sat right on the front page in bold type right above the picture of me carrying my partner on my back. Because it was newsprint, the picture looked a little fuzzy, but you could still see the horns. *Fuck.*

I fought back the tears burning in my eyes and took the pen Nerdy Guy held out like a carrot in front of me. At least one of us was a little excited about it. I tried not to look at the headline as I brought the tip of the pen down on the paper. "Who should I make this out to?" I asked it without emotion and without looking at my admirer.

"Jack, please."

To Jack, I give my first autograph, Ashlyn. The words flowed from my pen without conscious thought. Chills crept up my spine at the prospect of what I was doing, but I got through the first one. The second came a little easier. The third I hardly thought about at all, and by the time I finished the little Ashlyn autopilot in my head had taken over. Everyone who asked for an autograph got one. Everybody had been more than polite, though I don't know if they were just being nice, or were afraid I would go all demon on their asses.

I turned around, and Vic stared at me like I'd gone a little nuts. Viktor looked outright worried. I tried to shoot for unconcerned, but probably looked a little more like nauseous. I shook my head to clear it a little and sat in the nearest empty seat. My legs refused to support me anymore. Running into the fiery hotel had been less exhausting, at least on an emotional level.

"Come on, Vic. Let's go home."

"Yes, master."

The hotel was quiet as Vic and I showered (separately) and went to bed. She seemed hesitant about joining me, but I gave her a small wink that seemed to set her at ease. I really needed somebody to hold on to. Snuggle therapy sounded better than watching cartoons. I dressed in an oversized T-shirt and slid under the thick comforter. I really needed warmth. A chill radiated from my bones and spread through my body to the tips of my toes and nose. I watched Vic as she walked around the other side of the bed.

After getting out of the shower, she'd put on one of the robes provided by the hotel. I prayed she wore something underneath it, but knowing Vic, probably not. She pulled down her side of the comforter and turned the switch light off. It was a sweet gesture, but I could still see her perfectly. She reached to the tie on the front of the robe and pulled it loose. I debated closing my eyes. I probably would have if she hadn't been watching my face. I gulped as the robe fall open, revealing the front of her perfect body to me again.

She slowly pulled the robe off her shoulders and let it fall down her arms and pool on the floor. Like a cat, she slinked onto the bed and lay down next to me, with a stretch for good measure. She gave a little pout as she pulled the heavy comforter up over her hips and stopped it just below her breasts. Propping her head up on her hand, she stared at me with utter adoration.

I had to smile back at her from the sheer cuteness factor. That earned me a throaty chuckle. My nerves were rattled. She and I slept in the same bed every night. *What made this night so different?* I couldn't put my finger on it, but felt it in the air.

"Master?"

"Yeah?"

"Do you find me attractive?"

I couldn't help it. I lost it, and I think I might have spit on her a little when the laughter erupted from me like a geyser. As soon as it happened, I covered my mouth, hoping I hadn't completely crushed her feelings. I worried needlessly. She rolled onto her back and howled with laughter right alongside me. Finally, after what felt like the better part of an hour, the laughter died away to giggles.

"Thanks, Vic. I really needed that."

"You're welcome, master. I know you want me. I could smell your desire from the moment I danced in front of you. You've never even kissed a woman before me, have you?"

"Honestly, I've never kissed anyone. I never even knew I could find a woman attractive until I met you."

"That's good enough for me. We'll take it slow, and I promise not to seduce you until you tell me to."

"Thank you." I rolled over to her, laying my head on her shoulder, my hand on her taut stomach and kissed her on the cheek. She wrapped her arms around my shoulders and pulled me tight against her. I was the master, but right at that moment, I didn't feel that way. I needed her more than she needed me. I vaguely remember running my hand over her stomach as we drifted off to sleep. I sincerely hoped I was fully dreaming when my hand started to drift lower.

Chapter 19

The sound of the door opening woke me from a sound sleep. I didn't yawn, or stretch, or even rub my eyes. Within a second, I jumped out of bed and out in the main room ready to pounce on whoever had come in. I stopped in my tracks and blinked a few times. Thompson stood there with his arms crossed and a small smirk on his face. I gave a quick, "Woo-hoo," and launched myself at him. He caught me in midair and gave me a very un-Thompson-like hug.

"That hug wasn't from me, it was from my wife. She said she owes you big time. So do I, kid. Thanks for pulling my fat out of the fire, so to speak."

"Big guy, I would have run into hell to pull you out. Which, according to the news, I might know the way to." I rolled my eyes.

"I saw that. Nice job. I'm surprised they haven't called to set up a press conference."

"They probably have. Sander's is working with Marcel to come up with some sort of cover story. I signed autographs at the club last night. Before you ask, no, I wasn't out partying. I went to find Vic."

"Sure, kid," he said with a little wink. "I'm going to shower. I still smell like barbeque. The governor is giving a speech tonight at Cal State, so get ready."

"Are you kidding me? When did this happen?"

"As of last night. The original speaker called out sick. The governor was honored to be considered as a last minute replacement. With any luck, the bad guys won't have time to plan anything on such short notice."

"I doubt it. Knowing Greer, he's already called a press

conference. I'll go put on my stake proof vest."

"That's not funny, Ash. Sanders told me about the mall. You need to be more careful. Tonight, I'm riding point on the governor. You keep an eye out for bad guys."

"Um, I really hate to pull a *you're being stupid* card, but you just got out of the hospital, and a silver stake through you would most likely be fatal. No, I'll ride shotgun on the governor's ass tonight, but I do promise to be careful. If anybody shoots at us, I'll hold him in front of me," I added trying to make Thompson laugh. It didn't work.

"Fine, but if you get dead, my ass is grass. Remember that, okay?"

"It's a deal. Now seriously, go take a shower. You smell like a burnt hamburger."

"Funny, kid. Real funny."

I've always wanted to go to college. I was probably one of the few agents in the FBI without a degree. Maybe I would look into getting my degree online, just so I didn't feel like such a schlub.

The California State University Sacramento was beautiful. Most of the campus looked new. Students lounging around talking and studying gave me a little lump in my throat. Normal kids leading normal lives. Something I would never know.

The governor was due to arrive with his contingent of state troopers in half an hour. Thompson and I had to sweep the building before he got there. Maybe I'd get lucky and someone would attack his limo before he arrived.

Thompson pulled out his phone, checking the email giving the details as to the where and when of the speech, and then led us to the appropriate building. One thing was certain; the university's security left a lot to be desired. No one stopped us on our way to the main auditorium.

We walked in and the blast of cold air threatened to blow me back through the entrance. If they had cranked it down to subarctic temperatures, they must have been expecting quite the turnout for the governor's speech. We made our way into the heart of the auditorium. Thousands of seats faced a large stage complete with microphone and podium. I looked around at exits, entrances, and windows remembering points of possible danger to the governor. The place wasn't exactly Fort Knox, but it wasn't exactly a target range either. I sighed at the prospect of getting perforated by silver stakes yet again. My stomach did a little flip-flop, but I choked it down. What doesn't kill you often hurts like a son of a bitch. I didn't want to get shot again. Ever.

"I'm going to look around," I called out to Thompson as he checked out the people setting everything up on the stage.

"Good idea, kid," he called back.

I tried not to beam too much at his compliment. I could be a good FBI agent, I really could.

I turned and headed to the stairs leading up to the second level. I took them three at a time and made it up the flight rather quickly. I glanced around to see if anybody had caught me showboating, but they all seemed rather distracted setting everything up. The upper level itself was devoid of life as far as I could tell. I could walk around the entire perimeter of the ground floor and keep an eye on everyone and everything. Hell, if somebody tried to pick the governor off with another snuff rifle, it would probably be from up here. Thompson's idea of him guarding Greer sounded a little better. *If that son of a bitch who shot me shows up, I'm going to rip him apart. I don't even care if I get my shoes bloody.*

I went back downstairs and walked over to Thompson, who appeared to be going over security concerns with a gray-haired gentleman who held himself with an air of authority. You could look at him and know he was in charge. I waited in the distance until

Thompson finished and walked over to him.

"What do you think, kid?"

"If they're going to hit him, it'll probably be with a snuffer rifle. There will be too many people here to use explosives or incendiaries, or at least I hope they won't. That would just suck beyond belief. Don't roll your eyes, but I think you were right. You take bodyguard duty. I want to sit on the upper level and watch from there."

"You're learning, kid. I'll make you Deputy Director one day."

"Are you going to give me a full frontal lobotomy? The way I figure, you'd have to be partially brain dead to hold down that job."

Thompson's laughter echoed through the auditorium.

I watched from above the crowd as Greer entered the stage from somewhere within the bowels of the auditorium. Thompson followed behind the vampire governor and kept a wary eye on the crowd and the people who remained on stage. Luckily, the attending students and supporters of the governor weren't large enough to fill the massive auditorium. We got to close the second level as a result. I stood alone among the sea of empty seats and scouted the auditorium for trouble. Everyone sat and waited eagerly as Greer walked across to the podium amid a thunderous round of applause. The sheer enthusiasm of the crowd shocked me a little. Controversy surrounded the world's first elected vampire official, but you couldn't tell from the heartwarming reception he received.

When he stood before the microphone, the applause stopped, the eagerness in the silence of the crowd palpable as they waited for the Governor to speak. He smiled to the crowd and waved as he pulled some notecards from his jacket pocket. As he began his speech, I noticed one thing about Greer I hadn't before. When he spoke, there wasn't a single flash of his fangs.

Some of the older myths from a time when vampires

and werewolves didn't walk freely out in the open painted them as human-like creatures whose fangs sprouted forth like a snake's retractable fangs. This wasn't true. Just like the myths involving holy relics and not casting a reflection in mirrors. Vampires were full of magic. In fact, it's what kept them alive, but magic had rules just like science. To hide their true nature, vampires perfected speaking without showing their teeth. The older vampires, who had more practice, did so with minimal difficulty. Greer was a master, and to top it off, his diction didn't suffer at all.

Newer vampires, on the other hand, have a tendency to show a lot of fang when they speak. It takes a lot of practice to master it. I show fang more than any vampire I've ever met. It isn't my fault though. If I lived to be a thousand years old, I'll still show fang when I speak. Not only are mine longer and thicker than the average vampire, mine also curve. They're designed to pierce the flesh of my victims and hang on. I chalk it up to being a predator of predators. If it weren't for bad, I wouldn't have any luck at all.

Lost in my own thoughts, I missed the end of the governor's speech. The thunderous round of applause snapped me out of my reverie, and I saw a shape blocking out the starry sky through one of the windows on the second story. I gasped in surprise. There wasn't any ledge outside the windows up here. I'd checked to make sure they couldn't be used as a possible sniper location. The shadow looked definitely man-shaped, so my previous assumption must have been wrong. I turned and ran around the perimeter of the wall and crept below the windows until I reached where I had seen him.

Standing just before the window and looking out at an angle, I could see the shadow was definitely a man. How the hell he managed to hold himself just outside the window remained a mystery. It really didn't matter though, once I saw him raise the snuff rifle up and aim it at the stage, I jumped. The window shattered as I went through it. The shallow cuts became worth it when I briefly

Sean Hayden

saw the look of utter shock on the vampires face as I grabbed him.

I got my answer when I tackled him. Apparently, he had used his vampiric strength to dig hand and footholds in the side of the brick and mortar building. He didn't dig deep enough. When I grabbed him, he lost his footing and we both plummeted the twenty feet to the concrete below. A large crack echoed and I wasn't sure if my bones had broken, his bones had broken, or we put a serious hurting on the concrete pad outside the auditorium. I landed on top of Mr. Sniper, so I hoped they were his bones. I wanted to break the rest with my hands.

He had other ideas though. I'd hoped to at least have knocked him momentarily unconscious, but his fist connecting with my jaw told me otherwise, and so did the tree I crashed into. He took off as I slid down, almost comically slow. You know when the cartoon characters hit the walls and slide down with the *skree* noise in the background? That's what I felt like. As soon as my feet hit the ground, I took off after him.

I jumped a fire hydrant as his fleeting shadow rounded the corner about a block ahead of me. Adrenaline, or whatever it is vampires have, surging through my veins, burning as it flowed. I saw him ahead. He had no place to go except straight. The buildings in the area had been built with little or no room between them, and gave silent thanks to older architecture and overcrowding. I gave a burst of speed I didn't know I had left in me, especially after almost becoming one with a tree. I started to close the distance between us, but at the rate of speed we were traveling, the stretch of road ended shortly and he ducked around another corner. I didn't want to lose him, so I strained my limits to follow about fifty feet behind him.

When I got there, he was gone. Panic welled up within me, and I wanted to scream in frustration. I balled my fists, opened my mouth, and then saw him scaling the side of the building across the street. My scream of frustration turned into a *squee* of excitement as I launched myself after the bastard. I crossed the street in less than a second and started jamming my fingers into the concrete surface of the building. I never took my gaze from his back as he scaled the building, and within moments, my climbing skills proved better than his as I closed the distance between us. If the roof was his goal I would make it right behind him.

He cursed when he saw me right below him before he flipped over the side of the building and onto the roof. His footfalls echoed w h e n he started running again. I flung myself over the edge and landed on the roof with my feet already in motion. He looked over his shoulder and gave a little smile as he kept going. He didn't even pause when he jumped.

I can jump about four or five stories and he looked like he could do about the same. I debated jumping after him, but didn't know where he would land. I paused at the edge of the building to watch his descent, and the strangest thing happened. Once he reached the apex of his arc, he didn't come down. The night winds buffeted him, keeping him aloft above the building tops as he was carried away to safety. A cold chill ran up my spine. The fucker could fly.

Sonofabitch, I thought. Nobody told me vampires flew. I smiled a little. Maybe I could do the same thing. Then my smile turned back into a scream of rage. He'd gotten away. Again.

Sean Hayden

Chapter 20

I called Thompson on the way back to the auditorium. After hearing the glass crashing after I jumped through the window he'd grabbed the governor, shoved him in the limousine, and taken him back to the mansion. Basically, I killed the party, but got kudos from my partner for foiling the attempt before shots were fired.

Joy.

Thompson left the Suburban at the school, but had the keys in his pocket, where they didn't do me a bit of good. I debated calling a cab, but decided to take a walk instead. With a quick text to Thompson, I told him I'd wait for him at the college auditorium. Let him worry about getting us back to the hotel.

I hadn't been paying attention while I chased the bad guy, but I vaguely knew the way back to the university. Lost in my own thoughts, I passed street after street of closed shops without so much as a glance.

The Governor's Ball would be held in two days' time. I don't know why, but I had a feeling that if we didn't get the situation under control, Greer wouldn't live through it. For the fiftieth time, I wished the stubborn ass would just cancel the damn thing. Didn't he know he had a death warrant out there on him and he'd signed his own name on it? In a fit of frustration I punched the corner of the building I was rounding and felt a little guilty when a large chunk of concrete shattered into dust. I looked around, but the streets seemed to be deserted, too deserted.

The hair on my neck rose as a feeling of *oh shit* washed over me. I put my back against the wall and listened. I couldn't hear anything, but I could feel something wrong. I sidled along the length of the building and peered around the next corner. The trouble I felt stood in the middle of the street. He looked ordinary enough, except for the extremely long curls of blond perfection flowing over his shoulders. I'd seen him only briefly, but every detail of him had been burned into my brain. I'd been trained to remember details of everything and everyone around me, but the way the scene around the corner etched itself into my head had a completely different quality.

"Come out, little one." The timbre of his voice slithered over my skin and settled into my limbs. It forced my legs to walk and propel me around the corner to him. I closed my eyes and fought with everything I had. It didn't work, not even a little. Not only did my limbs refuse to obey, but they told me to shut the fuck up and do what I was told.

The closer I got to him, the more I could feel his power. I stared at not only his hair, but everything else about him. He wasn't pale like a vampire, but he wasn't tan either. He simply had perfect porcelain skin. He definitely didn't look undead. "Who are you?" It took me a few tries to find my voice.

He smiled and stepped closer when my legs stopped propelling me toward his presence. I expected him to strike and finish me off as I stood powerless, but all he did was walk a circle around me, taking in every inch with his eyes. I knew, because I could feel his gaze on my skin, soft and warm. I shuddered when he finally stopped in front of me again.

"We are cousins, you and I, Ashlyn. My name is Raphael. I simply wished to meet the creature I have been hearing so very much about the past few years." He didn't use his commanding voice, the voice that made me do things against my will, but every word he spoke sent a chill up my spine. I was a predator of predators, but I knew without a doubt, if Raphael wanted me dead he would have little or no trouble making it happen. I smelled my own fear before he did.

"What do you want?" I tried to sound as brave as I could. My voice didn't crack, but it was more than a little shaky.

He didn't respond, but he did close the gap separating us. He gave me the tiniest of smiles and raised his hand, slowly sliding his knuckles along my cheek. The gesture made me shiver in its intimacy, and at the same time made my stomach churn. He flexed his index finger, trailed that back up my jaw and over the arch of my brow until it settled on the spot right above the bridge of my nose. The build of power sent tingles throughout my head. "Miraculous," he said under his breath.

The world began to fade away and then burst in a flash of light.

I stood on a field of stone as the red clouds above rolled without spilling a drop of rain, and yet showered the tattered landscape below with bolts of yellow lightning. The thunder echoed, but the whole scene sounded as if the entire realm had been made of thin metal. There were echoes where there shouldn't have been and the sounds of battle had a sharper quality than should have come from the ring of sword on sword, and sword on flesh.

I looked down, seeing I wore a shift of the thinnest white linen. The sun broke through the clouds and beat down from above, yet did not burn. In awe, I lifted my head, and for the first time in my life, I gazed fully on its fiery brilliance. Our sun burned bright yellow, but the one above burned red. Not knowing if I would ever experience it again, I held out my arms and let its warmth flow over my arms and face.

An anguished cry stole my attention from the sky. Below me on the plain a battle raged the likes of which had never been witnessed before by man or monster. Men the size of giants fought hand-to-hand combat with magnificent swords made entirely out of fire and light. They stood twelve feet tall, and as they fought, they utterly devastated the landscape around them. Furrows formed in the dry soil from the sliding of their enormous sandaled feet as they wrestled and fought. I couldn't see as much as feel that those scars in the earth would never heal. Brother fought brother in a war that should never have been. Its very existence threatened the balance of nature itself.

Two of the giants closest to me fought ferociously. They didn't see my approach as I walked toward them. How could they? I stood barely to the waist of the shortest. I looked up and saw his face. Raphael swung his sword in a downward arc that his foe blocked with a blade of blackened night. Raphael's blade sank into the earth at my feet and both men stopped fighting to stare at the creature below them. The one holding the blade of night placed the tip of his sword into the ground and stopped fighting to gaze at me.

"What do we have here, cousin?" The one I didn't know glanced at Raphael.

"I think she might be one of yours, Asmodeus. She smells like you!"

"This might be the one who causes me so much distress so many years from now. I wish I could dispatch her now and be done with it. What say you, daughter? Would you take your own life and save your father some trouble?"

I shook my head and started backing up, one step at a time. "Father," echoed in my head like the metallic thunder around me. The blood drained from my face as he started to laugh.

Wings sprouted from both of their backs, Raphael's pure in their whiteness, and Asmodeus' so black they sucked the light from around them. Raphael said something in a language I'd never heard. It reminded me of someone singing pure tones of different pitches. Asmodeus understood and let out a discordant bleat in the upper register. The feathers of his wings started to fall with the grace of autumnal leaves from a tree. I expected to see what looked like a featherless bird wing, but stripped from its downy plumage, the wing resembled the stretched skin of a bat wing. His perfect teeth darkened and his canines started to elongate into a fang curved the shape of a sickle. A fang just like mine.

I screamed, and for the first time, I needed to breathe to fight back the fear.

Suddenly, back in the middle of the street, I spun in a circle. Raphael's absence came to me like a breath of fresh air. I had no idea who, or what, he was, but I gave silent thanks to whoever had sent him that he was gone. I really should have called the cab. Next time I would.

By the time I made it back to the University, Thompson stood by the Suburban with a curious look on his face. I felt like somebody had drugged me. It wouldn't really work if they did, but I imagined how I felt right at this moment would be similar.

"You okay?"

"Yeah, I just had a rough moment back there." "Sometimes they get away, kid. It's not a big deal." He opened his door and slid in the driver's seat. I opened the door and fell into mine. The SUV started and the cool air from the vents washed over me. I reached over and pointed the other one of mine, and one of Thompson's, full force on my face. I willed the cool air to wash away what I had seen. "You sure you're okay?"

"Just had an out of body experience and met my dad." "Excuse me?" He did a classic double take.

"Nothing. Never mind."

"Ashlyn…"

"Please, just let it go, maybe later."

The sign of a good partner is that they care. The sign of a great partner is they know when to let it go. Thompson was better than great. He nodded and became very interested in the operation of the SUV.

We rode in silence on the way back to the hotel while I rested my head against the back of the comfortable leather seats. I stared out the window at the starry night sky and thought about nothing in particular, or at least I tried to. I'd never known my mother, only her twin sister. I'd like to think they were similar, but it's still not the same. I had never, ever thought I would find out who my father was, let alone meet him. Finally, I'd met him and not only had he scared the crap out of me and asked me to kill myself, I didn't know if he was even real.

Chapter 21

The Governor's Ball was the next day and Thompson and I hadn't even begun to get everything prepared. The only good news we got was that he and I would be staying in the mansion for the remainder of the night and during the daylight hours of the big day. That gave us plenty of prep time to thwart the attack we were sure would come. Greer wouldn't be the only major political player in the vampire world in attendance either. Every master of every major city in California was on the guest list, and if I knew anything about vampire pride, few had turned down the invite.

Thompson and I walked the entire exterior of the mansion with legal- sized pads of paper making notes on possible weaknesses in the security of the governor and his guests. The list kept getting longer and longer, while my feeling of hopelessness got bigger and bigger. The words "death trap" kept crossing my mind for some reason. Thompson, on the other hand, kept up his positive attitude. I tried not to make gagging faces.

We did settle on who would be doing what during the ball. Thompson would play the role of orchestra conductor while I played inhuman shield to Greer. Thompson didn't see the other masters of the cities as potential targets (or at least important ones), but after visiting the dead master of San Jose, I couldn't help but feel a little sorry for those on the guest list. Thompson called it collateral damage; I called it more of my people I would have to protect if I needed to. I gave a little gulp at the idea that I was starting to think of vampires as *my people*. Especially after the walking, waking dream I had on the

Sacramento street the night before. That dream, or vision, had rattled what little I knew about myself and what I was.

"Ashlyn!" Thompson's shout snapped me out of my reverie. I looked up at him and blinked a couple of times.

"What?"

"Get your fucking head in the game, kid, or I'll have you sit this one out."

"My head is in the game. I was thinking about how hard it would be to get Greer to wear a stake proof vest under his tux," I lied.

"Good luck with that. Do you think four FBI SWAT agents will be sufficient to cover the rear entrance?"

"I think so; tell them not to engage unless they can get a clear shot from a distance and radio for back up immediately."

"I said that already, pay attention." He gave me a friendly slap on the head.

"Yes, Father."

He started to move on, and I followed him. I refused to go back to my thoughts, so I actually looked around for the first time that night. A hundred weak areas caught my attention, and I jotted them down on my growing list of possible avenues of attack. Shit, for all I knew, the vampires were going to drop a nuke on the mansion. How the hell do you protect against that?

"You see anything else?" I looked up and found we were where we'd started our rounds.

"Only about a hundred and fifty things."

"Yeah, me too. Let's go compare lists."

That's precisely what we did for the next hour and a half. Thompson saw things I hadn't even noticed. I'm ashamed to say almost every one of mine had already been marked down by him. At least I saw them. I might not be as good as Thompson, but I was getting better. Let's hope I would be good enough by tomorrow night. I really wanted this whole detail to be over.

A knock on the office door where Thompson and I had set up shop came just as we finished going over our lists. Thompson went to open the door, revealing a sheepish-looking governor. If a man who always expects things done for him ends up on your doorstep looking sheepish, you can bet your ass he wants something you won't want to do.

"Can we help you, sir?" Thompson stood back far enough to give Greer enough room to enter the smallish office.

"Actually, you can. Would you mind if I sat?" He entered the room taking Thompson's recently vacated seat.

"What do you need, sir?" I tried to keep the suspicion out of my voice. That didn't work out so well.

"You always get right to the point. I like that about you, Ashlyn. Let me be blunt. The master of San Diego has agreed to fly in tonight to show her support of my election. I gave my oath that nothing would happen to her. What I need from the FBI is her protection. Could you meet her at the airport and make sure she arrives here safely?"

Thompson's eyes shined with disbelief. "How are we supposed to protect you if we're out playing taxi service?"

"I'll go," I offered. The words flew out of my mouth before I could stop them. The reason was clear, at least to me. I'd indirectly caused the death of one master, was called in to see the body of another, and had been standing in front of another when he'd been blown to literal pieces. If I could stop just one more death from happening besides the governor, maybe this detail wouldn't be a total loss.

"Thank you," Greer said.

"Excuse me?" Thompson's question came out at the same time.

"I'll do it. You stay here and finish the prep work. You have a ton more experience than I do, and I'm better at keeping my ass alive. It'll be okay, big guy. I'll be back before you miss me." I smiled.

Thompson didn't return it.

"Fine, do you have the details of her flight?" Thompson turned to Greer.

"She is arriving at the Sacramento airport in little over an hour. Here's the flight plan." He handed me her itinerary while beaming. He got his way. "Esperanza Garcia Ramirez will be arriving via private jet at my hangar. At least you can avoid the traffic at the terminal. She will have two guests with her. Would you mind using the limousine?"

"Yes. I'm taking my SUV. I don't know how to drive your limo and don't trust anybody I don't know with safety right now. I drive, I keep us safe."

"I guess you're right, agent. Thank you."

"My pleasure, sir."

We pulled out of the hangar in silence. I think Miss Ramirez felt a little snubbed that she had to ride in a lowly sports utility vehicle rather than a posh limousine. I didn't care. She took an immediate dislike to the vampire FBI agent and decided to give me the cold shoulder. I made faces when she wasn't looking.

"Why did Greer not come and meet me himself?" Esperanza finally broke the silence once we hit the highway.

"His duties as governor kept him away, but he sends his apologies. I hope your flight was acceptable, Miss Ramirez." I smiled and did a little dance in the front seat. I was getting good at being polite.

"Dreary, but acceptable. Please hurry to our hotel. I am in need of a bath after traveling."

The incredulous look I gave her in the rear view mirror probably saved our lives. The headlights flying up on us were traveling too fast to be a coincidence. I gave the big SUV a little gas and made an unplanned right turn just to be certain. The road we turned onto led back to the airport and was more of a service road than an actual street. There wouldn't be a reason in the world for the car behind us to turn unless they were following us.

"Fuck," I said when the headlights reappeared. I picked

up my cell and speed dialed Thompson.

"Don't tell me, you've been attacked," Thompson said from the other end of the line.

"That depends. Did you send somebody to escort us to the hotel by chance?"

"No. Why? What's going on?"

"I have an unidentified car following us."

"Are you sure?"

"Positive. Track the GPS in my cell. I'm hanging up now."

"Got it, help is on the way in minutes."

I clicked the end button and put the phone in a compartment in the center console. If we wrecked, I wanted it as safe as possible. I reached over and grabbed the seatbelt I *never* used and clicked it into place. "Buckle up," I told my passengers who had been paying attention to my conversation with Thompson. At least they listened.

I slowed down and made like I planned on pulling over to the shoulder of the road, keeping an eye on the vehicle behind us as they closed the distance. I gunned the engine and gave the wheel a yank to the left. Not flipping a sports utility vehicle is difficult. Not flipping a full size Suburban is about fucking impossible. I managed to keep it from rolling, but I didn't keep all four wheels on the ground. Usually vampires and other supernatural beings are pretty fearless, especially as far as car wrecks are concerned. Unless the car exploded, the chances of a vampire dying in a car accident are slim to none. That didn't stop my passengers from giving little screams of surprise as I pulled a fast one-eighty turn.

As soon as we were safely facing the opposite direction, I gunned the engine. All eight cylinders pumped as fast as they could. Three-quarters of a ton of steel accelerates slowly, even with the finest of internal combustion engines pushing it. I turned and stared at the passengers of the strange vehicle as they sped past. Every one of them stared back in shock. I could make out the driver and a passenger in the front seat, and three others in the back. All doubts that they were following us vanished when they spun their vehicle in an almost identical move to the one I pulled off. Because they fishtailed on the shoulder of the road, slipping on the loose gravel, it bought us a few more precious seconds as they fought to gain traction. By the time they started seriously accelerating, I'd almost pushed the Suburban to top speed, barreling down the highway like a mini semi-tractor trailer.

The lead I'd gained over our friends didn't last long. Once I headed back to the main road, their headlights reappeared in my rear view mirror. I couldn't push the accelerator any closer to the floorboard, so I did the next best thing. I slammed on the brakes. The Suburban's tires screeched against the asphalt and the whole vehicle shuddered. Anti-lock brakes, my ass. I fought against the steering wheel as the mass of metal fought to fishtail out of control. The guys behind me weren't so lucky. They lost it and missed my rear bumper by inches as they swerved around me to avoid a collision.

I let off the brakes and gunned it. A small feral smile crept onto my lips. My headlights were now in *their* rear view mirror. I turned on my high beams. Twin shafts of illumination filled the smaller SUV, and the heads of the five occupants became visible. The three in the back seat glared at me, showing their fangs in the process. I smiled back, until the front passenger pointed a small cylindrical tube out the window and braced it on top of his shoulder.

I'd been standing in front of the master of Los Angeles when an anti-personnel rocket had hit him. I really didn't want to be in a SUV that got hit by one. He pulled the trigger and the rocket launched straight at the front of the Suburban.

"Look out!" One of my passengers saw the rocket and screamed. The others gasped in surprise.

I muttered a quick, "Oh, fuck," and spun the wheel frantically. The SUV spun ninety degrees and tilted over on its side just as the rocket impacted. We took the hit to the roof instead of the engine block. I didn't know if that was a good thing or not.

Fire filled the Suburban as we skidded to a stop. The concussion from the explosion had been minimal. I heard the *boom,* but the impact from the roof had set off the detonation. I thanked whoever might be listening that it hadn't pierced the roof and exploded inside the vehicle. Fire I could deal with. Being exploded might be a tad more difficult. Suddenly, the expression "pull yourself together" took on a whole new meaning.

I spun in my seat and looked at my passengers. They were on fire. I mean that literally. Not only did their clothes burn, but they appeared flammable as well. This day just kept getting better and better.

I forgot I had actually used my seatbelt for once and got a sharp reminder when I tried to kick open the passenger door. Mine would have been easier if the vehicle hadn't landed driver's side down. I quickly unbuckled and tried again with better results. By the time I made it out into the relatively (relative to the temperature inside the vehicle) cool air, my passengers' screams had reached almost unbearable levels. I stood atop the Suburban, reached down, and ripped off the door separating them from me. The blast of air magnified the flames, and I grabbed the first of Esperanza's entourage.

The tall blonde female vampire fought against my hand at first and then realized I was trying to help. She grasped my wrist, and I pulled. When she flew up through the mangled door, I frowned that she hadn't followed my advice and worn her seatbelt. My frown dissipated when I came to the realization that right at that moment, it might have been a good thing she hadn't. Once I had her on the roof next to me, she jumped off and started rolling around on the ground to put out the flames engulfing her.

Since Esperanza sat between the two female vampires of her group, I pulled her out next. She didn't seem as flammable as the other two and maintained her composure as I hauled her from the burning vehicle.

"Get out of here," I told her and she actually listened.

Jumping from the SUV and joining the tall blond.

Time wasn't on our side. I needed to get the last vampire out of the Suburban before the flames ignited the gas tank. Once Esperanza made it safely to the ground, I knelt down to reach into the Suburban to yank the last vampire out. As soon as my hand closed around the cool flesh of hers, the suburban exploded.

Flames licked my flesh as the vampire I'd been trying to save disintegrated in a ball of fire below me. One moment, I had her hand in mine, and the next it crumbled into nothingness. She didn't even have time to scream. I didn't have time to scream as the force of the explosion hurled me into the air with the force of some sort of medieval catapult. I saw everything below me as I completed the apex of my arc. I could see the other two vampires lying on the asphalt with their hands over their heads. *At least I saved the master.* My thought came as I started descending rapidly toward the hard earth.

I tried landing on my feet, but gravity had a different plan. Landing on my back with a resounding *crunch,* I didn't lose consciousness, but the pain wracked my body so hard I almost wished for sweet oblivion. Slowly, it ebbed, and I rolled over onto my knees. Spasms and the feeling of bones re-knitting themselves together still made it impossible to stand, so I crawled toward the flickering oranges and reds of the blazing SUV. About mid-way, I felt well enough to stand and slowly walk. About three quarters of the way, I had healed enough to run. By the time I got back, Sacramento's best had arrived and were frantically radioing for medical services. I fished out my FBI badge before walking up. One of the officers standing by the open door of his cruiser talking into his radio spotted me first. I held out my badge, and he dropped the radio and trotted over to me.

"Are you okay?" He looked me over. With the amount of burn holes in my new outfit, I couldn't blame him. I needed to invest in some fireproof clothes. Wonder if they sold those at the mall.

"I'm fine. The blast threw me over into the field."

"I'm sorry, what did you say?"

"The blast threw me into the field..."

"And you're fine?"

"Yeah, I'm a supe." I left it at that, and walked past him and over to the master of San Diego. Three officers stood nervously around her and her remaining companion with their guns drawn and pointed squarely at their chests. "Officers, these vampires are with me." I showed them my badge. They didn't look impressed. "Is there a problem?"

"No, ma'am," one of them said, and finally holstered his weapon. I noticed he was the only one without a flattop. I briefly wondered if there might be a correlation between haircuts and intelligence quotients.

"Thank you, officer . . ."

"Drake, ma'am," he supplied.

"Officer Drake, would you mind giving me and my friends a few moments?"

"No, ma'am, we'll be right over there," he said politely, and motioned with his head toward the ring of police cars a good distance from the blazing Suburban.

"Are you okay, Miss Ramirez?"

"Considering the circumstances, youngling, I'm fine. I wish Daria were alive, but I understand you did all you could to save her. Thank you."

I nodded and looked at the burning rubble that used to be my vehicle. I remembered my cell phone tucked safely away in the center console. I imagined a little piece of burnt plastic and glass and vowed to keep it on me next time. It might have made it. Hopefully, I would too.

The sound of emergency sirens in the distance drew my attention from the bonfire, red and white lights coming closer with each passing second. We probably wouldn't need the ambulance, but at least they could put out the fire. Hopefully, they had a brush truck with them. I doubted there were any fire hydrants in the middle of nowhere.

They pulled up in a flurry of well-practiced movement. Firefighters grabbed hoses and immediately started dousing my blackened Suburban with water. The EMTs grabbed their gear and gave me and my passengers a quick once-over. I heard more than one muffled, "Vampires," coming from whispering lips as they realized their services wouldn't be needed. I actually laughed at one of them when they pulled out a blood-pressure cuff. He gave a self-depreciating smile and put it away, quickly.

The crunching of gravel under tires behind me made me look over my shoulder. I could see Thompson through his windshield. He looked less than happy as he took in the scene. I smiled and gave him a little wave. He gave me the finger. I waited patiently for him to get out of the vehicle and join the party. *Maybe he brought marshmallows.*

"Kid, I hope you know you're filling out the report on this one."

"Hey, it wasn't my fault, chief. They had rocket launchers."

"Why is it with you, they always have rocket launchers?"

"Whatever works? They keep missing with the smaller crap."

He laughed, a little.

"Can we get a ride?"

"Not if they're still out there with more rockets."

Chapter 22

I swear I heard the sun drop below the horizon as I opened my eyes. I groaned inwardly, not at having to get out of bed, but because of the Governor's Ball in a few short hours. I could only imagine one outcome for tonight, and it had nothing to do with glass slippers and pumpkins. Bullets and blood, maybe. Sunshine and lollipops, I sincerely doubted. I'd stopped giving a crap about Greer three bodies ago. I just didn't want to end up one of them.

"Morning, master," Vic said sleepily from her spot next to me. I rolled over and touched the tip of her nose with my talon.

"Morning, Vic. What are you doing tonight while I'm out saving the world?"

"I'm going dancing with Viktor. Is that okay?"

"Of course it is. Your free time is yours to do whatever you want, and would you stop calling me master?"

"Sure thing, master." She stuck her tongue out at me.

I gave a girlish giggle as I got up and stretched. I had showered after the fire last night and slipped into bed wearing white cotton panties and a matching sports bra. I faced the wall as I stretched, but I could feel Vic's eyes trying to burn little holes through the back of my underwear. "Are you staring at my butt?" I said it without looking.

"Yes, master. Is that okay?"

I turned around and kneeled on the bed. I stared at her slit pupils and slowly lowered my face to hers. Without pausing, I gave her the gentlest of kisses on her soft lips. She moved in for more, but I had work to do. As she leaned forward, I leaned back. Breaking off the kiss, I smiled at her. "Duty calls. Don't stay out too late." I winked and wandered toward the closet to get dressed.

I was going to a ball, but I couldn't dress like it. A gown would be way too impractical. I hardly ever wore a gun since I was probably the worst shot in the FBI, so I wasn't worried about that. Chances were something or someone was going to get shot or blown up, and evening gowns didn't exactly say "combat." I pulled out my usual skirt suit and donned it without much thought.

Vic's soft, "*Hm hmm*," caught me off guard.

"What?"

"Take it off. You're going to a ball. I can't let my master be seen like that."

"I'm not wearing a gown." I frowned.

"You can wear a dress. It's possible to look beautiful and be dangerous. When you're not being frumpy, you are exquisite. Take it off, all of it."

"Vic, I…"

"Ashlyn, please?"

I'm not kidding. She gave me puppy dog eyes. Well, shit. "Fine." I rolled my eyes.

Naked as the day I was...whatever, Vic did my hair and painted my face with the skill of a professional makeup artist. By the time she finished I hardly recognized myself. She stood there while I took it all in, her shoulder against the wall, and a smile twice the size of mine on her face. I shook my head in disbelief and teared up a little. I'd never thought of myself as pretty, but the creature staring back at me from the mirror was positively breathtaking. Now I just needed to get dressed.

"Can I still wear my skirt suit?"

Vic rolled her eyes and threw her hands up in the air. She then took my hand and dragged me back to the closet. Every piece of clothing Marcel had bought her had literally gone up in flames with our last hotel, except one. That night she'd worn a little black spaghetti strap dress to the club. She'd been wearing my clothes until I could take her shopping again, but without a second thought, she reached in, took the slinky dress off the hanger, and held it out to me. On Vic, the dress's length bordered on obscene, but she stood well above my meager five-foot frame. I cocked an eyebrow as I eyed the dress and took it from her. I slipped it over my head and it fell around mid-thigh.

"You look amazing, master."

"I don't feel amazing. What if something happens tonight? I'm not going to be able to fight anybody in this."

"Stretch, and tell me different."

"Excuse me?"

"Bend, flex, or do whatever you want. See what happens."

Instead of arguing, I did what she asked. I couldn't believe the dress didn't bunch, hinder, or ride up in any way. I must have stared at Vic incredulously because she let out a quick giggle and gave me a little bow. The only problem I had would be in the footwear department. There wasn't a chance in hell I would be wearing Vic's heels tonight. I'd probably look a little fashion impaired in anything else, but I was putting my taloned foot down.

"Now you just need shoes. What do you have?" Vic asked. I needed to have her tested for ESP. Following my thoughts to the tee felt a little creepy, even to me.

"Mostly just flats. They'll have to do. I can't wear heels tonight, especially if all hell breaks loose."

She rummaged around in the bags of clothing I had bought at the mall and not gotten around to sorting through and putting in the hotel dresser yet. "Ha," she said, holding out a cute pair of sandals I had actually bought on a whim. They strapped around the ankle, but looked like a flip-flop made entirely out of cork. I'm usually pretty self-conscious about the talons on my feet, but I couldn't wear sneakers or flats everywhere, so I caved. The straps of the sandals had been crafted from black cloth and reinforced with something. My knowledge of cobbling bordered on nothing. I amazed myself by knowing they were called cobblers.

I put the shoes on and stood back from Vic. I didn't even need to ask how I looked. The hunger in her eyes said it all. I breathe, but it's just a natural process emanating from the primordial part of the brain stem. It's genetic even for me. After seeing the lust in Vic's eyes, I stopped cold. I didn't start again until I crossed the distance between us and took her in my arms. I didn't kiss her, but I wanted to. I didn't know where that would lead and didn't have time to find out. Instead, I put my head below her chin and pulled her as close to me as I could, and whispered, "Thank you."

"Trust me, master, it was my pleasure."

I looked up at her eyes and saw the truth in her words. I raised myself up on my toes and gave her a short kiss on her lips. She didn't lean into it, but still gave me a smile that threatened to melt me from the inside out. "Thank you anyway." I stuck my tongue out.

She laughed and stepped back a pace. "Time for you to go."

"Have fun tonight. Tell Viktor I said hello."

"I will, and master...please be careful?"

"I will."

The music wafting through the mansion threatened to make me regurgitate my last meal. I'm pretty tolerant in the music department, but chamber music tweaked my innards. The governor stood at the end of a long line of arriving guests to personally receive and welcome them. I guess the music was supposed to make them appreciate the snootiness of the extravaganza. I looked around at everyone in the enormous foyer. They looked bored, but apparently I was the only one who looked nauseous.

I stood on the stairs above the governor and had a bird's eye view of everything. The only thing that struck me as out of the ordinary was the sheer amount of jewelry draping the necks, wrists, and fingers of the governor's guests. If I wanted to, I could steal all of it, buy my own country somewhere, and retire. I'd probably start a new record, youngest person to retire. For a fleeting moment, retiring sounded almost perfect. No danger, no excitement, and no death might be a nice change.

Nothing exciting was happening anywhere in the mansion. The guests came in, shook hands with Greer, and entered the illustrious ballroom where they were expected to wait until Greer made his grandiose entrance. Even the tiny earpiece I had in my left ear remained silent except for everyone checking in periodically.

Just for the hell of it, I gave a, "Foyer clear." At least it gave me something to do to avoid looking down at the governor and old lady cleavage. I'm sorry, but if I were a ninety-year-old human, I'd dress a little less like a supermodel and a little more like a schoolteacher. Money does weird things to people.

Somebody waving at me interrupted my thoughts. I saw Esperanza and her remaining escort standing in line to present themselves to Greer. I waved back and gave her a little smile. Usually I just pissed people off when I met them. Making friends was a nice change. Marcel, Greer, and now Esperanza liked me. Three out of a million vampires wasn't bad, right?

I watched the exchange between the master of San Diego and the governor of California. My brows furrowed. Normally I can hear a flea fart from forty feet, but I couldn't make out a word Esperanza said to Greer. The noise level in the mansion had steadily increased since the first guests arrived and now had climbed above a dull clamor. I should have been able to hear them, but nothing reached my ears. I will say one thing; Esperanza Garcia Ramirez didn't look the slightest bit amused. In fact, my hand tightened around the staircase banister the longer the conversation went on. Before Esperanza finally gave a wan smile and moved on, I might have left a few talon marks in the polished wood. At least I didn't have to break up a fight before the ball started.

Esperanza glanced up at me as she passed and I shot her a quizzical look. She shook her head, and whispered, "Nothing." The whisper carried itself up over the staircase, and I heard it as if she had been standing next to me with her lips at my ear. *Neat trick*. I'd have to practice that one later.

The only problem with vampires is nobody has catalogued all the different variations, powers, and abilities some of them have. Vampires, overall, are often secretive and don't share information well, even with innocent scholars. Not that I blame them. When you let somebody see everything you can do, you might scare the shit out of them. Fear often makes humans destroy what they don't understand. If you've shown all your tricks, you're giving others the knowledge to overcome your skills. Kind of like teaching somebody to hunt, and then being the one hunted.

Esperanza entered the ballroom, and I relaxed a little. She might like me, but that doesn't mean I trust her. I don't think she was behind the attacks on the governor for the simple fact that she was the target last night, but that didn't mean she wouldn't start now. She'd been in Greer's territory when she'd been attacked. She might be suspicious of him, or she could even blame him for it happening outside his control. Vampires can be weird, too.

I shifted my focus back to the line of guests still waiting to meet the governor. This was going to take a while. The line reached from below where I stood and trailed outside the door. I could only imagine how many people were waiting outside.

I sighed in frustration and relaxed my stance. No sense being uptight. *If* something happened, it happened. I'd be ready. I just hoped I'd be quick enough to do something about it. I did make a silent vow not to step in front of any explosive projectiles.

"Greetings, James Branfield, master of Pasadena!"

Greer's exclamation below focused my attention back on him and his current hand shakers. The master of

Pasadena was a hunk. He towered over Greer by at least eight inches, but he wasn't gangly. Broad shoulders balanced his weight very nicely. Long brown hair swept down past his shoulders in beautiful waves that made you want to reach out and touch it. His face completed the package. Usually when you see a man with long hair, it compliments their face in a feminine way. Not James Branfield. His face was anything but feminine. I stood there with my mouth open and quickly shut it before anybody noticed.

"Cut the crap, Greer. I came because you asked, not because I wanted to."

"You sly dog, still ticked over the council denying you another territory? I assure you, I voted in your favor!"

"Bullshit." Branfield walked past Greer without so much as a handclasp. Apparently, Greer really was an asshole. Branfield didn't like him much, which made him a suspect. The list kept getting longer and longer.

"Call me, we'll do lunch," Greer said with a sneer toward the retreating vampire's back.

Branfield flicked him off over his shoulder. That alone made me hope the hunk of vampire wasn't guilty. I liked him.

Every vampire that greeted the new governor pretty much did the same thing. They were stiff, but cordial. None of them were friendly. That didn't shorten my list any. From the running tally I kept going in my head, every master of every city in the State of California must have shown up for the Governor's Ball. Tension thickened in the air. I hoped to get a "vibe" from at least one of them, giving me some clue as to who was behind the attacks. I didn't expect to get it from everyone. I recalled my conversations with Marcel on the new governor, and he had seemed almost amicable toward the vampire. Either he had shitty taste in people, or he got along with everyone. I suspected the latter.

After what seemed to be an eternity of handshaking and ass kissing, the last guest made their way to the ballroom. I quickly traveled down the stairs and followed the governor as he left the reception area and into the bowels of the mansion. He was headed toward the ballroom, his entrance had been staged at a different door.

As we neared, I saw Thompson guarding it like a bouncer. He just needed a velvet rope, a black T-shirt, and some sunglasses.

"You ready, kid?"

"Ready whenever you are, big guy."

Thompson nodded and opened the double doors, one in each hand. I stepped through, keeping the governor behind me. I gave one quick glance around at everyone seated at round tables. Nobody flashed a weapon or looked like they were about to attack, so I stepped to the right, letting Greer step into view. Everyone stood at once, and they brought their hands together in a half-hearted attempt at applause. I fought hard not to raise my hand and say, "Thank you." I don't think anyone would have appreciated my humor, especially the governor.

Amid the applause, the governor smiled, waved, and weaved his way to the large podium that had been set up for him to make his speech. I half expected him to pull out prewritten cue cards, but it looked like he'd either taken the time to memorize it, or he was just shooting from the hip.

"Ladies and gentlemen, I would like to thank you all, from the bottom of my heart, for coming. We've entered into a new era in the world, where humans trust vampires enough to elect them as officials! I can't even begin to tell you how proud I am to be the culmination of your trust." He paused after his introduction to a round of applause that seemed a little more genuine than from before.

He could play a crowd. I'd give him that.

"Too long has the vampire been painted as some sort of monster, incapable of common interaction with humans. Too long have humans feared what was once unknown. Many vampires in the world today will still disagree with me for saying this, but the time for truth is now. To further vampire and human relations, not only will I meet with human scholars, I will answer any and all questions they might have about the vampire race. We differ in ability as much as we differ in personality and it's time to set the record straight."

I quickly glanced around the room and saw hope in the expressions of every human there. Hope of overcoming prejudices that ran bone deep, for a better tomorrow. I didn't buy it for a minute. I looked around at the vampires seated at scattered tables amid human diners, and saw something else. Fury filled their eyes like fire in a lantern. They wanted blood, but not for consumption. They wanted Greer's blood.

"The great state of California," Greer continued, "has been riddled with problems since the day it joined the union. I know because I was there." A few people actually realized Greer made a joke and gave the appropriate chuckle. "The greatest quality this state has to offer is to know how to overcome these problems. One problem we've never had is acceptance of new ideas. Californians embrace change and new ideas like people embrace lost friends newly found. We're eager for them! Well, changes are coming, and I can only hope that the great citizens of California are ready for them!"

On cue, the lights dimmed and a faint waltz started softly in the background, but as Greer left the podium, the volume increased. Greer flashed me a look from across the room and walked toward me. I tensed, expecting him to tell me he'd seen something dangerous, but relaxed when he got closer, and I could see his smile. I tensed again for different reasons. I pictured the snake smirking at the mouse before he ate it. A shudder ran down the length of my spine when I realized I was the mouse.

"Agent Ashlyn, would you do me the honor of a dance?"

"Governor Greer, I can hardly keep you safe trapped in your embrace," I retorted. I felt quite proud of myself for my quick thinking.

"Don't be silly, we are completely surrounded by an army of your fellow agents. We couldn't be safer dancing in a vault at Fort Knox. Please, don't embarrass me in front of my guests." He held out his hand, and I couldn't say no. I wanted to, but I couldn't. I reached out and placed my hand in his, and he led me through the shocked guests to the hardwood floor.

Without releasing my hand, he held it up and out and encircled my waist with his free hand, pulling me closer than I desired. Without asking me if I wanted to lead, he took a step to the left and pushed me. Greer had taken lessons. He twirled and spun us around the floor like professional ballroom dancers. Hell, for all I knew, he could have invented the waltz or whatever it was we were doing. Gods know he had been around long enough.

I avoided conversation and concentrated on the guests staring at the homely girl dancing with the elegant governor. Nobody joined us on the floor, and my silent pleas for anybody to start dancing went unanswered. I finally saw Thompson, still at his post by the door. I held my breath, waiting for a look of disproval and he didn't disappoint me. He narrowed his eyes and shook his head before focusing his attention elsewhere.

"Are you not having fun, agent?"

"I'm just keeping an eye on things, sir."

"I promise you nothing will happen during our dance. You can relax."

"I've never danced at a ball, sir. I hope I'm not embarrassing you."

He gave a deep throaty chuckle and spun me from his chest, out to arm's length, and pulled me back. "You can relax, you're a natural. Being a vampire gives us a distinct edge over the humans. I've seen people who have been dancing for years who weren't half as good as you are."

I heated a little at the compliment. I didn't like blushing, at all. Pushing down the embarrassment, I focused instead on the crowd around us. About halfway through the dance, adventurous couples began flowing out onto the floor to join us in dancing hell. "Could they play something a little more modern," I muttered under my breath, forgetting the company I kept. The governor had no trouble hearing me.

"Be careful, young one. This piece used to be modern when I was young. I remember the first time I heard it."

I laughed, thinking he was joking, but he stiffened, and I realized my error. "I thought you were joking, sir."

"No, young one, I wasn't. As I said, I have been around a very long time. I have seen famine, flood, and plague. I have seen miraculous inventions. I have seen the humans of this world create wonders that give them ways to kill vampires and other immortals, which they should not have. Ashlyn, the world is changing again, and I fear it won't be in a good way. It is because of those changes, I chose to lead the people of this state. I like things the way they are right now. I intend to make California a Mecca of stability."

"Good luck with that, Governor. Change is inevitable."

"Not if you fight hard enough, agent. Not if you fight hard enough."

Chapter 23

"Governor, your guest is here," one of Greer's aids said to him as we walked off the hardwood floor after our dance.

"Ah, yes. Thank you, Michael. Tell her I'll be right there. If you would excuse me, Ashlyn, one of my people is here from San Francisco. I'll be back in a few moments."

"I'm going to have to insist on coming with you, sir."

"I'm going to have to insist you stay here and keep my guests safe, Ashlyn. I'll be fine. I'm going right across the hall to see one of the people I have trusted for the better part of two centuries. In my absence, she has been ruling San Francisco's vampires. She is here to make her report and join the ball. If you would like, call your friend Victoria and have her join us. No reason for you to be alone at such a festive occasion."

Before I could argue, Greer led his aid through the ballroom and disappeared through the doors behind Thompson, who gave me a classic "what the fuck" look. I shrugged and went back to keeping an eye out on the rest of the room. Wandering around, I stared at everything and everyone. I thought about following Greer's advice and calling Vic. Then I thought about what Thompson would do to me if I did. We were here for one purpose, and it didn't include dancing with my hot girlfriend.

I almost stumbled when the girlfriend thought crossed my mind. I did stop walking and stared at nothing in particular as I rolled the word around on my tongue. It didn't hurt, it didn't taste bad, and it didn't make me feel guilty like I thought it would. Either she was growing on me, or I was getting a little more mature about the whole thing. Either way, things were looking up. It was nice of Greer to offer up an invitation for her to come. It was really nice to…

I'd never had an epiphany in my short life, and this one caught me off guard. Immediately, my mind started piecing things together that had no correlation until that moment. Greer just offered an invitation by name to someone he'd never met, nor had I talked about her to him. Greer was the master of San Francisco. Victoria had been sent as a gift to the master of Sacramento from her abusive previous master. Vic was from San Francisco. Greer had every master of every major city in California gathered neatly in one spot. Greer had just left. Oh, fuck.

If I learned one lesson at the FBI Academy, it was never to show off my supernatural ability. Right at that moment, I didn't give a shit. I took off at full speed and burst through the door Greer had exited through, ran across the hall where he was supposed to be meeting with his vampire lieutenant, and came to a screeching halt when the room sat empty. "Son of a bitch," I swore as I heard Thompson run into the room behind me.

"What the hell's the matter?"

"It's Greer."

"What's Greer?"

"He's behind it all, and now he's gone. Radio everyone and have them close in. We need to get everyone out of here now. Thompson, it's about to get real ugly."

I expected him to argue and ask for a further explanation, but he nodded and put his finger to his right ear. "Everyone, converge on ballroom location double-time. Move it people."

I turned to head back to the ballroom. He fell in step behind me. The first of the agents rushed in through the doors at the far end of the hall and made a beeline to us. I didn't wait for them, I just ran back into the ballroom. I needed to get everyone out of the massive room; I just didn't know how to do it without causing a panic and getting everyone hurt or dead. Waving my gun in the air and screaming at the top of my lungs probably wouldn't be the best idea either. I searched around the room and spotted the massive podium Greer had used to deliver his double-edged speech. Inspiration struck.

Without drawing attention to myself, I wound through the multitude of guests and around the cherry wood pulpit. Greer stood taller than I did, so I lowered the microphone to a more acceptable level. I could see over the edge, but just barely. To get everyone's attention I poked the microphone with my talon three times. The audible *thump, thump, thump* did the trick. The music stopped playing, the couples stopped dancing, and the people sitting at their round dinner tables stopped talking. Everyone turned and faced the podium expecting more words of wisdom from the governor. A few turned back to their conversations after seeing me, ignoring the words of wisdom I was about to impart.

"Ladies and gentlemen, I apologize for the governor, but a situation has come to light that needs his attention. He regrets the unfortunate, unforeseeable incident, but I'm afraid the Governor's Ball has been officially cancelled. If you would find the nearest exit, it would be greatly appreciated. I and the governor apologize for the inconvenience." My voice didn't crack once during my announcement, and I smiled. Public speaking wasn't one of my greatest talents. I ate monsters with the best of them, but put me in front of a crowd and I usually sounded like an idiot.

The human guests started gathering their personal things looking quite indignant. The vampires started looking around nervously. I think they might have understood the truth behind my little speech—the shit was about to hit the fan. Esperanza Garcia Ramirez waved her thanks and took off toward the open door at full vampiric speed. A flash of light and a resounding boom threw her back into the middle of the room. I spun, expecting to see some sort of incendiary explosive, but the door and the entire surrounding area remained untouched.

A human couple had witnessed the entire thing and became frightened. The woman started screaming and her husband took off running, dragging her behind him toward the other exit. Again, a flash of light and a loud boom threw them back into the room just like Esperanza. There was one major difference though. Vampires are damn near indestructible, but humans aren't. The couple who had hit the trap lay there in a bloody, broken heap. Judging from the angle of his neck, he was quite dead. She wasn't moving, but the rhythmic rise and fall of her chest told me she hadn't bought the farm.

"Everybody, stay where you are," I shouted. One of the other vampires had stopped at the door and held out a tentative hand to the exit. Before I could say anything, he touched the threshold of the door. Because he hadn't hit the door at a full run, he wasn't thrown back into the room. But whatever kept everyone from crossing the exit knocked him on his butt with smaller pyrotechnics and a sizzle. The fucker trapped us.

I marched over to the vampire and offered him a hand. He accepted it, and I hauled him to his feet. "Are you okay?"

He nodded, looking a little embarrassed.

I pursed my lips and turned to the door. I didn't want to touch it, but I couldn't help myself. I raised my hand and put my palm out toward the door, slowly inching it forward to feel what was there. When my arm was halfway out the door, I raised my eyebrow and strode forward. Nothing happened. I stood in the middle of the hallway and turned around. The vampire who had been knocked on his ass, stood there looking at me in disbelief as Thompson came to a stop next to him.

"It must be gone." Thompson strode forward. He landed ten feet back from the door, trapped like the rest of them. I rushed back to him, but he seemed fine. He smelled a little like burnt cat, but wasn't injured.

"What the hell is it?"

"It feels like magic," the vampire next to us said.

Magic didn't affect me for some reason, so his statement made complete sense. I could be killed by magic, but only indirectly. Inspiration struck.

"Thompson, come with me."

He picked himself up and followed me to the door. I faced forward and motioned for him to stand behind me. I took his hand and put it on my shoulder and walked forward. I couldn't feel anything until Thompson's hand hit the threshold. He blew backward, and I flew forward into the wall on the opposite side of the hallway with a sickening thud. Well, so much for that theory.

"You okay?"

"No. Let's not do that again," he replied.

I pulled myself from the Ashlyn-shaped dent in the wall and turned around. A crowd had gathered around to see the results of our little science experiment. Great, I needed a crowd while I figured this out. I stopped at the doorframe hoping to find some kind of runes or something that might be causing the explosive shield keeping everyone in. I didn't see anything outright and stopped to think.

Panic started to creep along my spine. Maybe how could wait. The why seemed a little more important at the moment. I ran through the door and parted the crowd, looking around. I held up my hands for silence, but couldn't hear anything but heartbeats and breathing from the non- vampires in the room.

"What is it, kid?"

"We're trapped for a reason. Why?"

"So we can't stop him?" Doubt roughened his voice.

Feedback from the microphone at the podium began low and started building. I looked at Thompson, and he looked at me.

"Fuck," I said, earning a nod from my partner. We motioned everyone to get back against the wall while he and I strode to the ornate wooden structure. The closer I got to it, a feeling of dread seeped into my bones. By the time we got to it, I was ready to turn around and run out the door saying, "Fuck everybody." I didn't though. Thompson looked afraid, too. I took a little consolation from that. "You're touching it first," I said.

"Fuck you."

That made me feel a little better, and I gave him a half-smile. He hadn't taken his gaze off the four-and-a-half foot podium, so he didn't see it. Oh well, his loss. I eased around the back and looked down. The lower half of the podium was cabinet. I don't know how I knew, but I knew. The root of all the evil in this room, rested inside. "Thompson, I *really* don't want to open those doors."

"Neither do I."

I sighed and squatted down, rather than bending or kneeling. If I had to get away quickly, as I imagined I would, I could do it faster if I remained upright on my feet. I gingerly reached out with both hands and grasped the smooth wooden knobs, slowly pulling the doors open. I was hoping for a ceramic jar, or an artifact of some sort. What I didn't expect was the blackened skull of some sort of animal or monster sitting there. Evil poured off the thing in hot waves.

"Well, if I had to guess, I'd say this is it."

"Ya think so?" Thompson said it like I was in kindergarten.

"Give me something to grab it with. I am so not touching that thing."

Thompson stood from his leaning position and took off his suit jacket. He held it over my shoulder, and I grabbed it. I opened it and gently covered the skull.

One of the morons by the door must have figured that suit jackets magically dispel all traps in the vicinity and touched the empty space inside the doorframe with his. He landed with a crash and a groan on top of one of the round tables where everyone sat while not dancing. I rolled my eyes at Thompson and turned my attention back to the suit jacket-covered dead thing inside the podium.

"I'm going to grab it and smash it. Good plan?"

"I can't think of a better one. Go for it."

I reached in slowly and knocked the skull over, pulling the jacket underneath it like an Armani shopping bag. I pulled it out of the podium and stepped back, giving myself some room to work. I set it on the floor, reached over to Thompson's exposed shoulder harness, and pulled out his gun. I hardly ever wore mine anymore, and I sure as shit wasn't wearing one with my dress. I cocked the weapon and pointed it at the skull. "I owe you a new jacket." I shot the skull from less than three feet away.

The gunshot echoed through the room like a clap of thunder. Everyone stood silent and stared at us. I half expected somebody else to try the door, but they didn't. I glanced at Thompson and he nodded once. I reached down, grabbed the corner of the jacket, and lifted it, spilling the contents onto the floor. Dust, sand, and chunks of bone poured out in a scattered heap. I motioned toward the door when the pile of debris started to smoke.

"Kid!"

I saw the smoke, and stepped back several paces. The smoke continued upward until it stood about seven feet above the floor and began to pool together like some sort of insane lava lamp. It grew in thickness and took the shape of some sort of large humanoid. Legs formed, two arms, and then a head. Two large orbs, glowing red, formed into eyes, and then a maw full of sharp razor-like teeth smiled at us hungrily. I had Thompson's gun in my hand so I shot it, point blank. The bullets parted the smoky flesh but the wounds it left flowed together like water. Thompson packed silver ammunition in his weapon, most FBI agents did, yet it had no effect.

"Your silver cannot harm me, cousin," the thing hissed in a sibilant voice.

"I don't suppose you'll tell me what will?" I said it innocently, and he hissed a chuckle before striking.

I expected him to go for me, but he swung his arm in a vicious backhand that knocked Thompson across the room. The humans backed up against the far wall, and surprisingly enough, the vampires closed in around me, facing off against the thing. If we destroyed it, we could leave. Apparently, the vampires thought the same thing.

I circled slowly, not wanting to jump in and get my ass kicked like Thompson. One of the other vampires feinted and made a quick lunge before leaping back. He didn't leap fast enough. The monster grabbed the vampire's wrist. He fought bravely but his strength was no match. I lunged to help, but within seconds, the creature literally tore the vampire apart. I gulped in air, trying to hold back the guilt I felt for the untimely demise of the master of some city I couldn't remember.

The creature then did something unexpected. He brought one of the vampire's limbs to his mouth and started feeding on it like a human with a chicken leg. One of the other vampires thought that might be a good time to attack, but as soon as she got close enough, the vampire swung the leg like a giant bat. He caught her square in the head and knocked her out.

Two vampires down. Didn't leave us much to fight with. Seven of us stepped back while the thing continued to feed. I'd personally had enough. "Everybody circle." I started running around the thing in a weaving circle.

The vampires figured out what I meant and followed suit. We orbited the thing like electrons around a nucleus. The creature wearily watched as it ate. Even at the speed I traveled, I could tell it was getting more tangible. Its skin lost the smoky color and moved a few shades closer to onyx.

I decided to make a move, striking as I passed with my talons. I dug deep rivulets across the back of his leg, causing him to howl in pain and surprise. He swung the remnants of his meal and hit three of the vampires around me with one strike. They didn't go flying, but had to pick themselves off the ground before continuing with their distraction.

Every time I passed the back of his leg, I noticed the wounds weren't closing. He might be immune to silver bullets, but not Ashlyn talons. I leapt and grasped the thing around the neck with both arms digging my talons into his neck to hold on for the wild ride. I looked at his neck, and even though I didn't want to, I bit as hard as I could.

My fangs pierced the flesh and their curved structure slid in slowly. They went in, but not like they did through the flesh of a vampire or werewolf. He screamed in pain and reached up to grab me. He could hit my head, but couldn't reach back far enough to get me off him.

His blood hit my tongue, and I closed my eyes. It wasn't a pleasant taste, but there was power in it. I guess it would be like a human eating broccoli. Something that smelled like rancid feet while it cooked couldn't taste good, but it had to be good for you.

He pummeled me as I drank, but decided to switch tactics when he seemed to realize the precarious position I had him in. He fell backward and smashed me against the tile floor with all his weight. That fucking hurt.

More than one bone cracked and broke, but I didn't let go. I couldn't. I'd just begun to drink, and his strength hadn't even started to ebb. The other vampires leapt on him to pin him down. He kicked and threw the vampires off his legs and arms and spun on the ground, flipping me around. I tried to hang on, but inertia wasn't my friend. I hit the wall and slid down in a small heap. The strength of the thing impressed me more and more.

It leapt off the ground to its full seven feet and roared to the ceiling, flexing his arms. He shook off the lingering wounds and stomped his foot with a mighty thump, looking for someone to attack.

I didn't want to give him that chance. I charged him while he wasn't looking. It was cheap, but it worked. I hit him like a freight train, and he stopped me like a concrete barrier. I hit his chest, and he didn't budge an inch. His hand closed around the back of my neck as he peeled me off him like a wet towel.

The ground moved away as he lifted me and brought my face to his. "Your attacks are futile, cousin. Join me in my feast!"

"Why do you keep calling me cousin? You're a monster!"

"So are you," he said with a throaty chuckle.

I seriously didn't like this guy. The point became moot when he lifted me above his head and threw me across the room like a giant lawn dart.

I watched in horror as he grabbed another vampire and tore her throat out in a spray of blood. If the vampire had any vocal chords left, I'm sure the scream would have been ear-shattering. The choking gurgling noises failed to express the vampires torment. I wanted to puke.

I stood to attack when a giant werelion landed on the creature's back, raking claws tearing flesh, and spraying blood.

The creature dropped the vampire and spun in a tight circle, flinging Thompson off his back and squaring off. Thompson's lion form stood about as tall as the creature, but the creature had a definite weight and muscle advantage. They circled each other twice and after a few feints on Thompson's part, they started grappling like monstrous wrestlers. I saw the vampire on the ground beneath their feet and ran to pull her out of the way. I then turned to join the fight when the creature bit Thompson in the back of the neck. He shook his enormous head and Thompson's neck snapped as his body went limp.

The rest of the room went red as a haze filled my vision. I didn't see human or vampire, only the beast. Then he made the most serious mistake of the night–he smiled at me.

I lost control. My talons grew, my fangs elongated, and wet heat slid down over my face as horns sprouted from the sides of my forehead. I didn't need to reach up to know they were there. In fact, I welcomed them and the power their presence signified.

I let out a roar that shamed the greatest of his and charged. His movements seemed sluggish as I slapped his hands away when he tried to grab me before I attacked. I ducked under the third strike and raked the talons of my right hand along his ribs. I didn't go down, but followed the contours of them, feeling them slip in between as they finally hit a large bony plate and stopped. I pulled free and held up my hand in front of him. He looked down at my hand and snarled while I licked the blood from my fingertips and talons, never taking my gaze from him.

"I rightly named thee, cousin. I could smell it in you. Welcome."

"Fuck off." I struck him in the stomach with my fingers straight, feeling his flesh part as my hand slid in and grabbed the first warm wet thing I could find.

He kicked me and sent me flying away. I watched him look down in surprise when I pulled a length of entrails out of the hole I made. He howled and started stuffing his guts back inside. I wanted more as he ripped what I had from my grasp. I charged again and made it back just as he had stuffed the last bit inside.

I launched myself and straddled his neck and shoulders with my legs as I grasped his head in my talons. He'd stopped me like a wall before, but this time I'd caught him off guard and knocked him backward, riding his chest down to the ground. I slipped my talons under his skin and grabbed the back of his jawbone. I pulled with everything I had and twisted at the same time. His jawbone broke free, and I ripped it loose, tossing it to the side.

Anguish and fear filled his eyes as he stared at my face. I looked on in disgust without an iota of guilt. There wasn't much holding the remainder of his head on his body, and I quickly tore through that and held my prize above me like a gruesome trophy.

His body began to dissolve beneath me and disappeared back into the smoke from which it had been formed. I looked up at the head in my hands and once again it was just a skull. It had no jaw this time, but it seemed old and rotted like before the whole mess started. I dropped it where I sat and ran to my fallen partner.

He had changed back to human form, and I didn't know if that was a good sign or bad. I started to panic until

I saw his chest rise and his lungs filling with air. His eyes opened and smiled. "Did you get him?"

"Ripped his fucking head off."

"Next time, do it before he kicks my ass, would you?"

"You got it, old man."

Deceptions

Chapter 24

As soon as I'd killed whatever it was, the barriers between the ballroom and the rest of the world collapsed. The humans took off running in a panic-filled frenzy. I'm surprised no one got hurt on the way out. The vampires on the other hand, stayed behind to help those who had received near fatal injuries and mourn the one dead, the master of Bakersfield.

Greer had planned to kill every master of every city in California. He only succeeded in driving them together. I almost pitied the man if they ever got a hold of him.

The EMTs came and carted Thompson off to the hospital. He'd live, and he wouldn't be paralyzed, but they wanted to have the hospital test him for nerve and bone damage. Even though he's a lycanthrope, neck injuries can be dangerous and tricky.

I waved goodbye as they pulled away. I wanted to go with them, but *somehow* I ended up in charge. Thompson placed one phone call to the Deputy Director and every FBI agent in the area that wasn't already at the governor's mansion showed up with their guns drawn and badges out. Even Connors, the Special Agent in Charge of the Sacramento Field Office arrived and asked what I needed from him. Personally, I just wanted to go to bed and cry.

They brought in the local PD to take statements, help with the investigation, and basically keep everyone, including the press, away. They even had one of their practicing sorcerers inspecting the remnants of the skull. I wanted to know where Greer got it and learned how to use it. That thing needed to be packed in a wooden crate labeled "TOP SECRET" and buried in a warehouse next to the Ark of the Covenant. Talk about a nasty piece of work.

The police sorcerer knelt on the floor in front of it, not touching, afraid of triggering it. I described to him in detail what happened. He wasn't convinced it was dead, merely trapped again by the magic of the skull. Since I had absolutely no desire to ever fight the damn thing again, I couldn't blame him.

"What do you think?" I was standing behind him and winced when he jumped.

"It's old, whatever it is."

"How old?"

"Without someone carbon dating it, I couldn't hazard a guess. It's just a feeling I'm getting from it, old and evil."

"Yeah, I figured that one out when he ripped the vampire apart. Any idea on what it was?"

"I can give you my theory, but I have no way to prove any of it."

"What's your theory?"

"The skull belonged to whatever is trapped inside, that I'm pretty sure of. Here's the part I'm theorizing. The skull can be activated, don't ask me how because I don't know. It sets up a trap that keeps whoever is within a certain area there until they touch the skull. Once they do, the boogey man inside comes a calling. He either kills you, or you kill it, and then it goes back to being a skull. It's all very bad juju."

"Juju?"

"Magic at its most primitive, sometimes it can be more deadly than meticulously crafted spells. Sometimes it can be done through an innate ability, but more often than not, it's done through some sort of sacrifice."

"When you say sacrifice, why do I get the feeling you don't mean giving up chocolate for a week?"

"Because you're smart and beautiful, and I can't believe I just said that." His eyes darted between the floor and me. "I'm sorry. Sacrifice as in blood or more likely a life, in this case."

"Yummy." I shook my head in disgust. A disruption at the door made me turn my head from the Sacramento PD's resident sorcerer and stand on my tippy-toes to see what was going on. Several large men and one short blonde woman were arguing heatedly with Connors by the entrance to the ballroom. I would have let him handle it, but he pointed in my direction, and they started heading directly to me. They all wore plain black suits, so it couldn't be good.

"Can I help you?" They stopped about a foot from me. I looked around at all of them, trying to figure out who had the honor of being in charge.

"Are you Agent Ashlyn?" The blonde stood only a few inches taller than me so I didn't have to look up to speak to her.

"Yes, is there something I can do for you?"

"I'm Agent Carolyn Walters, Secret Service. We're here to collect that." She pointed at the skull at the feet of the resident sorcerer who had stood when the company arrived.

"But I haven't finished examining it," the sorcerer spoke up indignantly.

"Yes, you have," Walters said snidely. I didn't like her. Not even a little.

"Both of you can wait while I check with the Deputy Director. Could you give us a moment?" Sorcerer or not, I didn't want to get into a pissing match with the Secret Service in front of him. I pulled my new cell phone from my purse and dialed Sanders. He picked up on the third ring.

"Agent Ashlyn, is everything okay?"

"No, sir, it's not. I have several agents of the Secret Service here to collect a piece that is part of my investigation."

"Yes, I know. The Secret Service is responsible for dangerous magical artifacts, so there's not much I can do. How much time do you need?"

"Thirty minutes, sir, I have a local practitioner examining it now."

"Put the Secret Service agent on the phone and find Greer. I want his ass in a cell by tomorrow."

"Yes, sir, here she is." I handed the phone to a very annoyed Agent Walters.

I half expected her to have her conversation with Sanders in front of me. I frowned a little when she turned around and walked away with my phone. The rest of the agents just stood there and stared at me as if I'd just been caught counterfeiting hundred dollar bills. I smiled and bared a little fang. I couldn't help it. I expected to catch them a little off guard, but they didn't seem impressed. After about two minutes, Walters came back and handed me my phone in a huff. I smiled a little wider.

"You have thirty minutes." She left. I refrained from making faces at her behind her back, barely.

I whistled at the PD sorcerer before he left, and he ran back over, more than a little shocked. "You have thirty minutes to find out all you can about that thing."

"So far, it's not much, but I'll send you everything I learn."

"Thanks. Now get to work." I smiled to let him know I wasn't being a bitch.

I could have clocked the thirty minutes against a stopwatch. As soon as it passed, Walters and her cohorts walked back over to the skull and slid a metal box over it. The box had handles and must have weighed a ton because it took two of their heftier agents to lift it. Once they got it off the ground, the skull was gone. I tried not to cry out in frustration as they carried it away. The police sorcerer didn't look too happy to be shooed away, but to his credit, he didn't put up a fight or argue.

By the time the Secret Service walked out with their prize, the rest of us had just about finished sweeping for evidence, cleaning up bodies, and treating the injured. There wasn't anything left to do at the mansion, so I headed over to pick Thompson up at the hospital. We needed to find Greer. I'm sure he'd hung around the mansion, expecting his trap to neatly destroy his opposition and

217

witnesses alike. He could have then walked back into the ballroom and claimed to be the only one left alive, another foiled attempt on his life. He must have run as soon as he realized I'd kicked Mr. Nasty's ass. I hoped he was afraid. I wanted him to be terrified.

Thompson waited for me at the emergency exit. I raised my eyebrows, surprised he wasn't still being poked and prodded by the hospital staff, but knowing him, he'd probably told them what they could do with their medical tests and walked out. At least he had pants on and not a hospital gown. When he turned into a werelion, not much of his clothing remained intact. Thank the gods his pants usually did. That would be more of Thompson than I ever wanted to see, mostly because his wife would kill me.

I pulled up to the curb and he got in the passenger side without complaint. Usually, he insisted on driving, I guess he wasn't in the mood. "You okay?"

He nodded instead of responding, and I let it go. I stepped on the gas and drove back to the hotel. Sunrise would be in an hour, and I wanted to be showered and snug in my bed well before then.

"What happened after I left?"

"Not much. I got into a pissing match with the Secret Service, but I called Sanders and he straightened it out."

"They come for the head?"

"Yeah, how did you know?"

"Dealt with them before when they came to collect stuff from other cases I'd been working. Pleasant bunch aren't they?"

"Oh yeah, real charmers, they are. Where do they keep all the items they've collected?"

"Not knowing is their first line of defense. Nobody knows."

"Nice."

We fell into that comfortable silence for the remainder

of the drive to the hotel. I grinned when I found an empty parking space about three spots down from the entrance. I rarely found good parking spots. Thompson always did. I smiled triumphantly at him, and he rolled his eyes.

We left the car and headed into the hotel, through the lobby, pausing only briefly to hit the up button on the elevator. I noticed Thompson walking funny, but I kept silent about it. If he wanted to be a "manly man" I'd let him. I even vowed not to laugh at him when he fell on his ass.

As soon as we stepped off the elevator, chills ran over my arms. I looked at Thompson to see if he sensed anything wrong, and he seemed oblivious to everything, including me. I stepped off and raced down the hall, sure something wasn't right. I debated kicking open our room door, but it was already open about an inch.

My heart sank into my stomach. The door swung open with barely a touch, and a sea of devastation filled my vision. Couches overturned, tables broken, and doors smashed spoke volumes. Since there wasn't anything in our room worth finding or stealing, somebody had put up a hell of a fight. Only one other person shared our room.

"Vic!" Her name resounded off the walls in the suite, but no response came. I frantically searched every room, under every bed, and in every closet, but she wasn't there. I knew that already, but I had to check.

"Maybe she's at the club?" Thompson tried to sound hopeful behind me, but then I saw the blood on the floor in the bathroom.

I knelt down and touched my fingers to it. It was sticky and wet, but cold to the touch. It had been spilt a while ago. Whoever had taken her had a good head start. I knew who had her; I just couldn't say the name aloud. Wherever he had her, it had to be close. With the sun rising in less than an hour, he couldn't have gotten far.

"Greer has her. How the hell are we going to find him?"

"Kid, everybody and their mother are looking for him right now. Finding him won't be a problem–finding him in time might."

"Why would he take her?"

"Don't take this the wrong way, but he's probably pissed at you. You did just wreck everything for him."

I nodded and moved to the bedroom so I could sit on the bed. I needed to think, fast. "How do we find him?"

"Can't you use some of your vampire mumbo jumbo?"

I gave him a look that could have melted candles. Coming from a werelion, that seemed rather racist.

"It doesn't work like that. I couldn't find Cicero like that, why would I be able to find Greer?"

"Not Greer, you idiot, find Vic. She's your vampire. Find her."

I had a "duh" moment. I don't like them. Without looking at Thompson too sheepishly, I sat back on the bed and closed my eyes. "What if she's dead?" I managed to speak through the lump in my throat. "What if I can't find her?"

"If she were dead, trust me, you would know. What if you don't try?"

"Good point." I closed my eyes and thought of Vic. I remembered the first time I ever saw her and that was a mistake. Her naked form dancing inches from me brought a flush of heat to my face. I thought about her coming home shopping with Marcel, and it became a little easier to focus. Her holding out the bracelet with the curious stone that matched my eyes snapped her into focus.

I could feel her. Wherever she was, they had her bound and shut in the dark. She could see, but barely, even with her vampiric eyes. White cloth lined the box she lay in, and I knew it was a coffin. I pulled the memory from her mind. She used to sleep in one, they all did. In San Francisco and Sacramento it had been almost normal. Now fear crept up her spine and clouded her thoughts.

She could feel the sun coming up and knew there would be no rescue tonight. Not unless a miracle happened.

I tried to pull the memory from her thoughts, but couldn't find it. They'd covered her head after beating her nearly unconscious. The only clue I could find had been the smell of burnt wood and smoke as they came to their destination. That didn't help. I pulled myself from her mind and felt a tug to the north, but even that didn't help much. Saying "north of Sacramento" was like saying "over there somewhere."

"I can feel her, so she's alive. I just don't know where."

"You couldn't tell anything?"

"All I know is she's north of us, and in some place that smells like smoke."

"Smoke, like it had been burned to the ground?"

"Yeah, just like…" My voice trailed off. I could think of one place off the top of my head to the north that had been burned recently, "Bare Fangs," the lair of the former master of Sacramento. We needed to get there and fast. Facing off against who knows how many vampires would be a lot easier if they were sleeping.

"I'll call for backup," Thompson said as if he were reading my mind.

"I'll find something to hide in to get me over there. Can I borrow your suitcase?" I meant it as a joke.

"Daylight's in thirty minutes, kid. Why don't you sit this one out?"

"Vic is mine, mine to protect. Not a chance."

"Fine, I have a duffel bag that should be big enough. Go get ready."

Chapter 25

The duffel bag smelled like old gym socks and things I'd rather not think about, but it kept the light out, mostly. A few stray micro-shafts leaked in, but nothing that hurt too badly. Thank you gods, for military surplus green canvas. I felt worse for Thompson. He had to carry me to the elevator and out to the car. I felt really bad until he tossed me in the trunk like luggage.

I uttered a muffled, "Fuck you," and heard him laugh as he slammed the trunk closed like a morgue door. Bad analogy, but I've been in a morgue. It was what it sounded like.

The engine started and the Suburban lurched into reverse. The entire Sacramento Field Office would be meeting us at the dilapidated vampire strip club. I wanted to get there before they did and get out of the smelly body bag.

The drive lasted about twenty minutes. Tires crunched as they rolled on the gravel parking lot, letting me know we'd reached our destination. I just hoped it wouldn't be our final one. That would suck. I thought about it for a minute and rolled the idea around in my head. If I died and Thompson and Vic managed to get out alive, I'd be happy.

The car stopped and I felt the transmission, somewhere below the vehicle, shift into park. Thompson's door opened and I heard his size fifteen shoes kicking up the gravel as he walked around the back of the big SUV. The tailgate clicked and the heat from the morning sun poured into the vehicle, even through the military-grade canvas.

Ick, I don't know how people stood walking around during the day. The sun caused cancer and profuse sweating. I'd take the night any time.

The duffle bag stiffened as Thompson lifted me from the floor of the trunk and set me down on the ground. I hadn't been expecting that and gave a quick, "Hey," as I made contact with the uncomfortable stones.

"I need to grab some knives and shotguns. Hold on, kid."

I rolled my eyes as I waited for my personal chauffer to take me inside. We planned on waiting just inside the door for the cavalry to show up. That would limit the time I had to spend confined in a bag.

I closed my eyes and concentrated on Vic. I could feel her stronger than before. We'd definitely come up with the right spot. She was below me somewhere, and her proximity wasn't doing my patience a whole whopping lot of good. I wanted out of the bag, now.

After a few minutes of listening to Thompson rooting through the storage compartment I'd been lying on, he strapped on his weapons and lifted me off the hot gravel. He carried me gently, but walking produced a natural swinging motion even when you were trying to hold still. I bumped against his leg more than a few times on the short journey from the car to the burned building. The heat dissipated as we crossed the threshold from outside to inside. I started shifting in anticipation, and Thompson shook the bag to let me know it wasn't completely safe yet. Finally, he set me down on cool concrete.

I blinked as he unzipped the duffel bag. Light poured in bright enough to hurt my eyes. I must have winced because Thompson pulled his sunglasses off, and offered them to me. I reached up and slipped them on. "Thanks."

"Just make sure I get them back."

"The bad guys will have to pry them off my cold dead body."

"Not funny, kid."

I shrugged and looked around. The fire that burned the

place did an excruciatingly thorough job. The once somewhat decent-looking stage and bar were reduced to cinders along with most of the floor. Even the darkened glass comprising the majority of the building frontage either melted or shattered. We stood by the stairwell leading down, and still the sunlight poured in, making it quite uncomfortable for me, even with the dark sunglasses about two sizes too large for my head. I leaned against the door and tried not to look toward the daylight streaming in while we waited for the troops.

Luckily, we didn't have to wait for long. Black vehicles of every size, make, and shape poured into the parking lot one by one. Nobody waited in their cars either. As soon as the vehicles skidded to a stop, everyone started exiting and slapping on body armor and weapons. This was a vampire raid. Snuffer rifles, shotguns, and silver blades hung from every available space not occupied by Kevlar vests and armor made from the same material as the V-cuffs used to keep vampires immobilized. I doubted there would be any arrests today. We had writs of execution on any and all vampires with and including the former governor. Deputy Director Sanders was very efficient.

The FBI Agents and SWAT team poured through the broken doors and windows, all vying to be first into the building. They all converged around us in a semi-circle, waiting for Thompson or me to go over everything one last time. Connors nodded at me and gave a little nod for which I was grateful.

"We're certain that one hostage is downstairs, so we can only assume Greer is down there as well with an indeterminate number of vampires. We're here to rescue the hostage and kill everything else that's not breathing," Thompson spoke so everyone could hear, even the ones just coming through the entrance. "The hostage is a vampire, too, but one of the good guys. Let's make sure she gets out alive."

Someone scoffed at the alive. I glanced around, but every one of them looked embarrassed at the outburst, so I couldn't give anyone a dirty look.

"People, Greer is dangerous and evil. He set loose a creature so vile I can't even tell you what it was. Be careful and watch your backs." I continued for Thompson. "Do not hesitate to put silver in his heart. He is very old, which gives him strength you can't imagine. The silver in his heart probably won't kill him. If it incapacitates him, put some in his head, too. The executioners are on standby to come and cleanup. We just have to make sure nobody runs."

They all nodded in understanding. Without waiting around, I pulled the heavy iron door open. Cool air rushed out to surround us, and I blamed that for the visible shivers everyone seemed to come down with simultaneously, not the thought of an indeterminate number of vampires down in a very dark hole who wouldn't mind seeing us very dead. Amazing what a chilly breeze could do.

The smell of smoke and burnt wood permeated the stone stairway leading down into Santiago's lair. Or would it be Greer's lair? Right at the moment, I didn't give two shits as long as he ended up as dead as Santiago.

I hit the bottom landing and stared down the dark hallway leading to the cavernous main room of the lair. I could feel Vic's tugging presence coming from that direction, so I led the way. The other doors in the hallway were closed. I left it to the agents behind me to check and clear the rooms. By now, the sun hung fully overhead, so the odds of any vampires being awake were slim to none. Better to make certain than to get dead from behind, though. If all the vampires were sound asleep in their coffins, there wasn't any reason for me to be tiptoeing through the rough-hewn hallway, but I did.

Finally, we reached the entry to the main hall. I stopped breathing for a minute and listened. I could feel Vic behind the door and I fought the urge to kick it down. Greer had no idea we knew where he'd fled and had no reason to expect us to show up here during the day. We held the element of surprise and I intended to keep it that way. I tentatively reached out and pushed down on the latch holding the door closed. It gave a tiny little click and, I worked it open, praying it didn't creak like every door in every horror movie ever made. It didn't. Apparently, Santiago had been a firm believer in the miracles of WD- 40.

I expected a whole lot of things to be behind that door. I expected a pile of coffins containing vampires. I expected Greer to be sleeping peacefully atop a marble slab surrounded by a thousand glittering candles. I even hoped to see Vic standing there with a bloody knife, a smile on her face, and a dead ex-governor at her feet. I didn't expect the reality of what was actually in the room.

On the other side of the enormous cavern Greer stood with a tied up Victoria at his feet, holding a silver curved blade to her throat. At least a hundred hungry vampires were on either side of him, ready to start a war. I wanted to step back and close the door. Greer's evil sneer stopped me in my tracks.

"It's about time you showed up, youngling. I owe you a great deal of pain and suffering for what you did. Do you know how long I planned that final stroke? It would have given me more power than any vampire has had in centuries." He twisted the knife, and Vic tried to shrink away. "You owe me a life, and I'm going to take it. It's not yours, but I want to see you suffer like I am right now!"

I opened my mouth to get him to stop, but all sanity had left his eyes.

I stood there torn. If I moved a muscle, he would kill her, and I would never reach her in time. If I did nothing, he would probably kill her anyway. I pleaded with my eyes to get Vic to struggle or fight, do *anything*. She wouldn't even look at me. I guess she knew, too.

I cried out in anguish as he pulled the silver knife along Vic's throat. I could feel the cold silver as it parted her flesh, muscle, sinew, and finally bone. The wicked blade and vampiric strength of the madman did more than slit her throat. He pulled it clean through her neck.

Even being across the room I could see the light leave her beautiful eyes as the knife did its work. Her body fell forward in a lifeless heap as Greer held her head by the hair. He smiled triumphantly and threw her head sideways across the room. I closed my eyes as it rolled to a stop just short of the wall to my left.

My heart stopped. Then came the pain. A thousand needles shot out from the center of my chest and through my lungs. Explosions behind my eyes wracked my head in waves that threatened to destroy the very tenuous grip I had on my sanity. I probably would have welcomed the alternative. Insane people usually don't feel pain or loss, and that's exactly what my world had become. I dropped to my knees and grasped my head in my hands, futilely trying to stop the pain and the spinning room.

Greer's maniacal laugh anchored me. He thought he won, but it wasn't over. It would be over when I ripped his spine from his dead body and shoved it back in through his mouth. Then they could do whatever they wanted to me. I'd lay down on the cold floor and let his vampires tear me apart with no expression on my face. I had to finish him first.

"It hurts doesn't it, Ashlyn. It hurts to have a child of your making destroyed. I remember my first one. I loved her and made her just like me. That happened over a thousand years ago, and I still remember it like yesterday His footsteps brought him closer. "The agony is unbearable at first, but you'd get over it if I weren't going to kill you and all the humans in the hallway behind you. I hope they know that the minute they step into this room, my children will unleash a torrent of death upon them without even taking one step."

The chambering of ammunition echoed as Greer's vampires cocked the weapons they'd been holding when he'd decapitated my Vic. Apparently the SWAT team and the agents heard it too because the footfalls in the hallway stopped. The situation had gone from worse to horrid, and I couldn't even stand.

"Kid, what's happening?" Thompson's voice came from behind the wall housing the only entrance to the room.

"Stay back. Vampires…guns…" I managed to croak out through the haze, causing Greer to laugh even harder.

"Are you okay?"

"No, stay back."

"How fucked are we?" This time his voice crackled in my ear, reminding me of the tiny earpieces we'd put in before leaving.

I slipped my hand down and pressed the tiny button on the side. "Very," I said as softly as possible. I knew Greer could hear, but I didn't care.

"Don't respond. We're here. Give the word and we come in shooting. Try to stay down when we do."

I nodded to nobody, but the warmth that spread through me helped with the pain. I would kill Greer and they would come in guns blazing. None of us would survive, probably, but my friends knew it and didn't care. They'd give their lives and be happy, just as I would have to save Vic. Well that option was gone, but now I'd gladly give it to see Greer pay for what he'd done. I'd let him cut my head off as long as I got to pull his fucking heart out when he did it.

The anger began to build on top of the grief. It started as a small trickle that swelled into a creek and gave way to a raging river. The pain drifted away. My fists curled into tighter balls. My talons started to grow and they pierced the flesh of my palms, but I didn't care. It felt good compared to the throbbing in my head. The claws hit the bones in my hands, and I forced my fists open. I couldn't see the blood trickling into my eyes from my forehead because my vision hadn't returned, but I could feel it. The sting felt good.

"It's a good thing you're going to die tonight," Greer continued. "When Strozzini died, I knew you had something to do with it, I just couldn't prove it. I couldn't let an abomination like you continue, so I dispatched a letter to the Vampire Council, telling them all about you. What a shame, they'll never get to see your body. I'm sure they would have found it interesting." I could hear his shoes as he took several more steps while he gloated.

The pain in my hands had completely ebbed and vanished as I opened my hands. I rubbed them together and heard a strange scraping noise, like somebody rubbing pieces of sandpaper against each other. Frantically, I wished for my vision to come back. I wistfully wished for Vic to still be alive. That thought started the tears. I let them fall from my eyes and land on the back of my hands. Dimly, the room came back into view. I blinked twice at the scaly paws in front of my face. It took me a moment to realize they were mine.

My skin had been replaced by something else. Most of it had become a deep crimson color, but a myriad of tiny black shapes covered it like angular gooseflesh. It gave the appearance of reptilian scales, but they didn't overlap. I rubbed my hand over my arm and couldn't feel anything. I looked up and saw Greer had closed the distance between us.

He stared down at me with both hatred *and* amazement. I could only imagine what I looked like to him. Maybe he saw his death in my eyes. Maybe he just saw the pain and anguish I would be so willing to impart on his immortal ass.

I stood, and he backed up a pace. I could feel the weapons Greer's children were holding swing from the open doorway to target me. I took a step, and Greer took another one backward. I took a second step, and he frantically backpedalled, opening his eyes wide as he scrambled to get away.

The first shot rang out, and I yelled, "Now!"

I heard the surge of agents and SWAT as they frantically tried to shove thirty people through a space the size of Thompson. I focused my attention on my prize. The first shot hit me in the shoulder before I heard it. I felt the impact, but not the pain. I snarled in outrage and doubled my efforts to get Greer's neck in my hands. Nothing else mattered.

He gave up trying to run backward and turned to flee outright. I leapt on his back, pinning him to the floor. He screamed in outrage while I decided what to take off him first. I decided on his right arm when he spun, throwing me some distance away. He headed toward the door, the only entrance or exit to the room, and seemingly realized he had counted on his strength and that of his children a little too confidently.

He spun on me and pulled another knife. My friends finally started getting through the door and took positions behind what little cover they could find. Shots filled the room as the vampires answering to Greer returned fire. People and vampires fell, wounded or dead within minutes, with Greer and I in the crossfire. Bullets pounded into me, but I didn't feel a thing. Greer wrenched a smoking silver stake from his calf without breaking eye contact with me. I smiled and feinted as he swung his deadly silver blade at my face.

Power surged from him as he held up his left hand. I felt something, but not anything different. He looked at his palm and back at me as if he'd just discovered his lifeline had come to an abrupt end.

One of the SWAT members tried to get a kill shot on the governor, but got too close. Greer held out his hand again and thousands of bone-deep lacerations appeared on every inch of visible skin. Judging from the amount of blood flowing from his vest, shirt, and pants, those lacerations covered everywhere not visible, too. He fell dead before he could scream.

Greer held his hand up and smiled at me again. I braced myself for the impending rush of power from his palm, but nothing happened, again.

Greer comically looked at his hand and shook it before trying again. I smiled when it failed the third time. He looked pissed. I ran forward and he struck inhumanly fast with the wickedly curved blade. I didn't have time to dodge it, so I held up my forearm, willing to take the hit to get my hand around his throat. The blade struck with a shower of sparks and cut me even through my new spiffy skin. It hurt, but I smiled and bashed him open palmed with my right hand. I wanted to knock him on his ass, but he landed on his feet and launched at me again.

I braced for the impact, but he grabbed me where he'd cut me. This time I felt the surge of power from his hand as he released his curious over an open wound. Pain shot from the gash throughout my body like the roots of a tree. Everywhere it hit, my skin pain blossomed as well as a wound. My body became slick with my own blood. Greer smiled triumphantly. I spit in his face.

I lost an immense amount of blood before the lacerations closed. I could at least take satisfaction in the fact that Greer seemed shocked the wounds closed at all. I didn't waste any time. When I lose blood, I lose energy. The emotional damage I took watching Vic die, as well as the physical damage from Greer's power, weighed heavily in my limbs. My speed and strength sapped with every second that passed. I slowly circled him as he narrowed his eyes.

He'd figured out I was drained. He closed in for the kill and actually slipped the curved blade up through my stomach into my chest. If he'd been a hair to the right, it would have pierced my heart, and he might have been able to finish me off. Because he hadn't, I wrapped my hands around his shoulders. Too bad.

I leaned in close to his face before I killed him. I locked my gaze with his. I shouldn't have, but I wanted to see the fear I'd just started to smell on him.

As soon as our gazes locked, something clicked. The room spun around us as if we stood in the middle of a centrifuge. Within moments, the walls of the cavern flung away leaving a vast starry night. Greer wasn't in my clutches anymore. He floated above a calm ocean that had been electrified with living color, as if the rolling waves themselves radiated light rather than reflecting it. I looked down, saw my vast turbulent ocean, and knew I'd trapped his mind.

"You can't do this to me." He waved his arms and legs, trying to propel himself toward me.

"I can, and I have, you piece of shit. Look at me!"

He did and his arms and legs went limp. I wanted to tear him apart, piece by piece, but I couldn't do it here in this realm of the mind. He didn't look panicked; he looked like he had a plan. Wind that wasn't real blew me back as his ocean surged forward and pushed against mine. We both floated over his power now and fear gripped my chest. I closed my eyes and called my waters. I felt them trying to push his back, but couldn't. Sweat beaded on my forehead as his sneer grew more confident moment by moment. It couldn't end like this. Nobody would be left to avenge Vic.

She saved me. The moment I thought of her, my power didn't push his back, it split in a V shape and worked itself around Greer's power. He looked from left to right and lifted his hands to call his to him. It wrapped around him like a cocoon, and he smiled at me from within the depths of his shell. A tendril of power shot out and tried to spear me, but purely out of reflex, I lifted my hand to ward it off. A wave of my power shot up and blocked his. He stared at me in disbelief. I looked back in shock.

My power seemed smaller than before and less reflective. Like the color emanating from it had dulled to a matte finish. I needed to end this quickly.

I brought my hands down like a child bowling for the first time. I think they call it granny-style. I lifted both my hands and called everything I had with one large pull. The waters below me shot forward and wrapped everything Greer had, along with him in a large wave. I watched him panic as he drowned in my power. I mentally squeezed as hard as I could. His power grew smaller and smaller, squeezing the very life out of him. I gave one final mental scream, and my waters went from matte to shiny black obsidian, freezing solid, trapping everything within it.

The room spun back into focus. The sounds of fighting around us still echoed off the stone walls of the cavern. I held Greer in my arms and had his neck in my mouth. I sucked and nothing came out of the empty husk he'd become. I opened my arms and he fell to the ground, quite dead.

Chapter 26

As it turned out, the moment Greer died the rest of his vampires stopped fighting and attempted to surrender. The FBI agents involved in the firefight, including the members of the FBI SWAT team, didn't wait for the federal executioners to come in. After the vampires had thrown down their weapons, everyone finished them without batting an eyelash. I stood in the middle of the room and watched silently. Vic deserved that much at least.

I had Vic's body cremated and flew back to San Francisco to spread the ashes over the bay. It seemed fitting. She loved San Francisco, and Sacramento had been a sort of punishment for her. I wanted her to be happy, even in death. As I dumped her ashes, with tears rolling down my cheeks, I vowed to never make another vampire again as long as I lived. Silently, I hoped that wouldn't be much longer. Everywhere I went, death followed, and if Marcel could go on without making companions, so could I.

We lost seventeen agents that night, and still the Deputy Director dubbed it a success. He said we walked into a trap and came out alive. Most of us had anyway. He chalked it up as a win. I wasn't convinced. A part of me died in Sacramento.

I had one huge problem other than Vic's loss. When I enveloped Greer with my power and drained him dry, every vampire tied to him as master of San Francisco, Sacramento, Los Angeles, and San Jose became mine. I knew right away, not only because I could feel every one of them, but when the FBI massacred the rest of Greer's vampires, I felt every shot, blade, and stake as they pierced their flesh. I took each one as a sort of penance for failing Vic at the end. I know, I'm a martyr, or at least that's what the therapist the FBI is making me see told me.

I received a commendation from not only the FBI, but from the Department of Homeland Security, too. I put them in a drawer and haven't seen them since. Thompson smiles every time he sees his medals sitting on his desk. Then he notices me staring at him while he's doing it and quickly starts shuffling papers.

True to his word, Sanders stationed Thompson and me back in Chicago. Reese was only slightly happier than Thompson's wife. The moment I walked through the doors of the Chicago Field Office, he hugged me for a half hour straight. He had another surprise for me as well. Completely going against my wishes, he used the story I'd given him about how I'd come to be and cross-referenced the data against fatal accidents at the time and discovered my last name is Thorn. It was the one thing about me I never wanted the FBI to know. But he figured out who my aunt was and saved her house from probate, much to the chagrin of the estate lawyers. He not only had all my records changed to Ashlyn Rowan Thorn, he had the house put in my name as sole heir. I don't know how he did it, but he did. At least I didn't have to rent an apartment while I'm staying in Chicago.

When I wasn't doing FBI stuff, I'd spend spending all my free time with Marcel learning how to be a vampire. He took Vic's death hard. I guess he figured if he'd stayed, she'd still be alive. I passed along what my therapist told me. I hoped it helped. It was easy to be around him. He helps me forget what I lost and what could have been. I also passed along Greer's revelation of the letter he'd sent the Vampire Council. He wasn't too happy about that. I told him we'd get through it. *He* didn't seem too sure.

I visited Michaels' grave six times since I've been back. I smile every time I see him. I told him all about Vic and how much he would have liked her. I buried her cat's eye bracelet at his grave. I hope he didn't mind, but now I could say hi to both of them at the same time.

I also introduced myself to Michaels' parents. His dad is the spitting image of his son and has the same sense of humor. Even though I inadvertently caused his death, they not only didn't blame me, they sort of "adopted" me, and introduced me to all their friends as Pete's partner. I try not to cry.

For now, I'm living day to day and learning all I can. I know the Council will come looking for me and knowledge is power. Hell, it might be the only power I have against them. We'll see.

Epilogue

Asmodeus sat on his throne contemplating a solution to his problem. The All hadn't placed a time limit on fixing his latest indiscretion, but one didn't dally when commanded by the All. They hadn't provided him with a way to remedy it, but that was his problem, not the All's. He had his seneschal scouring all the tomes in his kingdom looking for a way for him to enter the mortal realm without being summoned. Humans had long ago severed all ties to his kind and burned most of the tomes in their world on how to summon even a minor demon, let alone a demon lord. Sometimes being one of the fallen had more than its usual share of disadvantages.

As he sat, he felt a shift in the power that permeated every corner of his kingdom. Someone had arrived in his realm unannounced. He hadn't summoned anyone, so he could only assume it was his annoying cousin, Raphael, or one of his ilk. He rolled his slit eyes in annoyance as he ran his taloned finger over the top of one of the hundreds of skulls adorning his throne.

"My Lord," Vizier said in his sibilant voice from the shadows.

"What is it, Vizier?"

"Your servant, Belial, has returned."

"That's impossible! What do you mean?"

"He is here, my lord, I have seen him myself."

"Bring him to me at once!"

"Yes, my lord."

Asmodeus began tapping the skull in impatience as Vizier sped along on his quest. The tapping changed its force and tempo and ended with Asmodeus pounding on the top of the skull with his closed fist. The demon lord had never been patient, even when he'd been mighty among the ranks of the Angelic Host rather than the Fallen. He snorted in disgust at the memories of those times flooding his mind. He'd been happy once, but that changed quickly.

"Belial, my lord."

Asmodeus nodded at the wispy servant and trained his vision on who had once been his favorite of servants. They had enjoyed many hunts and torments together until his accident. He never thought to see the young demon again. "I thought you were lost, my friend."

"So did I, my lord. To say these centuries have been long would be a bit of an understatement."

"I think it has been longer than that, Belial. How did you free yourself from the skull?"

"You knew?"

"I saw it when it happened, but since it was your offspring who trapped you, I couldn't retaliate. It was his right by blood. I saw him when he took your head and then trapped you within it. I didn't think he had the prowess in magic to complete such a task. I also felt you deserved it for losing your combat against your son."

"Pah! You know these damn offspring of our kind, unpredictable to say the least. It is not the talented swordsman the master fears, it is the novice. So much power, so little discipline, and a fierce temper can be the downfall of the greatest of us."

"You better not be foreshadowing, my friend. Apparently I have sired an offspring."

"Who do you think sent me home, my lord?"

"She bested you?"

"Yes, just as she now battles my offspring. I don't put much faith in him against that one!"

"Is she that strong?"

"My lord, she beat me barehanded. I fear what she might become."

"So do I, Belial. So do I."

"At least I am free of that damnable skull!"

"Do you still have ties to it?" Asmodeus excitedly slid forward on his throne, watching Belial step back in fear from the fire in Asmodeus' eyes.

"I can still be summoned through it, but no longer am I bound to it. The humans of the realm have secreted it away under heavy guard."

"Belial, you will get the offspring of your offspring to find it. You will get them to summon you back to the human realm, where you will summon me. I have an indiscretion I need to correct. Your life depends on it."

"Yes, my lord." Belial bowed down to Asmodeus.

Did You Enjoy Deceptions?

Please let the author know by leaving a review!
And be sure to watch for

Abominations

Book 3 of the Demonkin Series
Coming soon!

Other Works by Sean Hayden

RISE OF THE FALLEN SERIES

A VAMPIRE STEAMPUNK NOVELLA

About the Author

Born the son of a fire chief, Sean naturally developed a love of playing with fire. His family and friends quickly found other outlets for his destructive creativity. Writing is his latest endeavor.

Always a fan of the macabre, mythical, and magical, Sean found a love of urban fantasy and horror. After writing several novels in this genre, he found, fell in love with, and immersed himself in steampunk. He has always wanted to rewrite history and steampunk gave him that opportunity.

Sean currently lives in Florida as a fiber-optic engineer as well as an author. He was blessed with the two most amazing children he could ever hope for, has met the absolute love of his life, who coincidentally is his partner in everything. His hobbies include grand designs on world domination as well as a starring role in his own television sitcom.

www.ingramcontent.com/pod-product-compliance
Lightning Source LLC
Chambersburg PA
CBHW070917180626
46817CB00003B/1103